Also by Andrew K. Stone

All Flowers Die

12/3/04

To Steve Kramer,
with all best wishes

Disappearing Into View

a novel by

Andrew K. Stone

SO THERE BOOKS
Cambridge, Massachusetts

Copyright © 2001 Andrew K. Stone

ISBN 0967907314

Printed in Canada

Published by SO THERE BOOKS
www.sotherebooks.com

For David Cashman,

My teacher, my friend, and the noblest of the noble.

Chapters

Chapter One
The Legend of the Squab

W hen I was fifteen years old my home was blown up, but that's not the reason I'm homeless. After the explosion — and the subsequent aftershocks — that shattered my world, I made a conscious decision to remove myself from society. I don't regret that decision. My ten years on the street have been an invaluable experience and I've learned many lessons, most particularly how wrong I was. But I never would have realized this had I not run away. Before I left society, questions and doubts enshrouded me like a second skin. However, the transience of street life makes it difficult for too much moss to gather, and I suppose it was only natural that eventually I would have stumbled upon larger revelations. These came at a cost of pain and loss but the alternative would have been much worse. Remaining stagnant, my second skin would have solidified and, as a result of this emotional alchemy, I would have been sealed off to the point of suffocating inside of myself. I never would have felt a thing....

Technically, I told myself, there was nothing dishonest about it. If you order squab at a restaurant, it stands to reason you know what you're getting. Therefore, you're probably not going to ask where it came from; after all, how many times have you inquired about the slaughterhouse which produced your steak? Most people have a notion that a cow was slaughtered somewhere near Chicago, and they leave it at that; no one

1

really wants to think about the details. No one *ever* worries that their food might be, in any way, substandard. But the restaurant owners know everything about the food they serve. They've got the upper hand and, unless you ask probing questions up front, you put your trust in those hands.

Deep down I knew it was wrong, but it was a case of survival. I had to permit myself to believe in the technicalities of the transactions. If I didn't, I couldn't have gone through with it.

But it was more than just survival. I once saw a headline in the *Herald* peeking out from the window of a yellow newspaper box. The accompanying article related how the suspected Unabomber had been living in a shack in the middle of nowhere. I envied him. I thought it must have been wonderful to live like that — free from society. But now I've realized that society is the one thing we cannot be free of. Its boundaries are like the glass walls of an aquarium: invisible and impenetrable. It is our whole world and we are the fish swimming inside. We can swim solitarily but we cannot pass through the glass; it holds our world together and without it, life would drain from around us all.

But at fifteen, I had thought differently. I thought I could detach myself from society and only duck my head through its door when absolutely necessary. It was those times when I'd show up in the alleyways of some of the finer restaurants in Boston with my little canvas sack. A transaction would be made, and I would walk back through the door, weighted down by some cash and my technicalities.

This worked for years until the evening Sid picked the wrong bird out of my bag.

"I don't think you'll want that one, Mr. Sid. I was going to throw it away. It didn't look very good."

"Aah, I'll do you a favor," he said. "I'll take it off your hands half price, seeing as you were gonna toss it, anyway."

"It may have been sick."

He laughed, the tip of his ever-present cigar glowing like a brake light.

"Always the salesman, Cole," Sid chuckled. "Okay, then I'll give you two bucks. What's the use of throwing it away?"

"Well...."

He laughed again and handed me two more crumpled bills. Although the brake light flashed between his teeth, I thought about the pack of cigarettes I could buy and put the money in my pocket.

Of course he survived. After they pumped his stomach, he called the Board of Health, which performed an unannounced inspection on Chez Sidney. Pigeon feathers were found in the kitchen and the restaurant was closed down. Then he came looking for me but, oddly enough, he wasn't out for retribution. As it would be some time until he proffered his "business opportunity," the morning he found me on the green, wooden bench in the Common, he merely asked a bunch of questions. All during that first meeting, my mind clicked like a misfiring gun. And the thought that repeatedly refused to fully discharge was that it would have been better had he died.

Actually, that's not entirely true. Another question pulsed through my brain. For the first time, I also wondered how it tasted. This may seem odd, but I'd never met anyone who ate one before. This guy who showed up in front of me, with his long shadow blanketing me like an extra section of newspaper, was the first. I didn't have to guess that it was him, just as I didn't need to imagine the food poisoning or the stomach-pumping. I knew him by the way he dressed. His bruise-colored sweater tucked into his black, woolen slacks. The tops of his leather shoes displaying an intricate pattern of holes like some crazy Chinese checkerboard. And, of course, the trademark gel-slicked, black hair. The epitome of Eurotrash, he was just the type to be drawn to Chez Sidney. The longer I looked at him, the more vivid the scene in my mind became. A candlelit table, soft music, wine, and Eurotrash trying to impress his date: "To the common man, it's pigeon; to me, it's a *delicacy*." I wondered how delicate the doctors had been when they were evacuating his stomach.

Eurotrash stood above me. Black tufts of chest hair, like spider legs, crawled out from the top of his sweater. I started to rise. My own hair was sticky and my spine ached where the wooden slats of the bench had embedded themselves like railroad tracks. A big maple tree provided a chilly, leafy canopy against the sun and I shivered under it. As I drew my plaid flannel coat around me, some stuffing fell from the ripped sleeve, reminding me of an unexpected snowfall I'd once woken to on a particularly cruel April Fools' Day.

"I always thought it was just a myth." He spoke as if the letter 'h' hadn't yet been invented. "A legend."

"No. It's true."

He nodded slowly and, while he ran his fingers through his gelled strands, I was reminded of another front-page story about the Exxon *Valdez*.

The clicking in my head continued. I wondered how he knew it had been me. There were thousands of homeless people in Boston; how did he arrive at my park bench?

4

"How do you catch them?" he asked.

I said nothing. We looked at each other for a moment, and then he offered me a cup of coffee. I was dubious. I'd never had Starbucks before.

"Go ahead," he laughed. "It ain't gonna hurt you."

He held out the cup to me, almost threateningly, so I finally took it and drank.

"It's not so bad. Thanks."

I stretched and then took my canvas bag from the bench and strapped it around my waist. At night, I used it for a pillow but I kept a few items in it that I liked to have with me at all times — cigarettes, some change, and my little tool. During the day, I wore it like the small fanny packs I'd seen attached to bicyclists as they cruised down Beacon Hill.

I started walking towards the Public Garden. I had to piss, and there was a clump of bushes I could use without being seen. Sometimes I'd use my clients' bathrooms, but none of the restaurants were open in the morning. Eurotrash followed me to the little duck pond where the paddleboats were and I sneaked behind the bushes. A few flies buzzed around me as I let loose, carving small yellow trenches in the dirt.

"Poison?" I heard him ask. I stayed quiet. "I know. You snare them, somehow."

I wasn't afraid that he'd have me arrested; after all, they got Sid. I was small change. And if he wanted to beat me up, he would have done it already. Instead, he had stood in line at the forever-busy Starbucks (one of two nestled between the historic buildings and antique shops which lined the cobblestone sidewalk of Charles Street) and bought me coffee. I thought he must be psychotic, and I envisioned his dark eyes screwed up as he plotted an intricate revenge while puking pigeon.

I finished pissing and walked out from behind the bushes, vaguely aware of the flies which still followed me.

Eurotrash was sitting on one of the benches in front of a freshly landscaped flowerbed. The new blooms looked like an artist's palette. Eurotrash watched me with the expectancy of a cab driver waiting for a traffic light to change. He seemed to know, intuitively, that I'd answer his question, so I finally opened my bag, rifled through it and brought out my tool.

He laughed in that condescending manner parents use when they don't have the answer to their kids' questions.

"You're kidding."

"I don't get 'em all this way. The one you ate was already dead on the sidewalk."

His smile twisted slowly like a lemon rind.

"You asked."

"Yeah."

We sat down on a small grassy hill and drank our coffee. A young mother walked by, pushing her scream-filled stroller ahead of her. Eurotrash watched her pass and then said:

"Ten minutes of pleasure for a lifetime of aggravation."

Then he turned to me. Although I shivered in the eighty-degree heat of early June, his bruised sweater looked horribly warm.

"Let me see you do it."

"Sorry. I can't."

"What do you mean, you can't?" It was the first time he raised his voice, although his next sentence was a quiet hiss like a truck's airbrakes early in the morning. "After all the trouble you caused?"

"That's not the way I see it."

"Oh no? Well, just how do you see it?"

"I warned Sid. I told him. But he bought it anyway." He looked at me with doubting eyes, until I added, "Look, I'm just trying to make enough for an occasional meal."

"Oh, so that makes it all right?"

In the sun's glare, his gelled hair looked tenuously brittle, like fresh tar just before it dries. He pulled out a silver cigarette case and opened it. Late one night, I'd seen the same case behind an alarmed shop window on Newbury Street. Up close, his unmarked cigarettes lay there in neat rows, looking like Arlington National Cemetery from the sky. He handed me one, and stuck another between his lips. A flare from his lighter ignited both, and he exhaled a huge sigh of smoke. Crossing one leg over the other, he idly fingered the little tassel on his loafer. I looked past the barely scuffed soles of his shoes and watched his fingers play.

"I went to that restaurant with this beautiful chick," he said, drawing out his sentences nostalgically. "Her name was Amanda. I met her at the M.F.A. Ever been there?"

"I slept on the steps once."

He squinted at me dismissively, and then continued.

"We were both there for the Monet opening. But I was kind of bored, so I started talking to her. To make a long story short, we go to Sid's the next Saturday. We had a great dinner. Good wine, good conversation. Then, we headed to my brownstone in Back Bay. We started up the four flights to my apartment and I began to feel a little queasy. I poured some more wine and suggested we sit on my terrace, 'cause a cool breeze was blowing. I started feeling a little better and we continued our conversation. Then, after another sip of wine, we bent towards each other and started to kiss. I ran my fingers through her hair. Fuckin' silk. Must have cost her a fortune to keep up. Anyway, she put her arms around me, holding me tight. Unfortunately, she held me too tight. I felt a gurgling in my stomach, but it was too late."

He stopped playing with his tassel and looked me straight in the eye.

"That's disgusting," I said.

"No shit. So you see? It *is* your fault."

"Why? You were the one who ordered it. A guy like you probably knows every five-star place in this city but you go into Sid's and order the squab. And you even told me you've heard all about it. You 'thought it was a myth' but you ordered it anyway. You're the one to blame."

I thought it strange when he smiled and asked:

"You really feel that way?"

"Absolutely. Like I said, I'm just trying to make my own way. I've got to look after myself. I'm not responsible for anybody. Anybody except myself."

He nodded and kept smiling.

"Good," he said. "I like that. I'll see you around."

He got up and started walking away, but then turned back.

"Something's funny."

"What?"

"You...you don't talk like a bum."

I shrugged.

"No, no, I mean, you talk...educated."

"So what's funny about that?"

He scratched his head again.

"I don't know."

And he turned and walked towards Tremont Street.

I sat for another few minutes and, finishing my coffee, thought over what he had said about my speech while abolishing old memories. Then I stood and walked through the Public Garden towards the Ritz Carlton

Hotel. The buds on the trees had popped open a month before like small traps I'd never noticed. The tulips and crocuses had already bloomed. As kids, we used to say the crocuses had croaked. I smiled at that as I crossed Arlington Street and walked up Commonwealth Ave., passing the old brownstones that, unlike so many things in Boston, never changed except in value.

I pulled my tool out again. It was an old slingshot. The wood was marble-smooth with age, but the elastic bands were new. I had to constantly replace them, which meant grabbing them from magazine bundles in front of the newsstands early in the morning. The leather pouch was as old as the slingshot, made from a scrap of a jacket that I still wore in the cold weather.

Strolling in the median of Commonwealth, where people walk their dogs and the kids play on the statues, I approached an immovable statesman. Oxidation had colored him the same blue-green as the Statue of Liberty. My prey was on top of this statue, its shit dripping down onto a metal placard which was also blue-green. Bending down, I picked up a small stone, stuck it into the pouch and fired. I heard the familiar reverse-sucking noise as the rock hit the bird's breast. The pigeon fell from the statesman's head, following the trail of its last shit to land in the bright green grass. I picked it up and wiped off a bit of the white droppings from its hind feathers. The pigeon's eyes were glassy and vacant. I watched them for a moment, as if they might suddenly open, then put the dead bird in my sack and moved on.

———

A few weeks later, I dreamt I was a prince living in a fairytale land. The King came to me with a treasure chest and said, "All of this is for you." He opened the chest and I saw it was filled with jewels. Myriad colors gleamed from within. But as he handed the chest to me, I began to grow, taller and taller and into the clouds, dwarfing the King. He couldn't reach high enough to hand me the treasure. Finally, I stooped down to take it from his elfin hands. But as I lifted it up, the jewels changed into oval, brown beans.

———

My first night sleeping on the streets was in Copley Square, in front of the Boston Public Library. When I awoke in the morning, conflicting feelings pinned me to the sidewalk as if I were a footprint in the cement. People walked by, their glances drenching me in shame. If someone I knew had seen me, how would I explain? I was also scared. Had I been molested in the night? Had I been robbed? I moved slightly and felt for my wallet. It was still in my back pocket but, to my initial surprise, this did nothing to comfort me.

In those first moments, I had hoped for a convincing way to get up and walk away. But then I was flooded by images of the circumstances that had put me there — my once-heroic father; my destroyed home; the crime I still couldn't quite believe. I realized I was as *away* as I could ever hope to be. Melting into the sidewalk was the only option that would have been more preferable.

From that moment, I began to live up to the vow I had made to myself. The day before, the life I thought had been promised to me was revoked. Like a roller coaster out of control, the world had spun about and thrown me off. Now I was on my own, and I had resolved to remain that way. I was officially a non-person. Visibly invisible.

But it wasn't easy getting to this point. I was constantly prodded by temptations to abandon my life on the street. A few days without food, a rainy night without shelter — like taunting school kids, the elements of life continually nagged at me. However, the more I struggled against them, the stronger I became. I soon realized that instead of real alternatives, the temptations only offered more questions. It was when I finally gave up struggling that I was able to believe I was no longer anybody. And then an incredible rush of freedom rained through my body and dissolved my fears and shame.

After a few years, this freedom simply became a way of life. I rarely heard the people around me and, when I did, I didn't care what they thought of me. They were movie extras passing through scenes in my existence. Once I got used to sleeping on the streets, I felt as if I never really woke up; I just moved from unconscious dreaming to conscious dreaming.

The morning I dreamt of the beans, I felt a gentle prodding in my ribs. The hot sun massaged my eyelids and numbness nagged my lower back. Although half-asleep, I was aware of my body's usual contradiction of shivering in the heat. I blinked and then looked up. Eurotrash was standing above me, with his head framed in a green halo of spring leaves and his patterned sweater tucked into his pants. He looked like a Roman soldier off to a disco. I blinked again and inhaled. The aroma of coffee pulled my head to the side, and I saw a Starbucks' cup sitting on the base of the statue I'd slept under.

"Morning," Eurotrash said.

I sat up slowly. We were in the median on Commonwealth Ave., not far from the place I had killed the pigeon the first time Eurotrash and I had met. Straight ahead was the Common; to my right and left rose the brownstones. Some of these building were luxury apartments or townhouses, while others were old-time social clubs like something out of a Salinger novel. Taking up entire city blocks, these buildings were all three and four stories high, with many of the window frames and gutters stained the same blue-green color from oxidation. Some of them had wrought iron fences that surrounded curt, manicured courtyards.

A dog barked and I saw some children squealing with delight, playing keep-away with the mutt as their two Irish nannies looked on. Both were plainly dressed, and one wore a faded kerchief around her throat that looked as if it could have been an heirloom. I could hear them talking, their lilting voices playing musical chairs with their sentences, moving words around to fit their native vernacular. They were speaking of some boys they had met at a local pub and, while one girl was advising against sex before marriage, the one with the scarf mockingly let her rosary beads slip in her fingers. They both collapsed into giggles.

Eurotrash gestured for me to take the cup. I wasn't used to eating first thing in the morning — usually my stomach was empty until well into the day, so as soon as I took a sip, I was famished. I began to gulp at the coffee.

"This is how you make your own way, huh?" Eurotrash asked.

Slowing down, I said, "It's not so bad."

He grunted.

"By the way, my name's Vince."

I watched him as I drank, warning myself to be careful.

"And you are...?"

I didn't answer. He laughed and ran his fingers through his ever-oily hair.

"Okay. You're Birdman. You're the Bird."

"Larry or Charlie? I don't play basketball or sax."

Vince squinted.

"Where the hell are you from, anyway?"

"Here," I shrugged.

"You mean here, Boston?"

"More or less," I answered, sucking down more of the coffee. I needed food to go with it. My body was reacting violently; hunger pangs bit into my stomach. I wondered if this was anything like the feeling a vegetarian might experience after eating a chunk of beef.

Vince rocked on his heels, looking around at the tops of the buildings. The nannies walked by and he stepped back in mock gallantry to let them pass. "Good day, ladies," he said. The girls giggled and walked on. Then Vince turned back to me.

"So, how long you been catching pigeons?"

"A while."

"Like...a coupla years? Or longer?"

"A little longer," I said, sucking up the last drop of coffee. When I put the empty cup in my sack, Vince gazed at me questioningly.

"You never know when it might come in handy," I answered.

"What would you use it for?"

"Lots of things. If I get thirsty, there're plenty of places to get a drink of water. The duck pond, a puddle in the street, a gutter. But I don't always have a cup. Now I do."

His brow furrowed in a slight wince.

"It's part of making my own way," I reminded him, and got up to collect my few belongings.

"What say we go get a bite to eat? We can go to Downtown Crossing. Grab a sandwich."

It had been a long time since anyone invited me to "grab a sandwich," and temptation dueled with hesitancy. As a rule, I tried to avoid downtown during the day because I don't like the crowds. But, more importantly, I didn't want Vince to see how vulnerable

I could be. I didn't know what he wanted, but he didn't strike me as a philanthropist.

"Well...," I said, affecting reluctance.

"If you got other dining plans...?"

"No," I said, as my body betrayed me. "Let's go. Thanks."

We walked through the Public Garden and the Common. As we wended our way along the tar-black pathways, I avoided conversation by surveying the day's activities around me. In the distance, I saw the State House on Beacon Hill. A few dark-blue State Police cruisers were parked in front and the crew from a television news van was readying for a broadcast. Their satellite dish was raised and a guy was setting up a camera tripod. In front of us, the path darkened under the canopy of the drowsing oak branches. Sparrows pecked along in the dirt under the trees, unconcerned as they looked for worms. Up ahead, a little boy cried as he watched a flock of pigeons maniacally devouring the popcorn he'd just spilled.

"You're not the first," Vince mused.

"The first what?"

"Pigeon catcher."

"No."

We walked through the flock, sending them flying in a haphazard beating of reluctant wings.

"There goes what — twenty, thirty bucks?"

"You can't catch them in daytime. I mean, not when everyone's around."

"What then? You just chalk it up as a loss and don't think about them?"

"You can't lose pigeons," I replied. "Eventually they'll land again."

Vince scratched his cement head thoughtfully.

"So, where did you hear about it?" he asked.

14

"Hear about what?"

"The legend. Where did you get the idea?"

We had reached Park Street Station where the Red and Green lines of the subway — the T — intersected underground. Across Tremont Street, I noticed the wall of four-story buildings. A small convenience store and some fast food places had seeped between the cracks, trying to choke the indiscriminate shops which looked as though they'd been there for hundreds of years. The clash of time and place always made me question permanence. As we crossed the street, I answered Vince:

"I heard about it from some other homeless guys. Not many do it, but it's been going on for years. There are a few others...."

Vince laughed.

"For years bums have been passing pigeons off for squab and nobody's the wiser. Fuckin' great! What I've been missing out on."

"You eat a lot of squab?"

"Not really."

He kept laughing as we headed towards Downtown Crossing.

———

There was a little outdoor stand that sold wrap sandwiches. This was something I'd witnessed as the newest rage. It seemed people would roll up anything in pita bread, and the more outrageous the food, the better. Vince thought it would be best to buy the sandwiches and walk up the street to a little brick rotunda. We would eat on the benches there.

"I don't think you'd fit the dress code of the places I normally frequent," he chuckled.

We got our wraps and made our way through the crowd. Shoppers with full bags bustled by; teenagers stood on corners with radios the size of small trunks playing loud, bass-heavy music; businessmen passed each other while talking on their cell phones, gesticulating wildly as if in negotiations; vendors showed off homemade jewelry and scarves and dresses and leather goods they sold from wooden carts; cops sat on horseback, surveying the street as they flirted with the meter maids and chatted with construction crewmen. This was downtown in the daytime: a circus in which most people unwittingly performed. I preferred it at night, after the carnival had packed up and left. That's when I would normally venture down the stained sidewalks of Downtown Crossing and hunt the pigeons which roosted in the nooks of the gray buildings. I liked the feeling of the deserted streets. They exuded the same comfort that's earmarked for autumn nights when you're wearing your favorite sweater. At night, the streets always felt as if they were mine, as if someone had created a giant playground solely for my purposes. I was always the King of the Hill. I alone had possession, and I alone belonged.

We sat. The sandwich in my hands was called the Thanksgiving Special. Steaming, hot turkey breast wrapped around cornbread stuffing with cranberry sauce spread on top. The smell alone almost made me faint and my mouth watered as if my tongue had exploded. This was the closest thing to a Thanksgiving dinner I'd had in more than a decade. I quickly began unwrapping the sandwich, my fingers twitching with anticipation. It was when I momentarily glanced up that I noticed the middle-aged woman. She was walking towards us and, though it only took a millisecond, it was enough time for our eyes to lock. She quickly turned, as if she'd realized she had forgotten something and hurried across the street to retrieve it. My fingers slowed down like an engine sputtering out of gasoline.

"You okay?" asked Vince.

"Yeah."

"The sandwich is good. Eat before it gets cold."

I finished unwrapping the foil and bit into the pita. The sensation of warm food was wonderfully alien and, like one who speaks a foreign language for the first time, I had to get used to forming new chewing motions. I remembered how different it was to eat hot food. My mouth was quickly going through a type of unconscious physical therapy to remind me how to properly get the turkey to my stomach. But that wasn't what made me put the sandwich down.

"What's wrong?" Vince asked.

"I'm just not used to this place in the daytime. I'm not used to...to the people."

"Ignore 'em. That's what they do to you, isn't it?"

I snorted.

"What?" he said. "People ignore bums whenever they can. You think I didn't see that bag who wouldn't walk past us? But I would think you'd be able to tune her out the way she tuned you out."

"It doesn't happen like that. She didn't tune me out. She's probably still thinking about me."

"Aren't you flattering yourself a bit?"

"It's true. People feel guilty. They think they should help me — they feel obligated to do something."

"But you make your own way."

"That's right."

"So, why do you give a shit what other people think?"

"Because," I said, "there's no way around it. Their thoughts may stay with them for an hour, a day or may leave them as soon as they pass me, but they always occur. If you look in the people's eyes, you can see it.

17

Sometimes I feel as if I have a whole store of averted eyes in my mind which I could bring out and look at like the world's largest collection of marbles. And they're all the same. Behind each set is the same feeling of guilt. The truth is, I don't care if people pretend to ignore me. And I *don't* care what they think of me. I just care *that* they think of me."

Vince cocked his head. The sunlight reflected in his gel, giving his hair the appearance of ice-filled cracks in asphalt. He took a bite from his sandwich and, after chewing, said:

"There's not a lot you can do about it, is there, Birdman? It kind of comes with the territory."

"Yeah, I guess it does."

"Well, you're smart. You'll figure some way out."

"It hasn't happened yet. Not in ten years."

"That how long you been out here?"

"Yes."

He looked at me, up and down. His eyes scraped against my unshaven chin. They watered at the smell of the two mismatched shirts I wore. Over every inch of my body, his eyes roamed, probing like fingers reading Braille. They wondered about the blisters on my feet, how often I ate, what bathrooms I used, and what I did when a bathroom wasn't available. Vince looked at me as no one ever had — not with sympathy, but with genuine interest.

This was frightening and consoling at the same time. I imagined it was not unlike what the young boys on the street felt when the vans came around. Every winter night, city-funded vans cruise the streets in hopes of picking up homeless people and bringing them to the shelters. Some go, but many refuse out of fear. The young kids are the most scared. They know that no matter how cold it might be outside, and how hungry they may be, they're safer on the street than in some shelter where they might be raped or killed. It's not an irrational fear; it happens to the kids. They're defenseless against the bigger, stronger men. I've seen them refuse the van drivers with tears frozen in their eyes. They want to go; they want to believe they will be safe. But despite the guarantee that the pain of freezing and starving will stop, the possibility of a worse pain is enough to make them turn the vans away.

As I bit into the sandwich, I squirmed under Vince's gaze and saw many conflicts arising behind my own eyes. The most prevalent was the same that the young kids felt — the battle between the possible and the guarantee. I tried to fight it, but felt myself slipping. For reasons I wasn't yet aware of, Vince was tempting me and he was backing up his propositions with real guarantees. As I took another bite, I felt myself starting to give in to the guarantees, regardless of the promise I had made to myself ten years ago. I was astonished at my sudden irrational lack of will. I was astonished, too, at how good a turkey sandwich could taste.

Chapter Two
Sometimes You *Do* Need a Weather Vane
to Know Which Way the Wind Blows

It was night. Vince and I were heading for Union Square in Somerville where, presumably, he was going to show me a new place to hunt for pigeons. Usually, I don't travel far from Boston proper, as I can't afford to ride the T and the walk is too long; besides, there are enough pigeons in and around the downtown area. But Vince talked me into going to Somerville "for my own safety."

"I know that bastard Sid and, if he has to, he'll nail your ass to protect his own." We were driving in Vince's Lincoln, cruising down Massachusetts Ave. A little cut-out pine-tree deodorizer hung from the cigarette lighter, and a playing card with a naked woman where the Queen of Hearts should have been, dangled from the rearview mirror.

"He's connected," Vince continued. "When he gets it all sorted out — and he will — you'll have to be careful. He's not going to admit to anything, but the bottom line is, somebody's got to take the fall for his serving me that pigeon. So this time, he'll blame a busboy who conveniently happens to be in this country illegally. He'll say Pablo must've forged his papers. He'll tell 'em the little wetback tried to make some extra cash by buying some pigeon but lucky for everybody — 'cept of course Pablo — he got caught. That's a big enough bust for the fuckin' cops to be able to make a deal. 'Course, it's not like they don't know the real story. But if Sid can give them an illegal alien to fork over to the

Feds, the cops'll look like fuckin' All-American heroes, Sid'll be clear, and they'll all be in his back room drinking Chivas together next week. But you, my friend, will have to watch your ass. Keep outta sight. Because the cops aren't stupid. They'll have to start looking for you and your slingshot because, eventually, someone will end up worse than me and somebody else will have to catch shit for it."

He took a last drag on his cigarette and flicked it out the window. I watched as it trailed down the street like a small bottle rocket. We were passing through Central Square, a neighborhood which always looked as if fireworks were exploding from every crevice. Because of its wide diversity, this section of town used to remind me of New York City. Its one constant was an overwhelming sense of claustrophobia; everything was squeezed together, creating a visual cacophony. The shops pushed against each other like a line of children trying to fit into a school picture, and they resembled one another only in that each looked as if it belonged nowhere else. Economic outcasts, they took refuge together while selling a wide variety of merchandise and food. Unfinished furniture, used records, and cheap clothing stores, Indian restaurants, Asian restaurants, coffee houses — these were the staples of Central Square. Multi-colored awnings, like war-torn flags, hung over doors. Some were faded and ripped with their cloth tails wagging in the breeze. There were also bars and nightclubs, and the street poles were plastered with loud, overlapping colored signs, each one a child trying to out-scream the others in the street. These posters announced the bands that would play the various club stages, and were reinforced by placards in front of the bars which had cover charges, brands of beer, and schedules of afternoon sporting events scrawled in magic markers. This over-stimulation made Central Square a giant kaleidoscope that you didn't move, but rather moved through.

As we drove by a group of dread-locked men playing African drums in front of the glass doors to a bank's ATM machines, I asked Vince:

"You think I'm in danger?"

"I just think you need to expand your territory a little. At least for now."

"But I can't work out of Somerville."

He chuckled.

"Look, I know it's a step down from Back Bay, but who the fuck are you to be complaining? Beggars can't be choosers."

"I mean, I don't know anyone here. Who am I gonna sell to? I can't catch the pigeons and take them back to Boston."

Vince smiled.

"Don't worry, Birdy. I got friends."

We passed out of Central Square but its claustrophobia had hitched a ride.

———

There were a few reasons why I had allowed Vince to get close to me. I knew he had a motive and, while I didn't know what he wanted from me, I needed something from him.

Since that day he'd bought me lunch, Vince acted as if he were trying to gain an animal's trust. He'd appear every few days and buy me food or cigarettes. A few times he brought me soap, shampoo and razors and then paid for a room at the Y. I was able to get a good night's sleep and bathe in the morning.

One afternoon, we headed down Tremont Street towards Chinatown. As we walked, Vince probed for information while solidifying the hazy dependence I had begun to feel towards him. Crossing Boylston, we headed towards the theater district, meandering down the long gray block that used to be known as the Combat Zone, Boston's own little red-light district.

"It's a shame what they've done to this street," he said.

"What do you mean? They've gotten rid of all the X-rated bookstores and strip joints."

"Yeah. Now you gotta go all the way out to the fuckin' suburbs. And them places aren't as good as they were here. The girls are fat. And the peep shows are all pretty vanilla."

I kept quiet and Vince stopped and looked at me. Then he smiled.

"Don't tell me you never went in and checked it out?"

"Never did."

"Not even once?! I mean, I know you're on a limited budget, but you can see a movie for a quarter. Didn't you ever want to...I mean, at least once?"

"Well...I guess so. I just never...."

"Well, Birdy, there're still one or two places left. Here, look." We had stopped in front of a doorway that had three 'X"s over it and a neon sign in the shape of a woman which moved in colored robotic jerks: her legs closed in green and then opened in red. "You wanna go in? My treat."

I shuffled bashfully.

"I'll wait outside if you want," he offered.

"No. Thanks anyway, but...no."

"They got lesbian films. You know, a girl I once dated asked me why all guys get turned on by lesbians. You do, don't cha?"

"Sure."

"That's what I thought. All guys do. Well, I had a few lesbo flicks around the house, and this girl said,

'Vince, why don't you have any boy-girl movies?' So I told her to do the math."

"What math?"

"Figure it out, Birdman. Let's say a porno flick runs for one hour. And to make it easy, let's forget about any props or storylines. Just straight sex. Now, if you've got two or more chicks in it and no guys, you've got a full hour of naked girls going at it. But if you throw a guy in there, you've suddenly added a pussy-to-cock ratio where, before, you had a hundred per-cent pussy screen time. So in a one-hour boy-girl film, you've got thirty minutes of a naked chick and thirty minutes of a naked guy. And that's *minus* props and plot. It's simple economics."

"Supply and demand."

"Exactly. So, you wanna go in?"

"Maybe another time."

"You sure?"

"Yeah. But thanks all the same."

"Hey, my pleasure."

We walked on, taking a left into Chinatown where the crazy streets all seemed to begin and end at the same place and the tiny red, white and yellow shops all looked alike. I used to walk through Chinatown at night and, as I passed the restaurants with names like Wang's, Yum-Yum's, and Wu's, I wondered how non-Chinese patrons could tell them apart. I remembered telling one of my Chinese clients that if I owned his place, I would name it Antonio's so that it would stand out.

"What do you know about standing out?" he had snapped. "You blend in."

At the time, I had easily shrugged off his comment, but now I was confused at how the memory of it had stung.

Vince stopped in front of a small market. In the window, the bloodied, skinned bodies of five or six small ducklings hung on display. For a long time, he looked at the dead birds while I surveyed the street around us. The next morning must have been trash day because garbage-filled cardboard boxes lined the streets. At my feet lay a box of cabbage leaves, paper plates and damp, black mounds which I assumed were old tea grounds.

"Reminds me of this guy I once knew," Vince finally said.

I looked up.

"What, the dead ducks?"

"Yeah. This old bastard I did time with. In Walpole." My shoulders involuntarily shrugged and Vince added, "I hope you don't think any less of me."

"No. Not at all."

"I got caught stealing a car when I was seventeen," Vince explained as he walked away from the window. I took one last look at the ducks and then jogged to catch up with him.

"So what happened?"

"They put me in a lock-up for a few months, but I got into it with this kid from Southie just before they were gonna let me out. So, they gave me another few months. Then another fight. You know. By my eighteenth birthday, I was doing a two-year sentence."

"I was on the streets for three years when I was eighteen."

"No shit?"

"Yeah."

We continued on through Chinatown and passed under the multicolored archway at its main entrance.

"Anyway, this old guy named Clem had been locked up for about twenty-five years. Seriously. He'd been in

26

and out of jail all his life until he finally got caught for offing some guy. Bad scene. They put him away for life.

"I met Clem...it must have been in the mid-eighties. He was about fifty by that time. He pretty much ran the place — he had the respect from all the cons. He had this certain way about him...."

"What do you mean?"

"Well... Clem just seemed to belong in jail. I think he secretly liked it — the monotony, the routine. He didn't want change. He didn't want anything. I think even living or dying was all the same to him. Prison's the perfect place for a guy like that. Clem didn't give a shit so no one messed with him because if you *did* cross him, he had nothing to lose."

"You really think he preferred prison to freedom?"

"For some guys, prison is freedom," Vince said. "Clem was one of those guys."

We were at South Station now and were turning back towards Downtown Crossing. It was nearly five o'clock and the human river had started pouring into the South Station T stop.

"I remember one Saturday, the prison had a concert for us. We'd all been good — no riots or anything — so they had this local rock band come and play for us. Some band out of Boston. They were called Brian's Sandbox. I still remember the name because it was so strange. They were kids and they did all their own music. 'Course, Clem didn't give a shit about them, but he went out and listened for the fuck of it. Anyway, they did play a few songs by other people. The singer seemed to like Elvis Presley 'cause they played 'Heartbreak Hotel' and 'Jailhouse Rock,' although that might have been their idea of a dangerous joke. But Clem liked those tunes, and when they finished playing, he went to the front of the stage and requested a Bob Dylan song.

'Blowing in the Wind.' Jesus, you shoulda seen the expression on the singer's face. You could tell he knew the song, but not well enough to really play it. But Clem wasn't the kind of guy you said no to. So they struggled through it. The whole band sweated more on that one song than during their whole performance."

"Clem was happy. He told me later the song was timeless, but he didn't mean it in a way most people do when they talk about a song that way. Clem meant in a way that time didn't exist. He said it was timeless, like death, which was a pretty typical kind of thing for Clem to say."

Vince was silent for a few moments.

"Why did you remember Clem in front of that store?"

"Oh, no real reason. He used to love a good chicken dinner. The ducks reminded me of chickens in a way."

"I know what you mean."

Vince laughed.

"You should, Birdy. With your talents, I bet you could make any bird resemble a chicken."

"No," I said seriously, stopping near the benches where we had eaten the Thanksgiving wraps. "I mean I understand."

Vince sat down. As the sun started to fade, the streetlights popped on around us.

"Then, maybe I should call you Clem," he said.

Though it was my reflection in Vince's eyes, it was Clem I saw. Although I had never known the man, his ability to discern no difference between prison and freedom made him painfully familiar to me. Clem was personified in my shoes, which were a size too small, and the sooty rain that spilled over the balconies to cushion me from the sidewalk as I slept through a storm. I felt as I had at school, when the answer to a math problem miraculously revealed itself: the relief of finding the solution, along with the fear of losing whatever gift provided it. To me, this defined Clem's world and, on some visceral level, I felt I belonged to it.

Another streetlight popped on and I heard the sound. The *déjà vu* that never failed to accompany it shifted the gears of my mind. A pigeon which had been roosting on top of the light had been scared by the sudden surge of power and vibration, and took off in flight. Though that sound of wings beating the air still held an ugly memory for me, there was another force at work, holding a juxtaposition of optimism and despair. In vain, I searched Vince's face for a sign of possible relief, and although I was unsure how to read him, I finally said:

"My name's Colin."

Vince just nodded.

I was grateful that Vince never called me by my given name. He understood I had run from something — he didn't know from what, but that wasn't important. We all have a back story, a past which we may not think much about if we've done nothing to be ashamed or proud of. Still it lurks in our history with the power to emote Time. Whether we agonize over the past, fear the present or dread the future, we do so because our history is irrevocable. Vince was smart enough to see this. He realized that any homeless person who wasn't retarded or a drunk was on the street for a reason, and as that reason must be powerful, there were many ways to channel that power.

I had done a fairly good job of burying my past. For ten years, my only connection with society had been selling pigeons to fancy restaurants that would, in turn, pass them off as squab. I was able to tolerate this connection because there had been a clear distinction —

I caught pigeons, sold them, and a transformation that I never saw, was made. Once the birds left my hands, they ceased being pigeons. I never witnessed what the restaurants did with them; I only knew that somehow they were changed and sold as squab. For me, this change was like emotional plastic surgery. It allowed me to detach myself from the entire transaction and negate the human contact. This was my survival tactic.

However, when Vince appeared, the distinction dissipated. I was forced to acknowledge my interactions with society because, in Vince, I was suddenly faced with the pigeon *and* the squab. Before, I just saw the present, but now I saw the *result* of the present. It was only logical that, eventually, my past would find me.

And so, I needed to go back, and the way to do this was to put the idea of a pigeon in one place and a squab in another and view them separately. I would then understand the transformation enough to put it all out of sight. There are two ways to completely dismiss an experience. One is by never encountering it, and the other is by having an encounter so intimate that every variable is known. Then the experience can be tossed aside without question.

As the person who had already exposed me to some of these unwanted variables, I felt Vince would be able to give me the insight I needed. My existence would never be perfect again, but it would work. Vince had the experience of both the before and after, the pigeon and the squab, and I resolved to do whatever was necessary to gain this experience. It was the only way I could get back. It was my only chance for survival.

We parked on the street in Union Square. It was late enough where we didn't have to find a space as much as

choose the closest one to our destination. After I closed
the car door, Vince aimed the little black box on his key
chain at the car and pressed a button. The door locks
shrugged downward as the two-note alarm squeaked.

Vince started walking across the street towards a
row of darkened storefronts. I followed him, realizing
that one of the stores was, in fact, a Chinese restaurant.
We went up to the window and Vince looked at the
menu taped to the inside of the glass.

"You thinking about Clem again?"

"Yeah," he said. "A little."

He ran his finger down the glass, listing the various
dishes as he went. He started with the poultry, "Curry
Chicken, Chicken and Bamboo Shoots, General Gau's
Chicken..." and then went to seafood, "Spicy Seabass,
Hot and Sour Shrimp, Octopus...," and continued until
he reached the end. Skipping the wine list, he started
back at the top and surprised me as he read:

"Shiang hi chee, Woo sha moo, Gon gon ding wong...."

"I didn't know you spoke the language."

He chuckled.

"What makes you think I do?"

Confusion tripped from my mouth but Vince cut off
my stammering.

"Did you ever take Chinese in school, Birdy?"

"No. It wasn't offered at my school."

"Really? You know, that always amazes me. There's
over a billion fuckin' Chinese people in this world. More
people speak Chinese than any other language. But they
don't teach it in school. Why do you suppose?"

I shrugged.

"I took Latin."

"Latin?" His frown was stunned, but amused.
"Lemme ask you this, Birdy. When was the last time —
apart from maybe being in church — that you actually

spoke Latin? I mean have you ever *used* it? Did it ever come in handy, for instance, when you had to order from a menu?"

His grin was teasingly malicious.

"No...it was a requirement at my high school. Latin and French."

"What about Spanish?"

"You could take Spanish instead of French, if you wanted."

"Spanish is the second most spoken language. Think where you'd be today if you could speak it. But you only *parlez-vous* a language spoken by the Pope and a few guys at the Mint. Hey, maybe there's a coincidence there," he laughed.

"Maybe. But you're right. Neither one of them has gotten me anywhere."

Vince returned to his original thought.

"Birdy, if you could speak Chinese, you would know that I was talking gibberish."

"That wasn't really Chinese?"

"Come on. I barely fuckin' speak English."

"So...."

"So, that's my point."

Vince put his arm around me and we walked over and sat on a bench pock-marked with initials, misspelled graffiti and hardened bird droppings. In front of us, a solitary blinking traffic light panted like a trick candle.

Vince continued:

"Obviously, you're an educated guy. At least more than me. And you couldn't tell the difference between real Chinese and gibberish. Well, how many other people you think are in the same boat?"

"I don't know. Probably — "

"Probably fucking all of them. Except for the Chinese people. You go into a Chinese or Spanish or French restaurant and people are speaking a different language, ya gotta assume they're speaking in the same language that's written on the sign out front."

"I suppose. But...so what?"

Vince snarled.

"The 'so what' is this — you've been doing the same thing with your pigeon routine. You see, it's all illusion, isn't it? You don't speak Chinese, so when I start clucking in front of a menu, you think I'm fuckin' Chiang Kai-shek. Me, I go into a restaurant and order squab. I ain't never eaten Boston pigeon before, but with the right sauce and atmosphere, I may as well be overlooking the Riviera with a fuckin' accordion playing in the background."

I shuddered and tried to draw away. Vince relaxed his grip and laughed.

"Don't sweat, Birdman. You think I wasted all this time with you just so I could off you in Somerville? Jesus. I was just illustrating the possibilities."

"Which are?"

"That things aren't always as they appear." My eyes twitched and Vince stood and patted me on the back. "Come on. I'll show you."

I followed him across the street towards the car. Panting flashes of caution lit our way.

Chapter Three
I Used To Be Somebody

When I was a kid, I felt guilty because my family had money. We weren't rich, but we were very well off and, at an early age, I was conscious that I had a different place in the world from the majority of my friends. Even though it would be years before I understood the concept of money, I had a visceral sense that we had "more" than others.

The obvious big things, such as my father being a surgeon, didn't really make an impact on me. Every evening, he drove his Mercedes up our long driveway, walked in and put his leather briefcase on the marble countertop. I would jump up so he could kiss me, and he would playfully rub his cheek against mine, like sandpaper against dough, and ask me about school while he kissed my mother hello. We would stand in the open kitchen as my mother stirred the simmering pots and told us dinner was almost ready. Then, I'd follow Dad into the den where he'd make a drink at the small wet bar, turn on the national news, and listen to Tom Brokaw while he opened his stack of mail. I'd always watch for him to momentarily look up from some long, meaningless sheet of paper at the mention of the day's stock market report. I liked to try to guess whether his eyebrows would wrinkle into a frown or raise with interest. But these events held no real significance for me because, as a child, I had nothing to compare them with. I didn't know the difference between a Mercedes or a Ford, or a leather briefcase or one made from vinyl, and I gave no more thought to these nightly rituals than I did to blinking my eyes. It was the smaller things which held importance for me. Events such as Christmas.

My best friend in the neighborhood was a boy named Josh. We went to school together and were inseparable. Josh's father sold insurance and his mother worked in a dress store. Their house was always neat and orderly as if they didn't live there but instead locked the door when no one was looking and went somewhere else to preserve the museum–like semblance. There was something almost antiseptic about the house. We'd make a sandwich and instantly wipe up any crumbs; we'd put toys away as soon as they were played with; even outside, we'd carefully line up our bikes like dominos in the driveway.

Josh's family had an artificial tree which they assembled each Christmas. Though I thought it detracted from the holiday spirit, it did maintain the cleanliness of the house — no stray needles were sprinkled on the carpet in Josh's living room. His house was always elegantly, although conservatively, decorated. Rows of lights were strung on the bushes with obsessive precision while each window held an electric candle that maintained a perfectly glowing vigil. Glass bowls of candies sat on the end tables in the living room and Christmas cards were displayed around these bowls like floral arrangements. The artificial tree was the real centerpiece, though. During the year, I would occasionally see it in a box in the cellar with its amputated limbs sticking out like oversized pipe cleaners. But at Christmas, it was fastidiously trimmed and stood in the center of a campfire of gifts, all wrapped in an array of colored paper and bows. It was the mythical cake that looked too good to eat.

Our house was a different story — one of opulence and chaos. We always had a huge, live tree. Around it, seemingly hundreds of gifts lay, all wrapped in two or three kinds of paper. Because there were always so many presents, my mother bought paper in bulk, and the two or three patterns she would purchase added to the illusion of overindulgence. While there *were* more gifts under my tree, there were only a few styles of paper, and this added up to what appeared to be an even larger amount of presents.

So, I started to understand the idea of *more*. Even though my family was not snobbish and we didn't flaunt our money, it became apparent that we were better off than most people I knew. This somehow set us apart from other families — in a sense, I felt poorer than many of my friends. The day our house was blown up, I knew for certain how poor we were.

––––––––––

We weren't home, but that was the whole point. Gillatano, the woman who paid to have our house blown to bits, knew we were skiing in Park City, Utah.

I used to be a great skier. This was because I was tall *and* had grown up skiing. To really be a good skier, you have to "grow up" doing it, like ice-skating or swimming. You start just after you begin walking, and by the time you're five or so, you're zipping down the hill, scaring the hell out of adult beginners. My family went to Park City each year, usually during my February school break, so I was quite proficient at the sport from an early age.

I had a great time pulling daredevil stunts. I would fly down the mountain and aim for an adult learner, then delight in his panic as he slipped and slid in an attempt to get out of my way. To add to the fun, I'd expertly veer off just in time to avoid him as he fell over, face first, into the snow. It gave me enormous pleasure knowing I could ski better than so many of my elders.

But what gave me even more pleasure was that my dad would always get in on this act. After the guy fell, Dad would ski over and tell him not to worry because he was a doctor. He would make the guy lie still while he pretended to exam him. After about ten minutes, he'd let the guy get up — all wet and cold — and tell him he'd be okay and that he just sustained a snowjob.

We would only pull this routine once each year because we didn't want to piss off too many people. And it didn't detract from the fun in the least if Dad bought the guy a drink afterwards or, if he was *really* mad, dinner. For me, "snowing" a guy was the highlight of our vacation. I felt so close to my father as we plotted together on the airplane. He'd sit with me and, together, we'd plan who our victim would be. As we decided the characteristics of the snowee, Dad would jot it all down in a small, brown notebook.

"What about a fat guy?"

"Yeah!" I'd enthuse. "With a really stupid hat!"

"Good idea, Cole. I'll mark it down," and Dad would nod, repeating the words "stupid hat," as he wrote them. Then he'd ask, "What color?"

"I don't think it matters, as long as it's really dumb-looking. Like with a big pom-pom on top."

"You mean like a little kid's hat?"

"Maybe — oh, how 'bout a big ski mask?" I'd suggest.

"Ooh, I like that." My dad rubbed his chin in thought. "Something a jewel thief might wear. Something that the guy *thinks* looks good, but really makes him look like he just saw snow for the first time."

"Perfect!" I'd laugh because, of course, it was. Dad knew what to look for in amateurs, and there were always so many amateurs out there to pick from.

"Like shooting fish in a barrel," he would say.

We would have the entire plan in place before we landed. Dad had all the details written down and even a list of dinner entrees we might offer the man afterwards. I could hardly contain myself as we hit the slopes and began looking for our unsuspecting target. But what I liked most about it wasn't my part in the scheme, but rather my dad's role. The complete confidence the fat guy would have in the surgeon who had come to his aid, then the anger he would show at being snowed, and then the relief of realizing there was nothing wrong with him and finally his jovial attitude when he was offered his free drink. I marveled at how my dad could conjure all these emotions in a stranger in only a matter of seconds. With a few words, he could completely enrapture a person, totally altering their feelings. It reminded me of when he listened to the news, and looked up at the mention of the Dow Jones. I felt as if my father possessed the power of Tom Brokaw.

Dad was funny and generous. In many ways, he was like a big kid and he had a way of treating us as if we were all in a club together, with him as the undisputed leader. I remember when Josh and I had taken an interest in biology. After doing some reading, I caught a frog and we sat on the lawn in my backyard, debating whether to dissect it.

"It's gross!"

"No it's not. I read about it in a science book. You can see all the insides and stuff. They even show you where to cut."

Josh wasn't quite convinced.

"I don't know. I don't think the frog would like it."

"You kill the frog first, ya jerk."

"How do you kill it?" Josh asked as his eyes expanded with guilt and fear.

"Well..., the book says it's painless. You just stick a needle in the back of its head. It dies instantly."

As I said this, I could feel the pin penetrating my own scalp, and quickly rubbed the vicarious sensation away.

Dad came outside. He looked at the frog squirming in my slimy hands and the scalpel from my biology set lying in the grass.

"What are you guys doing?"

"We were gonna dissect this frog and learn how it all works."

"That's very studious of you." He looked from me to Josh and to the frog, then sat down in the warm grass. He was wearing shorts and, as he sat, the hair on his legs flattened like tiny, coiled snakes. "If you're really interested in biology, you'll want to start early. Dissection is important — I'm glad you guys are gonna get used to it all now."

Josh's face turned in contemplation.

"What do you mean, 'get used to it,' Dr. Franklin?"

"Oh, I was just thinking back to my first time in the O.R., Josh," Dad laughed. "I didn't realize there'd be so much blood when I sliced the guy open. Lucky for him, I turned my head before I threw up. 'Course the nurse next to me wasn't so fortunate...."

I swallowed hard, trying to keep myself steady. I was thirsty for air and I started to sweat. I knew if my Dad kept talking, I would throw up right then.

"Tell you what," Dad continued. "I'll make the first few incisions, just to start it, then you can take over. How 'bout that?"

He reached over for the scalpel. Josh's eyes were trembling and his face turned to porcelain.

"Well...I don't know, Dad.... Maybe you shouldn't...."

"It's no problem. Come on, give me the knife. Don't worry. I'll let you two have your fun. Cole — you jab the sucker in the head with the pin."

I began to loosen my grip on the frog. Dad smiled and stood up, releasing the snakes as his shadow eclipsed us.

"I'll be right back," he said, and jogged into the house.

We just sat there. I opened my hands further and the frog poked his head out. Its skin was sticky as the slickness had dried quickly under the hot, summer sun. Dad came back holding a small glass jug. As he came closer, I saw what looked like a still replica of the frog in my hands, but its body was translucent and it was floating in a yellowish liquid.

"This was a science project I did way back in high school," Dad said. "By taking a frog that's already dead and putting it into a mixture of chemicals, the skin eventually peels away and you can see inside without having to cut it open. After I did this, I realized that I wanted to be a doctor."

Josh smiled.

"Look at that, Colin. That's cool!'

Dad handed him the jar.

"It's also lucky for the guy in your hands, Cole. Just don't take the cover off, guys. It's full of formaldehyde, and you don't want to touch that."

As Josh took the jar and turned it around and around, I let the live frog hop out of my hands.

"Thanks, Dad."

"Sure thing. After all, why cut up a perfectly good frog when you don't have to?"

41

Dad smiled again, and we looked at the bottled specimen from a variety of angles. Meanwhile, the live frog made its escape.

———

One night close to my fifteenth birthday, the police called the house to inform us that Dad had been arrested. As my mother listened, her face twisted around the phone receiver like clay in an angry child's hands. Then she hung up the phone and became an efficient blur. She quickly called my aunt to drive her to the police station and then filled a large envelope with money she retrieved from a small safe hidden in Dad's office. A mechanical precision had overcome her. I wanted her to scream, to cry, to offer some evidence that the world had not suddenly stopped spinning. But her enforced grimness wouldn't let go of her. *Like death*, I thought. *This must be what it's like when you're dead.*

I had no idea what was wrong. I only knew my father was in trouble. Recent hushed conversations between my parents had produced a spider's web of expectancy over our house. Now the trap held us all.

The next morning moved in a slow-motion rehearsal of every other morning. Each aspect — from the way Mom made breakfast to the manner in which Dad walked into the kitchen — was caked with a heavy theatrical make-up. It was surreal. We were both the actors and the audience. My mother, in her floral-print flannel dressing gown, stirred the oatmeal just fast enough to keep it from burning. Dad tried to say something to her, but the only sign of recognition she gave were silent tears that dripped into the pot. He sat next to me.

"'Morning, Cole," he recited.

"Hi Dad."

"Colin...listen...."

He was struggling with his lines. As if to get a cue from my Mom, Dad stopped and glanced quickly towards her. But she walked out of the kitchen, leaving the wooden spoon leaning in the oatmeal on a slow moving tilt.

"Cole. Last night, there was an...incident."

"I know. You weren't here and Mom got a call, then left with some money."

"Yeah, that's right. Now, listen carefully. You're going to hear a lot of...a lot of stuff over the next few weeks, or maybe even a little longer."

"Like what?"

"Well, you're going to hear lies about me. And I know it's going to be hard, but I need you to try to ignore them. Just try not to listen."

"What sort of lies, Dad?"

He sighed heavily so that his cheeks puffed out.

"People are going to...accuse me of some things. They may even ask you what you know about it. But just don't pay attention, okay son?"

"All right. But...what's going on, Dad?"

The disappointment on his face was similar to that which surfaced when I would show him a bad report card. But strangely, his expression was not meant for me.

"People are going to say that I did some things which were wrong; things about my work. But I want you to understand that they don't know the truth and won't know it for some time. So you have to be tolerant of them. You have to realize that...the things they'll say are just things that they've heard. They're all rumors...lies."

I was frightened — not because of what my father was saying, but by the tone he used, the voice reserved for conversation with adults. He wasn't the club leader now; we were no longer in the same club. We were

43

displaced peers and our conversation held a bit of the "father and son" tone that was overshadowed by an unexpected role reversal. My father wasn't lecturing me as much as he was confessing, and I wasn't questioning him as much as trying to believe he was innocent of whatever he had been accused of.

The doorbell rang. Dad looked at me for another moment with strained reassurance, and then went to the door. His old friend Mr. Peterson was standing there. The two whispered in the hallway, and then Mr. Peterson said, "Are you ready to go?"

My Dad answered yes, and they left the house. I wondered why Mr. Peterson wasn't at work. I only saw him when he and Dad played golf. But now I watched from the dining room window as the two of them got into his car and drove away. My dad was carrying his briefcase with him, not his golf clubs. Besides, he only played on Friday afternoons when he didn't have any patients to see and when Mr. Peterson wasn't in court. My dad's friend was a lawyer, and the two had known each other for many years. Mr. Peterson and his wife would frequently come over for dinner, and he and Dad would tell us about the various stunts they'd pulled when they had been college roommates.

As I watched them drive away, I couldn't help but hope that this was some stunt, too. Some crazy, intricately plotted game involving both my parents and Mr. Peterson. My birthday was coming up — was this all meant to throw me off the trail; was this going to culminate in some big surprise?

The answer came to me in the sound of the newspaper slapping on the cement porch step. The paper boy — the kid who had, over the years, delivered stories of war in unpronounceable countries, natural disasters and corrupt city, state and national politicians, seemingly without paying attention to the headlines at all — lingered in our driveway after the paper had hit the porch and produced that sound which I still hear in the flapping of wings. Then he saw me in the window and he sped away on his bike. I went to retrieve the paper. As I did so, I noticed the wooden spoon had completed its descent and was smothered by the ruined breakfast.

———————

I was greeted by a slight chill that intensified as my bare feet touched the cold, cement porch. The newspaper was upside down on the step, and I quickly picked it up and then hopped back inside, shutting the door on the frigid, outside world. I carried the paper upside down, afraid to turn it over or even look at it. My stomach felt like a sack filled with nausea. Finally, I made it to the kitchen table and sat down but as I reached to turn the paper over, it flew up in the air, as if by witchcraft.

"You're not to read this paper, Colin," said my mother. She had crept into the kitchen and had snatched the newspaper away from me. There were three sections to it, but she crumpled all the day's news as easily as if she were kneading a meatloaf. "This is garbage. You're not to look at it."

But I saw a copy at school. It was almost impossible to comprehend — my Dad's picture on the front page and the story printed about him. The kids at school seemed to be in shock, and didn't say much. Whenever I came near, they grew silent, as if I were walking away rather than towards them. After a few days of this, Christmas break started and, for the first time, my parents decided to go to Utah for the holiday. It was my first Christmas away from home, and the usual warm holiday spirit was shrouded in an unnatural loneliness, like wearing a stranger's favorite clothes. But it would turn out to be even lonelier as it would be my last Christmas with my family. We received a phone call on Christmas Day from Mr. Peterson, and had to fly back immediately to the twisted, crumbling debris which had been our house. Gillatano had admitted to blowing it up and, as a result, she would sit and die in the same jail as my father.

——————

These memories of long ago were a stark contrast to the realities of the present. Vince had driven me to a dilapidated housing project. The image of closing the front door to my childhood home was still at the forefront of my mind as Vince unlocked a dark, veneer door and gestured for me to enter the apartment. The main room was nearly bare. Some of the strips of paneling were pulled slightly away from the walls, exposing tiny finishing nails or, in some places, pinprick holes from where the nails had long vanished. A small, cracked window faced Somerville Avenue, and the view was partially obscured by a tattered cloth that was taped above it and served as a curtain. Jutting from underneath this cloth was a broken curtain rod that dangled like a fractured limb towards the linoleum floor. Dim light peeked in from a street lamp and hinted at the dark squalor of the apartment.

In the far corner was the bathroom, with a rusty toilet and a leaky sink that clung desperately to the wall. Opposite the bathroom was a Formica table and a counter littered with empty beer cans and dirty utensils. Other than that, the room was barren, except for a mattress on the middle of the floor and an old black-and-white TV set with a shaky picture that blared the white-noise hiss of static. The TV sat on top of a wooden crate with a cheap VCR inside the box. Vince went over and turned the set off.

"You can stay here."

"Whose place is it?" I asked, hopeful yet uneasy.

"You saw me unlocking the door, didn't ya?"

"Yeah, but...."

I looked at the now-silent television set.

"Don't worry. I let Domingo stay here."

"Who's Domingo?"

"Domingo works for me."

"What does he do?"

"Listen, Birdy, ask him yourself when he gets back. He probably went to the packy. And lucky for you, Domingo took English in high school. Latin. Fuckin' Christ. I'll see you later."

Vince left the apartment. He gave no further instructions, but he knew he'd find me whenever he returned. Where else would I go?

Chapter Four

Working for the Man

M y eyes had to adjust to the apartment. Various images from it — floorboards, the windows, the corners where the ceiling met the walls — surged and receded in a hazy tide and I felt as if the place might vanish around me like an interrupted dream. It wasn't just the physical structure that was so disorienting but the emotions that clung to the place like pictures hanging on the walls. This was a home, something I'd not been in for a decade. And Vince was allowing me to live here.

On every level, this meant more than an occasional room at the Y. Vince was further sucking me into whatever plan he had, and while part of me was grateful for the initial benefits, I knew that the further I went, the harder I'd need to work to get out. As I walked about the room, the sound of Vince saying "beggars can't be choosers" rang in my mind with bronzed irony.

By most standards the apartment was decrepit, but it enveloped me in a type of warmth that I'd forgotten existed. I'd been on the street for so long that I had developed a perpetual chill. I had always attributed it to my physical homelessness, but once the reality that this room was mine to live in had solidified, I understood the emotional aspect of it. As I walked through the room, the chill began to slip away from me like a coat shrugged from my shoulders. In its place came warmth and, like the change of seasons, its appearance was both astonishingly slow and quick.

Conflict raced a collision course around my head. This was a sanctuary; I was suffocating. The walls were protecting me; the walls were closing in on me. The ceiling would keep off the rain; the ceiling would fall down on me in my sleep. And yet, there was a comforting familiarity to the apartment which I had felt when crossing its threshold. I had stepped into another world, but it wasn't an entirely new one. With nostalgic cajolery, Vince had brought me back to the joys of my childhood.

Finally, the room stopped swimming and I was able to take in its details. My eyes settled on a brown dial on the wall. After a moment of wonder, I remembered what a thermostat was, along with the luxury of having control over the temperature. I touched it, feeling the power in my fingers as I turned the dial. I listened to the heat that I conjured, obediently crackling through the pipes and radiators.

After a few revolutions with the dial, I sought out the bathroom. Not the *facilities* which some of my clients had graciously let me use. There were no signs on the wall, no graffiti, no pink liquid soap in a plastic pump. There was only the decadent privacy of a toilet seat that hadn't known every ass in the city. The towel hanging to dry would be cleaned rather than tossed into a large plastic container. But most wondrous of all — the strongest personification of home I'd seen that night — was the single toothbrush nestled in a chipped porcelain holder. I gently touched its bristles but quickly pulled my fingers away as if I'd been shocked by an electric current. They were still damp! This wasn't like the dried-up, abandoned toothbrushes I had occasionally fished out of the garbage. It had recently cleaned the teeth of this person Domingo, the man who lived here, who used this bathroom, who called this apartment home.

Undoubtedly, I would soon see this Domingo. I would watch him eat. Then I would see him cleaning his teeth and, later, he would use the bathroom, completing the cycle. The idea of sharing in the digestive process this way uncovered a layer of human contact I hadn't known for ten years. Images of other possibilities began to call out to me like children playing hide and seek. Watching television, after-dinner conversations, sleeping safely — these had all been extravagances in which I hadn't indulged since my youth. But they were indelible parts of this apartment, like the paint on the walls or the tiles in the floor. Furthermore, the lack of all companionship, which I'd sought out and embraced, was unnatural in the apartment. As I stood in that one room, I felt like a ghost haunting my childhood.

My thoughts were still on the toothbrush when I walked out of the bathroom and looked in awe at the floor in front of me. If the toothbrush embodied home, the bare mattress in the middle of the floor summed up all the comforts of that home. It was a magnificent sight, like the first glimpse of a sunrise. Tentatively, I walked around it, like a sniffing dog, before carefully lying down.

Unused to such a soft resting place, my back screamed in pain for a good five minutes. My spine felt as if it had been fused to accommodate park benches, and as I lay there, I thought my bones would break from the comfort. Though the mattress smelled of stale beer and urine, for once I wasn't lying directly in the filth. I hovered elegantly above it, and that feeling frightened me. That I felt above something, even the dirt on the sidewalk, heightened my sense of the unnatural. I never wanted to be anything — not above or below, better or worse. But this desire was suddenly overruled by my inability to relinquish the soothing relief the bed was now providing.

I heard a police car passing outside. As it approached, its siren built in pitch and volume, stirring up fragments of self-doubt in the wake of its aural wind tunnel. These doubts rained down like the last remnants of a tickertape parade and, when they had settled, I looked over the empty, littered path I'd chosen and, for the first time, wondered if perhaps I had gone too far.

I was astounded by how quickly my world had changed, dizzyingly rocking on its axis in a struggle between the direction I'd been heading for ten years and Vince's version of magnetic north. But before I could think it through anymore, the door crashed open. I must have dozed, as my immediate fear was that an angry landlord had caught me sleeping on his steps. I jumped up to see a thick, brownish man with almond eyes and black hair, standing in the doorway. He was wearing a multicolored short-sleeved shirt, and a brown paper bag was pressed into the folds of the brightly striped cotton.

"What's this?" he shouted, in a swollen Hispanic accent.

"Domingo?"

His eyes narrowed as he lowered his bag.

"Who are you?"

"I'm a friend of Vince's. He let me in."

"No friend of Vince would be sleeping in my bed. And no friend of Vince would turn off my television. Why do you turn off my television?"

I looked at the corner where the silent wavy TV had been blaring. Domingo began to hop up and down, like a small child, and started to yell: "Turn it on! Turn it on!"

I had been stealthily moving towards the corner of the apartment opposite Domingo. But now, to quiet this lunatic, I ran towards the television set and pulled at the small metal knob, feeling the same confused nostalgia between my fingers. As the set hummed and crackled, I moved the knob all the way to the right. The humming got louder, and I saw a yellowish-orange light growing brighter through the plastic grates in the back of the TV. Then the picture came on; it was a test pattern that shook uncontrollably. The humming was now overpowered by the sound of white noise, a loud persistent rush of gravelly wind.

As the television came to life, Domingo slumped down in front of the doorway. He took a six-pack of beer from his bag, opened a can and began drinking, never once taking his eyes from the television. Then he started rocking slowly, like a toddler with his teddy bear. For a solid five minutes — during which I slowly retreated back to my corner — Domingo did nothing but drink and watch the TV.

Then he spoke.

"Have you ever been to Aruba?"

His sudden complacency lent the nonchalance of his question an even more unsettling air. His eyes never left the TV screen and his tone sounded as if he were conversing with a longtime friend. I squeezed myself into the corner as far as I could so that the opposing walls pressed my shoulders inwards.

"No," I answered.

"Nice. You should go to Aruba. Everybody should go," he said. "Maybe not everybody should stay."

He shuddered and rocked urgently, as if he were trying to move closer to the television. Then he opened another beer.

"Are you from Aruba?" I asked.

He looked at me for the first time.

"*Si*. But no more. In Aruba, the *agua* was good."

Then he turned back to the TV. I allowed myself to slide carefully to the floor as I contemplated this comment. I was used to seeing all sorts of people muttering to themselves in the streets. There was even one guy

53

who hung around the Public Garden, "feeding" the bronze ducks which stand in tribute to Robert McCloskey's *Make Way For Ducklings*. But I've always been able to stay away from these people whereas Domingo, who sat in front of the doorway with his beer, didn't allow me this option.

So I tried to make friends with him. A few weeks earlier, while dozing under a tree in the Common, I happened to overhear two businessmen discussing a vacation one had taken to the island. He was telling his friend that Aruba has the second-largest desalinization plant, next to Saudi Arabia, and the water tasted terrific. I thought that might be a way of starting a conversation with the lunatic, and perhaps engaging him to the point where he would move away from the door and I could get the hell out of there.

"Is the water *really* that good, Domingo?" I asked.

He screwed his head towards me and grimaced.

"The *agua* was very good! The *agua* saved my life!"

"Then I guess the coffee is great," I tried.

Domingo's face swelled unevenly like asphalt patches over potholes. He pried his eyes from the screen.

"Who are you? What are you doing here?!"

"I told you. I'm a friend of Vince's."

"Vince would never bring someone like you here. The water could have taken me but it brought me back! And you laugh!"

He started to get up, swaying from the influence of the beer or, perhaps, the hypnotic lines on the TV. As he staggered toward me, he reached into his pocket and pulled out what looked like a rusted spike with a prong sticking from it. He raised the spike above his head and lunged at me, but then his eyes were arrested with a momentary glare of surprise and anger. With the jerk of a Styrofoam cup caught in the wind, Domingo violently darted forwards and then back as his foot caught on the corner of the mattress. He hit the floor, knocking his head on the hard tiles.

I held my breath and looked at his chest. It was rising and falling and I was afraid he might be pretending to be unconscious. But then I noticed the blood trickling down his cheek. His head lay next to the mattress, and poking through the faded material was a bent, metal coil.

I sat shivering as Domingo's blood seeped past his ear and mixed with his thick black hair. It reminded me of pigeon blood sticking to feathers. Cautiously, I moved closer and saw that the cut was superficial and that he was out cold. With the spike balanced haphazardly across his limp fingers, Domingo looked like a man resigned to crucifixion.

I picked up the rusty spike and examined it. Long-ago images of Neptune's staff bubbled up in my mind, and I realized it was a fisherman's gaff, used for hauling a struggling fish into a boat. Its prong was almost completely rusted off, but there was still enough of it left to do serious harm. Had Domingo not tripped, the gaff would have peeled through my chest.

I tossed the spike towards the door and then studied Domingo. His mouth was open and his breathing was heavy. A small residue of beer foam had collected in the corners of his lips and, along with his wispy mustache and black eyes, it gave Domingo the appearance of a rat. Something about his hands caught my eye. I noticed his palms were covered with long, curling scars. They twisted viciously through his skin like a mass of clogged tunnels.

As I studied the Aruban, I heard the doorknob turn and Vince walked in. He looked casually at Domingo. "I hope you didn't kill him. He's your partner."

Vince walked to the television and turned it off. The room filled with the sound of Domingo's breathing. He seemed to be gurgling.

"I think he's dreaming." Vince noticed the gaff on the floor and bent down to pick it up. He tapped it against his palm, like a bored cop playing with his nightstick. "He told you about Aruba, didn't he?"

"Yeah."

Vince walked over and sat down on the mattress, between Domingo and me.

"Domingo was a fisherman in Aruba. You know them movies when they talk about 'his father was a fisherman, and his father before him?' Same thing with Domingo. For most of his life that was all he knew. Like his father, he married a local girl who just about nagged him to death. And just like his father, he spent all day on the fuckin' beach, casting out his line and hoping to catch enough to sell at the market with something left over for his supper. And then at night, just like his father and his father before him, he went home to his wife who would nag him until she got tired of nagging and fell asleep."

"So, what he'd do, run away?"

"Actually, you could say Domingo was pulled away."

"Pulled…?"

Vince glanced down at the gaff, as if he were suddenly aware that he held it in his hand.

"The cops will always tell you there are two sides to everything. The same thing's true about the island of Aruba. You know the beaches they advertise, the beautiful weather? That's one side. It's the other side they don't show you."

I used to lurk in front of a downtown travel agency to look at those posters. During the winter, especially, I would gaze at the tropical get-aways for hours before finding the warmest possible place to spend the night. It was exquisite torture, like the smell of warm muffins from a bakery, but it always provided me with much-needed support. Those large photos reinforced the fact that one of two things would happen — either I would find warmth or I would eventually die. This cold reality provided the harsh but reassuring outcome that, either way, I would have relief. I never needed to worry about *when* the weather would turn warm — in the present, you can't worry about the *when* of anything. The fact was, the weather would change. If I were still alive when it did, I would enjoy the sun but if I died, my suffering would also come to an end. In most situations, I've found the *if* to be more comforting than the *when*; it makes getting through the *now* easier.

Domingo began to groan and I moved away from him. Vince knelt down and put his hands on Domingo's bulging shoulders.

"Hey Dommy, wake up. It's Vince. Wake up."

Domingo's groans turned to a sudden sputtering, gagging sound. His head jerked about and he seemed to be spitting out air. Vince held him down the way I'd seen cops restraining violent drunks.

"It's okay, Domingo...hey Dommy, it's all right."

Domingo relaxed and looked up at the ceiling.

"I was dreaming."

"I know."

"But why?"

"'Cause you were asleep, Dommy."

"*Si*, but...."

And then he looked over at me, and his mouth twisted like a dishrag.

"It was him! What he said about the water!"

Vince held him tightly.

"It's okay, Domingo. Listen...it's okay. Birdy didn't know."

Domingo suddenly went stiff, as if his blood had turned to cement.

"Birdy?"

"Yeah. This is the Birdman. Birdy, come say hello to Domingo."

I moved over slowly.

"You are Birdy? You *like* birds?"

"Yes," I said, taking cues from Vince.

"I mean, you like what they stand for?"

Vince nodded and I agreed again.

"Birds are freedom," Domingo stated.

"Yes they are," I agreed.

"Because in Aruba, where the water is rough, it was the birds that delivered me."

I looked at Vince, but he just nodded, and I let Domingo continue.

"Where the water is rough, the undertow can come up at any time and drag a man out to sea. Every year, four...five fishermen drown like this. Their lines get tangled, and they know they shouldn't tempt fate, but they do anyway. They go out into the water to untangle their lines, and then the undertow comes. If you ever go to Aruba, you can see the dogs of these drowned fishermen. The mutts run back and forth at the place where their masters were pulled to their death. The dogs eventually go crazy and they die of starvation while they wait for their masters to come back."

"Dommy, that's not what happened to you though, was it? You lived."

"*Si*, I lived."

"Domingo was on the other side of the island — the rough side they don't talk about — and he snagged a big fish. He wrestled with the bastard for three hours, finally tiring it out enough so he could reel him in. He almost got the fish to shore, then he waded out — just up to his knees — to gaff the fucker with this little guy."

Vince raised the gaff slowly.

"*Si*, the fucker. He felt the spike in him and decided maybe he had a little more fight in him. The bastard started to pull me just when the rough water came. All I remember is the water rushing around my head. And the noise. Noise like thunder. I was being sucked down further and further until the fish got away. I had both hands on the spike because I was too afraid to let go. It cut me to shreds — see?" And he showed me his palms. "And then, suddenly, the water let me go and I shot up to the top, *psst!*, like a cannon. I could see no land and could only tell the water from the sky because the water was red with the blood of the fish. And then the birds came. Came to drink the blood and eat the flesh of the fish. And they circled around me and called to their friends and more came until a ship saw them and then saw me and picked me up."

I caught Vince's eye, and with a few small facial expressions, asked if Domingo was crazy. Vince gave his head a short jerk.

"It was a cargo boat which had left Aruba and was heading toward the Dominican Republic," Vince explained. "When they finally got Domingo on the deck, the captain told him he would radio for a helicopter to come pick him up. But Domingo said no. He didn't want to go back." Vince glanced at the Aruban. "Did you, Dommy?"

"*Non*. The captain said if I don't go back he would throw me overboard. I had no passport; it was illegal. But I explained to him my life. I made a deal that I would work for free transport and when they got to the island, they could report me as a stowaway. But they would let me escape, first. The captain felt bad for me and agreed. So before we sailed into the port, I slipped off the ship and swam ashore. And the water delivered me safely. And with the help of some friends I knew on the island, I was smuggled here."

"So, you see, Birdy? Domingo is grateful to birds. Birds saved his life. So you two have a lot in common."

Vince's voice was holstered in a threat but it also carried the promise that my "partnership" with this Aruban would help my own agenda.

"You and Domingo will get along fine. He's just got a few rules. The first one is to leave the TV on like it is. The static and snow remind him of being in the water, and this reminds him of his safe delivery from Aruba. Isn't that right, Dommy?"

"*Si*. Television stays on."

Vince stood up.

"The TV pacifies him, Birdy. Keep it like that, okay? Well, we're all friends now, right Dommy? You and the Birdman will be good friends."

"As long as he is a friend of the birds, he is a friend of mine."

"Good. Then tomorrow we start work. Right?"

"*Si*, Vince. Tomorrow, we work."

Domingo turned to me and nodded slowly. A delicate scab was forming on the side of his head, holding back the blood like a repressed memory. It made me think about how easily memories can be picked at until they flood the present. It made me think that no wounds are completely forgotten.

Chapter Five
A Rose By Any Other Name

Domingo was snoring in staggered gasps. He had finished most of the beer in the apartment and passed out. But, for me, the thought of sleep was unattainable. Hunched in the corner, I listened to the whitewash of fuzz coming from the television and tried to make sense of what I'd gotten involved with. The talk about work meant that Vince would soon reveal his motives. This, and having nearly been killed by Domingo, elevated my association with Vince to a fearful, dizzying level.

I was terrified at how simply Vince had unraveled the past decade of my life. Ironically, it reminded me of those long-ago family ski vacations and the ease with which my father had been able to manipulate our victims. Vince and my father shared a power of persuasion and both could easily disintegrate the permanence of belief. My father had guided my convictions until that day I became stranded, hopelessly abandoned. Now Vince had cast a brighter glimmer on what I'd become by overshadowing what I'd missed. He was so successful at this that a part of me wanted to believe that my isolation had, at the very least, served its purpose and it was now time to move on. But the memory of the crime held me in check. It would always be there, a defining factor in who I was. At this point, believing that I could ever truly reenter society was too farfetched. Still, I felt Vince's pull and its force was unwavering.

As I waited for the night sky to fade into translucence, I also wondered about the work — what it was and how long it would last. Although I always knew Vince had some plan in mind, it was no longer a vague idea, an unknown eventuality. There was now a realism attached to it and I began to think in terms of goals, methods and time frames. I'd always known there would be a point at which Vince's needs and my own would intersect, but now my concerns took on the aspect of time. What would happen when Vince no longer needed me? I left the present to search amongst the foggy future.

At the very least, Vince didn't know what my motives were. While it was true he didn't think of me as an average homeless guy, he also didn't know who I really was. He regarded me as smart, but he was smart as well, and he knew I wasn't merely going to throw away ten years of my life. So, while we would each help each other accomplish our respective goals, I would have to watch carefully for my opportunity to break from him. But this would have to be a vigilant watch as Vince had control over the timing. I would have to tread carefully.

So I didn't run that night. I sat hunched in the corner, breaking down all the parts of my world that Vince had already turned upside down. Squab is pigeon in a fancy dressing. A man can wear a sweater in the summer and not sweat. Language can sound meaningful and be gibberish. Vince also took this one step further by showing that it all made perfect sense. His upside-down interpretations of all that was around me were sheathed in rationality so clear-cut that they dissolved my perceptions of reality.

However, when my house was blown up, a series of events, like falling dominos, were set into motion, and they would shape who I would ultimately become. That long night in the apartment, I still didn't understand all the implications of these defining occurrences, but I knew they alone had empowered me with a reliable stability. On that night of uncertainty, I decided that regardless of what happened, somehow I needed my world to stabilize once again. I had to have a keel that I could rely upon. And in the end, I would have to create my own set of beliefs which I alone would have control over.

"How did you get here?"

I was sitting at the kitchen table when Domingo walked cautiously out of the bathroom. A damp facecloth was plastered over his thin, soggy hair. Although the beer had obviously frayed the insides of his head, Domingo appeared used to hangovers. He moved slowly, but was still able to speak without the noise of his own voice shredding him from within.

"Vince brought me," I answered.

"*Non*. Here."

"You mean in Boston?"

"*Si*."

"It's a long story."

"Vince says you are a friend of the birds. If that is true, the birds must have brought you."

"In a way, I suppose they did."

He was standing in front of me now, and I realized that he was actually shorter than he appeared the night before when he had held the gaff.

"You and me — we work together soon. If we do that, things have to be even, *non*?"

"Even, how?"

"You know where I come from. I should know where you come from."

I stared up at him. Domingo's wispy mustache grew like fine silk from his mocha lip. With dull eyes like black buttons and teeth that looked like nubs of hardened butter, Domingo resembled a rag doll that had become stiff with age.

"What kind of work are we going to be doing?"

"What does that matter?"

I screwed my eyes into his, trying to pluck at those buttons to discover what they were hiding.

"I need to know."

"Why?" he persisted. "You need the money. So why do you care?"

"The money isn't important."

From the noise he made as he laughed, I expected him to spit.

"Of course it is! We all need the money. Money is what makes us live."

"Not me."

"So how have you been living? You live on the street, but still you live."

"I only need so much."

"So much, but still you need," Domingo replied. He whisked the washcloth off his head triumphantly, and walked across the dulled linoleum floor to the refrigerator. It was a small box, like I'd seen college students unpack for their dorm rooms. Above the refrigerator was a small window with a torn screen. Instead of curtains, it was partly shaded by strips of newspapers and, when the breeze whispered, the paper would brush across the screen like a veil hiding an amused expression. Domingo took a beer from the small refrigerator and opened it.

"Vince has a business. It is good. We will all make good money."

"Doing what?"

"We are going to supply supper for people."

"What are you talking about?"

"You will see. It is a good business and not just you and me. There are many others. But that is all I say now. Now it is your turn to talk."

"Tell me first — what do you mean by 'supply supper'?"

But Domingo wouldn't answer. I looked past the broken screen. The breeze carried a tragic joke and rippled the newspapers that tried unsuccessfully to shield it from our window.

Gillatano had admitted to it all but, of course, that was part of her plan. She confessed the day we returned from Utah. My family was standing in front of the smoldering rubble that had once been our home. There was no semblance of order. Nothing was where it should have been; nothing belonged or fit any longer. The chimney stones were heaped in the center of a black field of debris surrounded by the once-sturdy walls which were now relying on strands of wallpaper to hold them together. The big picture window, which my mother had repeatedly warned us against playing ball in front of, was scattered like gleaming rhinestones around the yard. What had been an intricate maze of plumbing in the rafters was now a collection of viscously twisted pipe cleaners. Smoke rose from the kitchen but caused no alarm while water gushed into the living room to no one's concern. But these details failed to make my family cry; it was the larger unimaginable terror over which we wept.

Through the haze, I saw the police lead my father away in handcuffs, and again the world had turned upside down. My dad's hands were supposed to grasp metal implements to release people from suffering, but now metal was restraining him for causing pain. That's what the television news had said, and that's what we would have read in the headlines if we still had a front porch for a newspaper to slap upon.

My mother was unnervingly stoic.

"Colin, your father will be proven innocent."

"But that woman, Gillatano..."

"She is lying, Colin. She's...she's just out for money. Don't you believe that woman."

But she wasn't out for the money at all. Gillatano wanted revenge. My father had ruined her; because of my dad, Gillatano had to suffer two permanent losses. So now she turned the tables by forcing my father to experience a similar pain; although destroying our home was meant symbolically, it was as far as her subtlety would extend.

Gillatano had known that I had loved and worshipped my father unconditionally, but when she exposed his true self, there would be no medals I could pin on him which would stick. My father — the man with the power of Tom Brokaw — would be stripped of all validity for me. Of course Gillatano knew her revenge would be devastating, but she could have no idea of how far-reaching its effects would prove to be.

Gillatano couldn't have known how much I would suffer and I'm certain it was more than she could ever have hoped for. The simple truth was my father had been my idol; he personified all that was good and right. But Gillatano knew that once I saw him for what he really was, I would reject him, and that would be his permanent loss. But she could never have predicted the severity of what I would lose.

My father and I had been so close that, after this revelation, I felt poisoned by our association. To retain any purity that may have still been left inside me, I had to refuse not only my father, but also his world. And this is how I ended up on the street. This is the reason I ran away from my father's society and became a non-entity. No one knew me now. I didn't exist — not for my family or Gillatano and sometimes, not even for myself. So when Domingo asked me where I was from, the only answer I could truly give was: "I don't know...I can't even imagine it...."

———

"Domingo told me about your business idea."

Vince and I were sitting at the wobbly kitchen table in the apartment. Its Formica top was cracked in various places, and the small wrinkles, which were filled with years of dirt and grime, had spread out like rivulets of muddy water. As I traced my fingers along one of these murky streams, the frayed ends of my sleeves trailed behind like an anchor line.

"What did he tell you?"

"Not a lot. That we were going to 'supply dinner' for people."

"Yeah. That's right, Birdy."

"So what's the rest of the idea?"

Domingo had gone out to get some more beer and Vince sat back in his chair, somewhat conspiratorially, and looked towards the door. Then he spoke.

"Birdy, I've told you that I think you're a smart guy. And I meant it. With your brains — and skills — you're perfect."

"Perfect for what?"

"I've got a very large network of people working for me. And I need someone to help manage things."

I plucked my fingers out of the table's dirty rivers and folded my hands.

"What do these people do for you?"

"Well, it's kind of ironic, Birdy. They're all in the same business as you."

"I'm not in any business, Vince."

"Sure you are. You catch squab."

"That's not a business."

"It all depends on how you look at it, Birdy. You've got to think more globally."

I stared at him, nervously rubbing my fingers together.

"So you have a bunch of people that catch pigeons and sell them to restaurants as squab?"

Vince laughed, in the same sort of condescending manner that Sid used to regard me.

"I told you, you've got to think globally. The squab bit is just the tip of it all."

"What else is there?"

"Come on," Vince smiled and stood up. "I'll show you."

I followed him outside, leaving the dirty rivers to flow where they would.

The slate-colored building was too indiscriminate. With no sign, its dark windows, and a rusty door at one corner that was nearly hidden in the leafy shade, the building was an orphan. I remembered reading about the thousands of street urchins in India who beg in the night and populate the cities in such great numbers that, after a while, they become as unnoticeable as the stench in the air they breathe. Like this building, they finally blend in, are accepted and aren't given a second thought. I wondered how many people had driven by this building — some on their daily commute — and never even noticed it. This thought expanded in poignancy when I got inside. That's when I realized it's the orphans who really *should* be noticed.

Vince swung open the door and revealed the factory. It clanked and hissed in a strange symphony: the gigantic and hollow-sounding percussion of filling machines; the scurry of conveyor belts like eighth notes on a cello; a hurdy-gurdy horn section of whistles and screeches; the occasional solo of a bellowing foreman. As I listened, I noticed Vince's ironic smile. He had the look of the cocky artist who, after a string of bad reviews, has finally orchestrated the masterpiece that will force every critic to eat his words.

Vince surveyed the entire room, nodding at whoever happened to look up. Following his gaze from left to right, I blinked hard until my eyes adapted to the shards of fluorescent lights. Then I saw the workers clearly.

They all wore dark blue smocks, hairnets and rubber gloves, and stood at various positions along the connected conveyor belts which looked like a mini amusement park. At the beginning of the line, two women, one Hispanic and the other, a small Asian, were taking sixteen-ounce tin cans from a box and putting them on the belt. The cans traveled along until they were grabbed securely by metal clasps from another belt that turned them upside down like a roller coaster. When the cans were facing downwards, a jet stream of air blew into them, clearing away any dust. Then they came up the other side and were grabbed by a belt that brought them around the first corner of the line to a large, gray filling machine. Two men, both wiry and scruffy, spoke nonstop like carnival barkers as they made sure the cans lined up with the clear, plastic tubes of the filling device. When the cans were in place, the men would each give an order like "okay now," or "look it here," and down the tubes oozed brown globules in a dark liquid sludge. Then they would smile at each other, as if congratulating

Andrew K. Stone

themselves for a job well done, before turning to watch the next two cans.

After this, the cans with the lumpy soup continued towards a machine that was supervised by a tall, gangly man with bulbous eyes. He stared intently at each can, ensuring the machine properly sealed them before they rounded the final bend. Other fasteners then took hold and spun them around on the belt as labels were attached. When they approached the final stretch of the line, a pale, anemic girl with dark eyes picked up each one and smoothed down the label with a damp cloth. Her arms were so thin, I thought they would snap under the weight of the cans, but her muscles flexed each time she lifted, and her veins bulged from the effort. I followed Vince over to her. He had to shout to be heard over the noise of the room.

"Gloria, did you make the clinic today?"

She looked to the ground while subtly draping the damp cloth over her sweaty arms. But as Vince questioned her, shame dominated and exposed the woman.

"Barely."

"You got there, though?"

"Yeah, Vince. But you know there's always the line. I go there at five-thirty but still the lousy line." She had to shout, and that added to her humiliation. Blushing, she again concentrated on the gray, cement floor.

"Okay, don't worry about it. I'll have Dommy pick you up at eight-thirty instead of eight. Then you can make it up at the end of the day. How's that?"

"You mean it? 'Cause I'm trying, Vince. You know that. It's just the line."

"I know."

"Thanks, Vince."

"No sweat."

Vince nudged me and we walked over to the table where the cans waited to be boxed up. Two heavy men put the cans in boxes and taped them shut. One nodded at Vince and mumbled an incoherent greeting as he moved aside. His face was red and greasy with sweat, and as he moved away, he wiped his face on the sleeve of his smock.

Vince picked up one of the cans, petted it like a baby, and then held it up to me. I read the label. *Escargots.* Vince smiled proudly and yelled over the din.

"This is one of our product lines. We get them from Spanish and Oriental fishermen all up and down the coast. Whaddya think?"

"It's spelt correctly."

"Very funny, Birdman."

He put the can back on the table and motioned me to a door at the back of the room. As we crossed, the workers gazed at us sideways, like schoolchildren trying to avoid being caught by their teacher. I returned the glances, but my eye caught a steely blur, like a metallic sunset behind the workers' shoulders.

"That's our meat grinder. Come on, I'll show you."

A metal bulldog with revolving teeth, the grinder had once been used by a butcher's shop to make hamburger. But now, Vince told me, it had been modified so that any meat could be fed into its large mouth at the top. As the meat churned towards the machine's flared middle, it would be torn into an unrecognizable mass of red and brown strands.

"We use it to make sausage."

"Out of what?"

"You name it — squirrels, rabbits...even possums. It doesn't really matter what you put in. With the right seasoning, it all comes out sausage."

My stomach flipped and Vince laughed.

"Get used to it. It's our biggest product — we sell to people who use it as is, or mix it in with regular beef or pork. By adding it to the Grade A stuff, it's a lot cheaper for the restaurants."

"Jesus."

"Come on." Vince nodded towards the door and brought a wad of keys from his pocket. They cascaded over themselves, producing muted chimes until Vince found the right one and turned the lock. I heard the buzz of the fluorescent lights just before they lit with a fluttering spark.

"Welcome to your office," Vince grinned.

I looked around the paneled room. The green, shag rug was marred with grease-stained footprints like muddy tracks on a lawn. Bits of paper, empty bottles and other debris littered the floor, and an old wooden door propped up by a sawhorse on one side and a barrel on the other made a desk. There was no window, and the air was stale and thick like powder. I could taste every breath. In the corner was a small bathroom with a toilet of yellowing, cracked porcelain loosely pinned to the floor by rusted bolts. My office, Vince had said. Like the apartment, it was a dump by most people's standards, but for me it offered a second haven and another parcel of conflicting emotions.

"Take a seat." Vince pointed to a rickety chair behind the desk. It had a round base with casters on it; I sat down and could swivel and move the chair at the same time if I wanted to risk being dropped to the floor.

A curtain hung next to the door. Vince drew it open, revealing a two-way mirror through which we watched the factory workers as if they were the cast of a play. For a moment, Vince studied them like specimens under a microscope. Then he leaned against the wall, and his musing face was reflected in another mirror tacked just above where his shoulder rested.

"I like to be able to classify people, ya know? I like to look at a guy and pretty much figure him out. And I'm good at it. For instance, I used to put homeless guys into two categories: addicts and crazy. These people here — " and he gestured towards the window "— they all fit into those categories. Take a closer look. The girl I spoke to — Gloria. Obvious smack addict. I picked her up at the Boylston T station one morning. It was about ten o'clock and she was sitting on the steps inside. She offered to blow me for ten bucks. I took her to an alley in Chinatown. It was a short walk, but long enough for me to get her story. I found out that she wanted to get clean. I told her if she did, then I could get her a job. But she had to start going to the methadone clinic. So she's in the first category. 'Thyroid Charlie' there — the guy who stares at the cans — he's in the second. Found him babbling in front of Filene's Basement one rainy afternoon. He had a paper coffee cup and was trying to make enough for a bagel. I asked him when his last meal was, but he couldn't remember. He just stood there while the coffee cup fell to pieces in his hands. Then he started to cry — not because he'd lost the change that had been in the cup, but because he'd gone to so much trouble to get the cup in the first place. After talking to him, I knew I could use him, too. And so I gave him the job. I wouldn't say I'm a fuckin' Samaritan, but these people would all still be on the street if it wasn't for me."

"And you want to make me the same type of offer?"

"As I said, Birdy, I like to classify people. Until I met you, I thought there were pretty much just two catego-ries of bums. But I was wrong — you're different. Obvi-ously, there's another reason why you're on the street —

and you don't have to tell me what it is. All I know is that you're there. But I can get you a better deal."

"What if I don't want it?"

"What's your alternative?" he asked, and smiled.

It wasn't a threat, and Vince knew it. It was just another sharp turn on this roller coaster I was strapped to. My life had become a funhouse maze and the only exit lay beyond the carnival surprises, trick mirrors and trap doors.

"That girl, Gloria. Did she give you a blow job?"

"Of course. But I gave her *fifty* bucks."

Vince smiled again. I sat back in my chair. It squeaked under the excess weight.

Chapter Six
Working (Under) Class Hero

W hen Vince began laying out his business plan, it was distressingly apparent that he didn't take the idea of "thinking globally" lightly. At first, I couldn't believe I was hearing correctly — it was as if his English was as foreign to me as the phony Chinese he had spoken. However, as he described the operation, I began to understand that not only was it feasible, but Vince was accumulating a healthy profit from what was a major venture.

"You see, Birdman, we've got three main product lines — meat, fowl, seafood — that we sell mostly to suppliers overseas. They turn around and sell to restaurants, most of them, naturally, having no idea what they're getting. The thing is, a lot of countries are too poor to buy USDA. But the suppliers know they can get a deal from us, then mix our product in with better quality stuff and repackage it to look even more legit. So, when you figure that these restaurants are paying Grade A dollars for food that's...well, let's just say slightly below Grade A levels, and then you factor in our low overhead costs, it adds up to a pretty profitable operation."

"So a restaurant in China, for instance, thinks they're getting pork sausages, but what they're really getting is pork with rabbit and squirrel and God knows what else?"

"Exactly."

He beamed at me with arrogant pride filtered through danger.

"How are you able to get it out of the country — I mean, with customs and all?"

Vince's confident smile spread.

"I work for a large national network of people who take care of that end."

"You mean the Mob."

"I wouldn't use that particular word to refer to them, Birdy. They prefer to be called 'my associates.'"

Although I nodded, my head felt as if it were floating freely.

"This network is spread throughout the country. I'm not the only guy shipping out product — I could never do this alone. That's why we've got hundreds of operations exactly like this all over the country. To accommodate them, my associates have built another business — a completely legitimate, and also profitable, export business — that we use as a front to get product out of the country. Even with all their regulations, the government can't touch us. Here's the part that will interest you, Birdy. See, we have a number of built-in safeguards," and Vince leaned in towards me and said, "and the most important one concerns our employees."

My mind froze from my ears inwards to the core of my brain. Was I understanding Vince correctly? Could it be possible?

"You mean, this network hires only homeless people?"

"From all around the country," Vince smiled and leaned back. "Pretty fuckin' brilliant, isn't it?"

"Jesus Christ."

"What's the matter — you have a problem with employing the homeless?"

"No, but...it's just incredible."

"It's good business sense. Shit, it's like a human fuckin' services operation! Of course, everyone has to be screened carefully to meet the right criteria, but after that they've got themselves a pretty decent deal."

"What kind of people are you looking for?"

"People we can trust. People who aren't going to blow the whistle, who need a job but can keep their mouths shut. Most of the people we hire are mildly retarded, and we tell them only enough of the bare facts so they won't accidentally leak anything to the wrong people. Also, I give them a place to stay to keep them a bit...isolated."

"What, do you have a dormitory or something?"

"Not exactly. They're all spread around in various 'private' facilities — much better living situations than they had before they came to work for me. Dommy picks 'em up in the morning and drives 'em home at night. See, Dommy is another of my managers. He's an illegal alien, of course, but I was able to procure some paperwork and a driver's license. So it works out for everybody, you see?"

"Until they get caught."

Vince's tone hardened slightly.

"We've been in business two years and that hasn't happened yet, Birdman. But if one group does go down, nobody's gonna do any real prison time — these people don't have a clue that they're doing anything wrong. Think about it — they're retarded, homeless people going to work every day. They don't know there's anything illegal about it. So if they get caught, they'll be clear. That's why I don't tell them — I'm protecting them."

"That's real big of you, Vince."

"Don't be a wise ass. I'm covering myself too, of course, and you know it."

"So what happens to them? If their group goes under — they're back on the street."

"Sure. But you got to look at it this way — we kept them employed for a while, at least. Think about it in your own terms. You ain't doing so bad. I'm giving you decent food, a place to live and a middle-management job. And you didn't exactly walk in here with a glowing resume."

My world was reeling faster. The idea of a network of homeless people supplying substandard food around the globe was mind boggling, but here it was, all occurring in this little, barely noticeable building which people passed every day without taking any notice. How could I dismiss the idea that there were buildings like this spread out over the entire country with people doing the same thing? All the components were there — there were certainly enough homeless people, equipment, animals and savvy men like Vince to pull it all together. I looked at Vince's smiling face and realized there was no way to deny it.

―――――――

When I was a child, I once stuck a screwdriver into an electrical outlet. The shock traveled through me in waves of vibration that blacked out the entire world while it amplified my numb body. As Vince continued to describe the operation, a similar sense-altering shock rolled through me.

"Your job will be to manage the work force, Birdman. The whole operation is growing and I need you to help take care of day-to-day stuff here as well as working with our vendors."

"Vendors?"

"The people we get the product from."

"Who are they, anyway? Are they homeless, too?"

"Some are. Others are people who sell what they can't get rid of legitimately. It varies, but the one thing that stays constant is that none of them know us — we're completely anonymous so they can't turn on us. Of course, that makes it easier for them to try and cheat us.

"See, everybody really works for himself. I'm just one guy who buys from the vendors — they don't even know my name. It's a strictly cash-only, no-questions-asked operation and that cash nicely supplements the vendors' income. Look, I'll give you an example. There's a fisherman we buy from — guy named Santos. He's got to have legitimate customers or he wouldn't be able to fish — you can't just sail into a harbor with a bunch of product and not report where it's going. But if you're smart, you can smuggle a part of your haul in, and that's what Santos does."

"So it sounds like a good deal. Why would anyone try to screw it up by cheating you?"

"Because people get greedy. They always think there's better money to be made and they think they might get away with it. They know I'm not gonna go to the police if they cheat me. So, they gamble on trying to make that big killing. Of course, their gamble is whether I'll come down hard on them, but still some people take that chance, thinking they can clean up and get away. What you see here — this factory — is easy to watch. I know all these people so I don't hafta worry about them much. If they try to fuck with me, then *they've* got to worry about me. But these other guys, like Santos — they can be here today and vanish tomorrow. So your job is to protect the investment. Keep it all quick, clean and quiet."

Vince punctuated these last few words by raising his eyebrows and jutting out his chin in short, stringent movements like a conductor's baton. After his words had sunk in, I moved outside my numbness just far enough to ask a question.

"Vince, with all these vendors, how do you know who to trust?"

He leaned back in his chair, absorbing my question with amusement. Then, he righted himself with a thump and replied as if he were chewing the words:

"Don't you think I know what I'm doin'?"

"It's not that. But — "

"Listen, ya gotta have more faith in me, Bird. Everybody — from the vendors on up — is carefully screened. So don't worry about anything except doing your job. Okay?"

He got up, smiled briefly and left the office. As I listened to the muted symphony outside the door, Vince's last words came back to me — *except doing your job*. The motives were now clear and I had no choice. There would be no exceptions.

———————

Vince hadn't exaggerated the magnitude of his operation. As his business plan called for as much product as we could get, he had vendors spread out all around New England. Domingo and I made pick-ups in an old flatbed truck with wooden slats for sides and a heavy canvas canopy on top. We drew up a schedule of three or four pick-up points and each night we'd return with an eclectic truckload of product. Every few weeks, Domingo and I drove the truck into northern Massachusetts and New Hampshire. In Portsmouth, New Hampshire, there was a man who worked at a large bait store. In the back room, he kept a secret supply of frogs and turtles in a freezer. Because frog legs and turtle soup are considered delicacies, we'd make a quick stop and load up before heading inland to a wooded area on the outskirts of the University of New Hampshire. A commune of hippies lived there and, when they weren't smoking marijuana or putting down capitalism, they trapped squirrels, chipmunks and other animals which would all end up in the grinder. The hippies didn't have a freezer, but knew a guy in the nearby town who would keep the product fresh in exchange for some homegrown grass. We'd stop at the commune and the hippies would come out with cold bags that they'd lift onto the truck in a laughing haze of pot and midnight fogginess.

As for Vince's fowl line, ducks were always a versatile and valuable staple. They could be used for Peking duck, roasted duckling, *duck l'orange*, and, of course, as substitutes for chicken — albeit, dark meat. The same held true for geese, which were even more plentiful and versatile. Geese could be pawned off as duck *or* chicken, in addition to stuffed, roasted goose. No one guessed that they were caught around a variety of stagnant puddles throughout the Greater Boston area.

Vince bought the ducks and geese from a small band of men who lived in abandoned mill buildings in Lawrence, Massachusetts. At one time, Lawrence had been a thriving mill town, and its industry spawned great structures that rolled out a variety of textiles. These brick fortresses had labyrinths of wide hallways with dark wooden floors and great iron doors that hid musty rooms or revealed other mazes. Whenever these doors were opened, the dust and dampness stung the eye and throat. In prosperous days, the tar and blacking materials used for manufacturing were suffocating; now the ruins of these buildings themselves choked the men who squatted there until they were forced out by demolition teams. Hopeful new industrialists were always buying the old ruins, and the band of geese-catchers was forced to roam from one dilapidation to the next, sometimes just a few steps ahead of wrecking balls that would tear down and rebuild not only history but, for these invisible nomads, home.

The geese were easier to catch than ducks because they traveled in larger flocks and stayed mainly on land. However, because they migrated there were only small windows of opportunities to catch them during their trips between the north and south. But the mill-dwellers were versatile hunters and, depending on the season, would supply Vince with various components of the fowl product line.

Vince was curious about how the mill-dwellers caught the geese, so one night Domingo and I drove the five or six men from their latest shelter to a North Andover industrial park. It was the last place I would have expected to find geese but, as we drove up, we saw a large flock of the birds standing about a small man-made pond behind a converted mill that housed a software company. There were a few graffiti-covered picnic tables and some dented trash bins, making it obvious that the employees of the building enjoyed lunch outside in what was supposed to serve as a nature refuge. However, from the cigarette butts and soda cans which littered the ground, the space seemed more of a refuge for the workers in need of a diversion from computer screens and cubicles.

The leader of the geese-catchers was probably only thirty-five, but his grime-smeared face was aged like old leather. I'd found out he was a former lightweight boxer from the Bronx, but one too many punches and a few too many drinks had landed him out of the sport and onto the street. The arteries in his arms bulged like overflowing rivers around his still-hard muscles, but that was the only sign of health about him; when he spoke, a fluid cough wended around his words.

"'Kay, everybody got da sack?" the leader questioned in a hopeless monotone. He would have gladly heard no response from his bandmates. Not coming prepared meant disqualification from the night's activities and, of course, from sharing in the evening's profit. But the others all grunted as they held up dark sacks made from old rags and ripped clothes.

"Let's do it," the leader said in his same resigned manner. Then, looking at Domingo and me, he abruptly changed his voice to a resentful snarl. "Youse two stay back, if youse don't wanna get yer asses bit off. Dere very protective birds."

The men quietly fanned out with their sacks, nets and ropes. As I watched, I could only think of the old Keystone Cops movies I'd seen as a kid. Six men sneaked up on the birds and, on cue, grabbed, lassoed or ensnared as many as them as they could, and then ran, chased by the other hissing and honking members of the flock. The men ran a good distance until the geese gave up the chase, then they double-backed to where Domingo and I waited. Each had at least two birds; one guy had four. The necks of the geese were all broken — the experienced men broke them instantly while the newer guys killed the geese as they ran. I could tell which men were new by the number of bite marks on their forearms.

After the geese had been counted, and each man given the appropriate credit for the number of birds caught, they were thrown into a large plastic garbage pail that was lined on the bottom with chunks of ice. We then drove to another site and the process was repeated, and on to a third site where it was repeated again. After the third poaching, we went back to the first pond behind the mill building.

"Whazzit been, an hour or 'bouts?"

"Yes," I said.

"Good. Den dey'll have settled down now," said the leader. So the process was repeated at each site. By the end of the night, the men had caught over a hundred geese. In addition to the week's supply, which they'd kept on ice in the basement of the mill, we brought back almost eight hundred birds to add to the inventory.

The main supplier to the meat line was a mildly retarded Southerner named Joey. He was a pipe cleaner of a man with a peat moss beard that swirled down in tangles to the frayed collars of his heavy plaid shirt. Joey led a small group of men who all lived together in an elaborate fortress of rooms underneath an Amtrack train bridge. The rooms held ten men, and were separated by pieces of plywood and old tarps that the group had built out of debris they'd lugged from around the city. Joey had some electrical experience, so he was able to tap into a power supply near the train tracks. By burying a wire that ran from the power supply to their home, they effectively siphoned electricity from Amtrack.

Each night, Joey and his men rode the freight trains between Boston and Mystic, CT to supply us with hundreds of wild rabbits. Normally only a two-hour ride, to bring in their haul Joey's group extended the trip by a few days.

"Ya see," he explained, the first time I had met him, "there's five towns — Canton, Providence, Kingston, Westerly and Mystic. Now, in each of these towns — 'cept for Providence — we've got a place laid out with snares. So's ya really only got four places you're talking 'bout, right? Good, now we go out and at each stop — 'cept for Providence — we hop off the freight car. We got us our sacks and extra rope for fixin' up the traps, right, and we all head to the Places o' Plenty."

"What are the Places o' Plenty, Joey?"

I thought I'd offended him by my question. Joey began waving his fists in my face and bobbing around me, jabbing at either side of my head. I ducked a few times until he suddenly stopped and slapped his knee. He laughed with a shrill *hee hee hee* like a demented elf.

"I had you going! I had you going!" Then he straightened up, as if the last few minutes hadn't occurred, and answered my question.

"Why, the Places o' Plenty are the meadows and fields and woods along each stop — 'cept for Providence — where we get our little bunnies."

As soon as the word "bunnies" was out of his mouth, Joey began to maniacally pick at the swirls in his beard, as though the rabbits were hopping through his tangles. Then the spasm left him suddenly and Joey dropped his hands to his sides and continued.

"So at the first stop, after we get the little critters, I sends one guy back on the next train heading home, right? He might have four dozen or fifty rabbits and he brings them back and puts them in our freezer."

"You've got a freezer in the trestle?"

He laughed as if the idea of *not* having a freezer under the train bridge was absurd.

"'Course we do! How the hell else are we gonna keep them bunnies from spoilin'?!" Joey started scratching again, but his excitement kept him talking and his hands moved unconsciously. "So then the rest of us have to wait 'til the next train, so, while we're waiting, we reset all the traps and then jump on and head out to the next stop."

"Except for Providence."

As if he'd suddenly found himself at a funeral, Joey stopped moving and nodded gravely.

"Exactly," he whispered with wide, conspiring eyes. "By the end of about two days, we can go there and back — make all the stops — and bring home a coupla hundred, give or take, rabbits. Now, you multiply that by seven days, 'cause that's how many are in the week, and you've got a pretty darn good haul."

"How long have you been doing this, Joey?"

"Oh, a few months. Your boss there sent his dark brown guy, Domino — "

"Domingo."

"Domingo." He tasted the word, rolling it on his tongue like an olive. "Yeah, Domingo. He came to us a few months ago and we started then. I can't says the money keeps us off the streets —" and he laughed hard at his joke "— but it helps, it helps, right?"

"I hope so, Joey."

"Oh, it helps. There's lot's of Places o' Plenty. 'Cept Providence."

It was night. Domingo and I were driving down Route 495, heading towards New Bedford, Massachusetts, a small seaport town just northeast of Rhode Island. New Bedford is populated by many Portuguese fishermen who sail through Narragansett Bay to make their livings in the Atlantic. As a child, I would watch the ships in the distance and pretend to squeeze them between my fingers as the waves carried them home. Now, as each mile brought us closer to my home state, my stomach was squeezed.

We were making a pickup from Santos. Underneath the truck's canvas top were dozens of five-gallon jugs, each one secured in a square frame on the flatbed. They would be taken out of the truck and filled when we got to the docks. Domingo would shout orders to the men who would shovel chunks of ice into the flatbed before replacing the jugs, while I would deal with Santos, ensuring Vince's terms had been met exactly, and handling the payment.

"Remember to watch that guy," Vince had warned me, referring to the crew boss. "Make sure his scale is set right."

"How can I do that?"

"This weighs exactly ten pounds," Vince said, picking up a metal pipe from the desk. It was a short, blunt rod like a small axle. "You put this on the scale before and after he weighs out the buckets. If at any time it doesn't say ten pounds, check the buckets. It'll be dark and he's been known to mix fake product in with the real stuff."

"Fake...?"

"Rubber."

I chuckled as I remembered the rubber worms my dad and I used to fish with, the ones with small black hooks hidden where their spines should have been.

"You're kidding."

Vince's hand tightened around the pipe.

"It's gonna be dark. You'll never know the difference until you get back here. And by that time, it'll be too late. So watch out," Vince sneered, tapping the pipe against his palm before handing it to me.

Domingo and I arrived at the dock. As we drove towards the boat, I recalled how the life of a harbor exists primarily by sound. I heard the shadowy water lapping against the hulls of rocking boats as it tasted the remnants of salt. The wind exhaled from between the creases of the reddish-silver clouds and softly cried in the entangled cobwebs of rigging that dissolved into the night. Even the salty air reached our noses by the flapping canvas of an unfurled sail, waving the odor towards us. Every aspect of the harbor was filtered through our ears and all perceptions, real or imagined, were determined primarily by the sense of sound.

As we turned onto the dock, our headlights painted broad swaths of light along the side of the boat. I first saw the rounded curves of its starboard side, then the small engine room and finally the mast, which reached upwards to merge with the black sky. Domingo stopped the truck and cut the headlights. Then, the absence of light was more revealing as we saw the ship's crew scurry across the boat's gangplank and begin to work.

Business commenced almost before we had a chance to emerge from the truck. The men had already hoisted the skipjacks, mussels and undersized lobsters from their cargo hold, which they'd separated into large, black bins. They opened the back of the truck and, with only a few words of instruction from Domingo, started unloading the empty jugs.

I walked to the edge of the dock and took a long, memory-laden breath. The sea air blew open a mental scrapbook from my past; visions of days spent on the beaches of Rhode Island triggered myriad remembrances from my childhood. I hadn't smelt the sea since I was a kid, and the reeling flashbacks from my childhood were a tortuous luxury.

The most poignant memory was of a particular dinner I'd had with my family. It was my tenth-birthday celebration and we had gone to L'Apogee, an extremely expensive restaurant in the Biltmore Hotel, in Providence.

Everywhere I turned, the restaurant winked with glittering opulence. The brass railings on either side of the main entrance were cylindrical mirrors in which my face was reflected in oblong caricature. Large plants adorned every corner, and twinkling white lights, which my father said had been put there especially for my birthday, splayed across their boughs.

As the maitre 'd showed us to our table, I noticed the other diners dressed as if they were at a fairytale ball. The women wore sparkling jewelry and the long white candles flickering on each table ignited their fingers and throats. The music playing in the background was different from what I'd heard in other, less expensive restaurants. An actual string quartet played in the corner, their melody lines crossing and re-crossing each other like intricate sewing patterns. As I listened, I couldn't believe their music could exist anywhere else but in this room.

The food was fabulous and the waiter's ability to memorize each of our orders, right down to the salad dressing, amazed me. I was sure he'd make a mistake and bet my father a week's allowance that he would. But when he came back and put each perfectly ordered plate in front of us, my father called off the bet.

"I couldn't take your allowance on your birthday, Cole," he laughed and rubbed my head with his gentle paw.

Whenever we went to dinner for a special occasion, my mother would insist that I order something I wouldn't normally eat.

"Why not have the veal or the lobster, Colin?" she asked on this evening. So I looked at the menu and ordered the lobster tails, and my mother asked that the meat be taken out so that I wouldn't make a mess.

A pile of lobster meat sat between a baked potato and a silver container of hot, melted butter. I was able to dip the bite-sized chunks of red and white meat into the butter and eat it easily. There was something decadent about this; it felt taboo and secret. Just as the string players could only make music in this restaurant, I could only be allowed this luxury there, as well.

"Don't eat so fast, Colin," my mother warned.

"Let him enjoy himself," my father said. "You know, Cole, not every restaurant would take the meat out of the shell for you like that."

"Why not?" I asked, while chewing.

"Don't talk with your mouth full."

"Well, Cole," Dad continued, after an almost imperceptible glance at my mother, "this is special restaurant. It's very expensive and, because of that, they do extra nice things for you. And because today's the most special occasion that your mother and I can think of, it's well worth a little extra money to have the chef pull out the meat for you."

"Thanks, Dad. Thanks, Mom," I said, with butter running down my chin. "It's a great dinner!"

"You're welcome," my mother said, swabbing at my chin with a cloth napkin.

Standing on the dock in New Bedford, that birthday scene kept playing over and over in my mind's theater. Every detail was as vivid as if I were seeing it in the reflection of the black water, but it was the dull, rubbery-like lobster meat that stood out the most. The lobster had been delicious, but it was the centerpiece of my recollection because it was the only aspect of that restaurant which could have been removed without notice. The music, the diamonds, the brass railings — all these were integral components to the experience of the restaurant, but the lobster tails were disguised intruders. Their costumes were the lack of their shells and, cloaked in its nakedness, the lobster meat could have come from anywhere. There probably was a pound and a half of meat on my plate, but from how many tails? Two, which had been purchased from a commercial fisherman in Maine, or five, which had been procured from a slimy man on a dock in New Bedford who was selling illegal, undersized seafood?

My father's words mingled with the sounds of Santos and his crew, who were finishing the loading of the buckets.

"...not every restaurant would take the meat out of the shell for you like that."

As the crew shut the back door of the flatbed truck, I wondered if my father had understood all the reasons for the hospitality that could be found in restaurants.

———————

The drive back up 495 was dark and timeless. At three o'clock in the morning, the highway was deserted and, other than the black ghosts of the trees on either side of us, and the half mile or so of the road that continuously revealed itself to our headlights, I saw nothing. This void seemed to stop the world. There was only the noise of the truck, Domingo and me; we were somnambulists in a world that had died.

The deal had gone smoothly. Santos had given us the correct amount of fish and, after they had all been packed onto the ice in the truck and hidden under an oily leather tarp, I'd handed him the wad of bills. His smile was a broken picket fence of missing teeth. After counting the money, Santos said in a thick Portuguese accent:

"Tell your boss it's pleasure to do business."

And that was it. His crew vanished as magically as they had appeared and Domingo and I got back into the truck and headed home.

"That was pretty easy, Domingo."

"*Si.*" And then, after some thought, he added, "and *non.*"

I glanced at his brown face in the mirror. His teeth were clenched and the skin along his jaw line looked like it could be sliced with a fingernail. Domingo's black eyes pierced the windshield as if they, and not the truck's headlights, illuminated the road.

"Making the money is easy," Domingo continued. "But getting caught is not."

"Why do you think we'll get caught?"

Domingo continued staring ahead, but his face slowly relaxed, like a melting candle.

"We do not get caught. The fishermen. They will. One day, they will try something stupid. Then they will get caught."

"Maybe not."

Domingo snapped his head around as if a striking fish had jolted him awake.

"You do not know what it is." He struggled to keep calm while he glared at me. "You do not make money. But a fisherman is different. One day his catch is many, the next — nothing. But you don't know this."

He looked back at the road, his jaw tight again, his skin even tauter than before. In one respect, he was right — I didn't make money. But I realized then that we shared a commonality much larger than I would have ever supposed. In silence, I sat and wondered how and when to tell him.

Chapter Seven
Stripping to the Bare (Facts)

I never thought it would have been possible, but the phony food business was booming. Each day, the assembly line seemed to hum a little louder. As I watched various parts of the product line being ground, filled and packed, I made out address labels for their shipments. Sometimes my hand performed acrobatics as I spelled out the names of cities and countries I'd never heard of before.

Gloria was the foreman of the plant, and she was responsible for giving me these addresses. Like most of the workers, she distanced herself from me, although she had adorned me with a pet nickname. Each Monday, she would knock on the office door, calling "Mornin' Tweets," and hand me a list of the orders to be filled that week. The destinations varied. Vince had steady buyers, but new addresses were always popping up on the list. Many of these new names would start to appear more often as Vince built his client base.

One morning, Gloria entered with her usual greeting and handed me the list. There were six new addresses.

"Business is good," I said, looking at the sheet.

"Nothing wrong with that, Tweets. If it keeps money in my pocket, I don't complain."

"No?"

"Sure. All of us here — if it weren't for this job, we'd be back on our asses in the gutter."

"But you're not afraid?"

She looked confused.

"Afraid of what, Tweets?"

93

"What we're doing is illegal. You're not afraid of getting caught?"

Gloria laughed.

"Honey, getting caught might even be better for us — a solid roof over our heads, three meals a day."

Then her laugh dwindled like the final few fireworks of a July Fourth finale, and she slid into the chair opposite me. The circles under Gloria's eyes were darker than her pupils and her skin was pulled too tightly to wrinkle, giving her face the appearance of mask for her skull.

"Listen to me, Tweets," she said in a whisper that struggled to contain itself. "I don't know nothing about you but I do know Vince good enough. He wouldn't let nobody in here who would stir up trouble, so — you want to talk illegal? I got enough of my own stories. But just keep this one in your head. It's a fucking crime that we have to be here to begin with. Nobody's lifted a goddamned finger to help me, or any one of us, out. Yeah, the city promises you shelter for the night, but that's just a simple fix. And it doesn't last. If it wasn't for Vince, a lot of us wouldn't survive. We wouldn't eat, and I mean eat *every* day. So you want to talk illegal — shit, *that's* the real crime."

She twisted her head down, as if to put the floor in its place, too.

"Gloria, I'm not trying to probe. I'm sorry."

She lifted her eyes.

"That's okay, Tweets."

She stood up and retreated back to the main room. As I looked back at the list, conflicting emotions again nagged my mind. I had attempted to bury all aspects of this business in order to concentrate on my own needs. Working for Vince was a necessary evil that I tried not to give much thought to. Besides, I had no choice — I was between worlds, like an actor stuck amongst the folds of the stage curtain. And so I thought of my job as a transient stop I had to make until I could figure out where I really belonged. I tried comparing it to the way I used to choose a place to sleep on the street. There would always be times when I'd be awoken in the middle of the night and told to move on, but if I dwelt on that possibility I would never have gotten any rest. And so, like those doorways and park benches, I tried to block out all aspects of the job and only concentrate on the end result.

But looking at the operation through Gloria's eyes unlocked other facets — some which I had been unconscious of — and they sprung out, striking me in the face with stinging implication. The work was beginning to feel less transient and more a part of my off-balanced world. As other people began to populate that world, I was being forced to interact with society on a larger scale, and this frightened me. My world was growing more dense yet it was unraveling like a piece of fraying yarn. Still, I had to traverse it and I felt it was only a matter of time before the thin line broke.

The door opened and Vince walked in.

"Hey Birdy. How's it goin'?"

"Busy, Vince," I answered.

He looked at me, then at the sheet in my hand.

"New orders?"

"Gloria just brought them in."

He nodded and turned to inspect himself in the mirror on the wall. Without taking his eyes off his reflection, he said:

"I bet you're wondering about this operation, Birdy."

"I...."

"Save it. I talked to Gloria. Don't worry. She was just trying to save her own skin. Fact is, she likes you a lot. But you've got to see it from her point of view —

she doesn't know much about the business and she's worried about ending up on the street again. So she told me about your conversation. No harm done."

"No?"

"Gimme some credit," he scoffed. "I expected that eventually you'd have some concerns about the legal aspects of the operation. Remember, those people out there aren't like you. They may be from the same place but they don't understand like you do. So let's get some things out in the open. Even with all our safeguards, the workers aren't completely sealed off. The last thing we need is one of those retards out there babbling on to somebody about what we're doing."

"What about Gloria?"

"Don't worry. She can be trusted. Why do you think I give her the customer lists? But remember, the others all think this is legit.

"But the vendors? Now that I've seen how many people are involved — people who do know this is illegal — how can you be so sure someone won't talk? People come and go from these groups — there's a big risk."

Vince considered this for a moment as he re-tucked his sweater into his pants.

"Your buddy Joey, who we got some of these rabbits from. He ever tell you his story?"

I shrugged and shook my head. Vince chuckled.

"Joey and his guys traveled all the way up here from Georgia. They thought they could find work, given their backgrounds at home were...dubious. So they walked — can you believe that? It took them a hell of a long time, but they did it, camping out in the woods and hunting and fishing to eat. That's how come they're so good at snaring rabbits. Unfortunately they had the same problems up here as they did where they came

from. They're all retarded or addicts. And crooks —
but not really criminals."

"What's the difference?"

"The difference," Vince said, turning from the mirror to pace in front of the desk, "is in the way they were
perceived. You know what they do to kids who get in
trouble with the law down South? They put them in boot
camps. Work camps where they 'straighten them out.'
Hard discipline — it's worse than the fuckin' army."

"And Joey was in one of these camps?"

"Most of his guys were. But it was all wrong because Joey and his buddies are retards, see what I'm
saying? When Joey was thirteen, his neighborhood 'pals'
talked him into mugging this old guy. Joey didn't know
what he was doing was wrong, never mind illegal. He
thought it was a game. Unfortunately, he ended up taking the guy's wallet and bustin' his jaw. In broad day-
light with plenty of eyewitnesses. So they threw him
into a camp for a few years. But the camps don't
straighten kids out — they screw 'em up, especially kids
like Joey, who are clueless to begin with. When the other
kids realized he wasn't all there, they talked him into
stealing cigarettes from one of the guards. Again, he
thought it was a joke, but this time the guard beat the
shit outta him. Ever notice the way he talks? One of the
men in his group says he's got permanent brain damage from that run-in."

"Jesus."

"Pretty much the same type of story with his crew.
Joey's a smart guy from where he's standing — by that
I mean he's better off than the rest of his band of merry
little men. He's had some odd jobs since he got out of
the camp, but he could never really escape his past and
there wasn't shit happening in Georgia, so that's why
they ended up here."

Vince stopped pacing and stood in front of me.

"Look, I've said it before. I'm no Samaritan, but these people aren't gonna say anything 'cause I'm the guy who's keeping them from starving. But even if someone does talk, who's gonna believe them? Yeah sure, Joey can point out his rabbit traps and his home under the bridge, but he can never point us out. We're anonymous. And the people here — you think they're gonna talk? Take a look at Gloria and Charlie, there," Vince pointed through the mirror. "A heroin addict and a nut job. I'm their only lifeline. Besides, they couldn't even find this place — remember, that's why I have Dommy pick them up and drop them off. And Dommy, well he's an illegal alien who's found a better life in the US. You think he's about to screw me over? We're all anonymous, Birdy."

I hesitated a moment before speaking. Then, in as steady a tone as I could choke out, I said:

"But I'm not anonymous, Vince."

"No. No, you're not, Birdy. And that's why I just told you all this."

He walked over to the desk.

"But you're also too smart to let anything go wrong. So, you just be careful and everything will be fine. I'll see you later."

Vince smiled and then spun toward the door. As he left the office, I could feel my stomach melt.

A few days later, Vince came to me with a special assignment.

"Birdy, I need you and Dommy to make a delivery for me."

"A delivery?" I asked. "Why? And where?"

"To the North Shore. The distributor's regular guy got in a wreck last night. Totaled his truck."

I scanned Vince's words, listening for any baubles or stutters.

"This isn't how it works, Vince. Just the other day we were talking about anonymity and now — "

"Listen, Birdy," Vince pulled me into the office and closed the door, "sit down. Here's the deal. The customer is a good friend of mine. He's not even part of the network. He owns a club up in Revere and, because we go back a long way, I give him a deal on the food he serves. So you just go to this club, drop off the food and leave. You'll never even meet him, cause he's not there in the daytime."

Vince's voice kept me pinned to the chair.

"I'm just worried about it."

Vince smiled.

"Look, Birdy, all that stuff I told you the other day — I did it for your own good. So you know where you stand. But the fact still remains that you're too important to me to let anything happen. Don't sweat it. You just make the drop-off and get home. The whole trip'll only take you two hours at the most. Besides, Dommy'll be there with you."

"Okay. What's the club?"

He handed me a piece of paper with a name and address.

"Playland?"

Then he grinned like the frat guys I'd seen on their way to sorority parties.

"I don't know when your birthday is, Birdy, but consider this a little gift."

"You're kidding me."

"Hey, I thought you might like it. If you guys want, hang out a coupla extra hours and catch the action. It could do you a world of good, my friend."

———

After his trial, my father's license to practice medicine was, naturally, permanently revoked. The AMA unanimously ruled that the surgery he performed had been unethical; however, that was the least of his worries. My dad was also sent to jail for life on a charge of premeditated manslaughter. When Gillatano eventually died, I saw a small notice about it in the *Boston Herald*.

The news about her death didn't faze me. I was still horrified by my father's crime. The day I had read the headline, an old western I'd seen as a child unreeled in my mind. One cowboy had said to another "hanging's too good for you." It wasn't until I went to Playland that I fully understood the significance of that line.

———

Domingo and I drove into the parking lot of the strip joint. Even in the afternoon, four or five cars were huddled in front of the club's discreet façade. The building itself was painted a muted brown, and there was a white double-door and high, darkened rectangular windows. If not for the neon sign out front with its glowing promises of thick "X's," "topless" and "100 girls nightly," Playland could have been a hardware store or even someone's house.

Domingo drove the truck to the delivery entrance around back. The flatbed held five-gallon jugs of shrimp the size of fingernail clippings which would be chopped and used in the seafood salad, as part of the Happy Hour buffet. We also delivered sausages for the morning "legs and eggs" crowd.

Domingo pressed a button on the back door and we heard its insect-like buzz cutting through the muffled '70's dance music from inside, where Donna Summer was singing "Bad Girls."

"Jesus, Domingo. I haven't heard this song in twenty years. And it hasn't gotten any better."

Domingo gave a quick laugh.

"Not like a fine wine, then? But it fits the place. You will see."

"You've been here before?"

He looked at me dubiously, as if not visiting the strip club would have been unnatural.

"*Non*, Birdman," he said slowly. "But these clubs, they are all the same. Same music, same watered drinks, same everything."

The door opened. A jagged man with a sallow, suspicious face popped his head out. The perimeter of his eyes cried reddish-yellow tears, but his pupils were small and tight and fluttered back and forth like drunken hummingbirds.

"What is it?"

"We've got a delivery. Food for the buffet."

He squinted, arresting his eyes in mid-flight.

"From who?"

"Your pal in Boston," I said, using Vince's code.

"Wait."

He closed the door. A few moments later, we heard footsteps and the door reopened. The suspicious man walked outside, sandwiched between two large bouncers. The bouncers were identical, resembling a large claw between which the suspicious man was lodged. When they were a few yards from the truck, the man snapped his fingers and each half of the claw broke away and followed Domingo to the flatbed. As they began to unload it, the suspicious man smiled as if at a private joke.

"Why don't you come in and have a beer?"

"I don't think so…."

"You'll come in. I've been told you would."

He held the door for me. I entered and followed him down a short, low passageway. A few dim bulbs hung from the ceiling like limp marionettes, and they seemed to create more darkness than light. Then we turned and came to a room on the left. The mirrors that hung from all the walls tripled the size of this dressing room and large bright lights dotted the perimeter of each mirror like snowballs reflecting against a sheet of ice. Four bustling women were rapidly getting changed. One was completely nude, two topless and the fourth was zipping up a lacy white wedding gown. The zipper was in front, and I followed it from her thick thighs as it traveled upward, showing off black panties, which protested against the slight bulge of her stomach, and over her thin breasts which looked like deflated balloons. She hadn't yet put her veil on, so I got a good look at the heavy makeup which frosted her face.

The completely naked girl was the best looking of the four. As we paused at the door, the suspicious man, who had put on sunglasses somewhere in the dark hallway, asked her who was on stage at the moment.

She floated over to us. Her breasts were full but sagging. They swayed as she moved and my eyes were tethered to them. "Candy's just finishing up, Ritchie," she grinned devilishly, and quickly flicked her gaze across my trousers. I had a bulging erection and my attempts to hide it only made her grin wider. She was so much at ease without her clothes that I felt naked. As she gave Ritchie the schedule, I noticed her nipples looked like tarnished silver dollars. I peered closer and saw that each one was crossed with tiny pieces of masking tape.

"After Candy, Stella is doing her turn, then me and Jill."

"You two doing the double?"

"Yeah, Ritchie. It's the only way we're gonna make any cash — there ain't no one out there 'cept that Jap businessman. He's good for some, though."

"Okay, Roxanne. When Candy gets back, tell her to work on him."

Roxanne turned back into the room with slightly more effort than she needed, and giggled teasingly to the other girls. Then Ritchie and I continued down the hallway. With every step, the music got louder until we came to a curtain at the end of the hall.

"May I ask you a question?"

Ritchie glanced at me.

"Depends."

"Why did she have tape on her?"

I thought he might spit through his nose.

"They all do. We ain't got a license to be a topless joint."

"But this *is* a topless club. It says so outside."

"Sure," he grunted. "It's what you call a technicality. You can't see the tape from the stage — it's the same color of the skin so the girls *look* topless. But *technically*, they ain't."

He chuckled thinly as if bored by an old joke, and opened the curtain to the main room. It was dark, and the windows which I'd seen from the outside were hidden amongst the furls of shadows and cigarette smoke. The music was blaring "Hot Legs" by Rod Stewart, another song resurrected from my youth. The stage was rectangular, like a large pool table, with a wooden floor and a mirror in back. Black vinyl bar stools, like mushrooms, conspicuously sprouted in front of the stage. Anyone sitting there was visible from the whole room, but the four or five men who were in the place didn't seem to mind if they were recognized. They all nursed their drinks while dollar bills were splayed out in front of them like poker hands. Velvety curtains hung on either side of the mirror and two brass poles jutted up from the floor to the ceiling. On one of these poles, a girl was swirling around and around. Naked, except for the tape and a red thong that matched her hair, she was upside down, holding onto the pole with long, bronzed legs while her arms stretched out helplessly and her long red hair burned a campfire around the stage.

After a few revolutions, she jumped down, and started bouncing to each corner of the stage like a billiard ball to its pocket. She danced to her own rhythm, paying no attention to the music. It was incidental, clinging temporarily in the air like the cigarette smoke until it would eventually waft out of the bar and leave her behind. I wondered if this was why she ignored it. However, because she was dependent on the music, her dancing was defiant, almost in competition against it. But, no matter how violent her steps were, the music would always win and she knew it. Although she danced to her own beat, the songs kept time over her performance and when they stopped playing, Candy would have to leave the stage, regardless of how much money she made in tips. Knowing that the music could come and go with the freedom of a prison guard, Candy danced in fluid contradiction.

As the song was reaching its final verse, Candy began desperately streaking, her hair cutting gashes in the air as she rebounded from corner to corner, enticing the men who tried to decide whether to give up one last bill or wait until the next girl. Candy worked them, cajoled them into changing their minds. When an elderly man handed her a dollar with trembling fingers, Candy blew him a kiss as she nonchalantly dropped the bill on the stage behind her. Then she went back for more, trying to earn as much as she could before the song ended. If I had been sitting there, she could have had everything in my pocket. Something made her more deserving of it than me and when she looked up momentarily and caught my eye, I realized what it was.

The club operated on a topsy-turvy class system. Candy was middle-class, and the lonely, sick bastards who fed her dollars for a thrill were her peasants. Yet, when I looked at them, I couldn't help feeling that, in a bizarre parallel, they were emperors and she was their geisha. I realized that it all depended on the vantage point — the stage or the stools.

Candy began yelling at the Japanese man.

"Hey you, slant-eyes, show me watcha got there!" Grinning widely, she slid her tongue around the insides of her lips.

The Japanese man obviously spoke no English and smiled back as Candy berated him.

"Come on, ya yellow bastard!" she shouted, bending down and pushing her breasts close to his face. "You think it's for free? Go back to your fuckin' country if ya want it for free! Here ya gotta pay!"

The other men roared.

"She's hot for ya, ya Nip! Give her your yen!"

"Yeah! Maybe she'll suck-ee your cock-ee!"

The Japanese man gave Candy a five, which she took with a wink and put the bill in her cleavage. She mashed her breasts together so that they held the five in place, and looked at him with a little girl's pout.

"Ain't cha got anything more, Papa-san?" she mewed.

"Come on! She wants ya baaad, Hirohito!" another guy yelled.

Now he gave her a ten and, hearing the music was about to end, she got up and finished her dance with a few quick gyrations. The men roared and whistled, throwing dollar bills at her. Then the music crashed to oblivious silence and the spell was broken.

Somewhere in the ceiling a voice boomed:

"Let's hear it for Candy! Candy! Yes, gentlemen, she'll be back later. Give it up for her."

Candy gathered the bills that she'd dropped on the stage, and yelled, "thank you." Her voice was flat and drained of the passion she had used to coax her audience. The men applauded half-heartedly and looked at her — the illusion of her majesty had dissolved with the stage lights and now she was just a naked woman scrambling to pick up the money like a street beggar. And the men, now exposed in the darkness in which they sat, squirmed and hid behind their beers, more naked than Candy.

As another girl was readying to take the stage, Ritchie offered me a beer.

"On the house."

"No thanks," I said, looking back at the curtain.

"I can't let you take one of the girls. Sorry."

"What?"

"The boss didn't authorize that. I'd have to pay for it myself. But I can arrange a discount if you wanna go upstairs."

"No. No thanks. I'm going to go help them finish unload."

I turned and, without listening to Ritchie's protests, found my way through the dark corridor until I reached the disillusioned freedom of the parking lot.

"How did you like it inside?"

Domingo's tone was gilded darkly.

"It's hard to say."

"Why is that?" he pushed the truck forward.

"The women were...."

"Pretty, *non?*"

"Yes. Very pretty. Even the ugly ones."

Domingo laughed.

"It has been a long time since you have seen a woman."

"Yes, it has."

We were driving down Route 1, towards Boston, and were approaching the Tobin Bridge. As we entered the onramp, we became mired in the bridge's usual traffic congestion. Like a serpent, the cars and trucks inched their way over the bridge. In the truck, we were like a single piece of food in the belly of a giant snake.

"Do you go to those places a lot, Domingo?"

"Now and then. Being so far from my wife...it gets to a man."

"You miss your wife, then?"

He shrugged.

"*Si.*"

His lazy fingers tapped along with the rhythm of the gearshift.

"And going to a strip club doesn't bother you?"

"*Non.* Why should it bother me?"

"I don't know....I felt kind of pathetic."

He looked over at me.

"What does that mean — 'pathetic'?"

"It means...pitiful...shameful."

Domingo had been picking at his butter teeth, trying to dislodge a remnant from lunch. He stopped, and took his fingers from his mouth.

"You were ashamed? Of what?"

I stared ahead at the cars and trucks that had been swallowed by the serpent.

"Of myself, I guess."

"Why? You were working."

"Yes. But when I saw the girls, it made me feel...less."

"I do not understand you. You haven't seen a woman in years. Now you do and you feel less. You should feel more. If you didn't feel more, I don't think I want you sleeping in my house."

I chuckled and said, "That's just it, Domingo. I *was* attracted to the women — that's why I felt bad."

Consternation screwed into Domingo's face. I didn't know how to articulate the way I felt until I cast my mind back to the posters of Aruba I used to see in the travel agency.

"Domingo, in Aruba, they have some pretty fancy hotels, right?"

"*Si.* Very expensive."

"I once saw a picture of one of them. There were these couples eating dinner outside. All around them were palm trees with cages hanging from them that held parrots. And there was a stream that winded around their table and ran out among the other tables."

"The hotels build those eating places. Tourists. They like to think they are eating on their own little island. It does not make sense — they *are* eating on a little island just by being in Aruba."

"So, the hotels build the whole scene — the streams, too?"

"*Si.* Is stupid."

"Okay, let me ask you this. Are there any fish in those streams?"

"Of course. Just like the parrots in the cages, the hotels put the fish in the streams."

"Well, would you ever go to one of those streams and try to catch the fish?"

"You would not have to try very hard. The fish are like pets. You could almost pick them up with your hands."

"Well, that's sort of how I felt today in the club. The men and the women weren't real — they were all playing a game. But they were all trying to fool themselves into thinking that they were different. The men thought the girls really wanted to be with them, when the girls just wanted money. And the girls thought the men really wanted them, but all they really wanted was a cheap thrill. After the place closes, they'll all go home to their wives or girlfriends while the dancers will go home with their money. There's nothing real about any of it, so you tell me what the point is?"

"Why does it have to be real? If the men like it and the girls get paid, what does it matter?"

"It matters because none of it is true."

Domingo rubbed his silky mustache.

"Perhaps it is untrue, Birdman. But then, perhaps the real question becomes this: if you felt so...pathetic, why did you stay inside so long?"

"That's a good question."

"*Si*, that *is* a good question," Domingo shook his head, staring at the snake of cars in front of him. I followed the snake, too, watching how the brake lights in the distance affected those on the cars right in front of us. I knew my answer to Domingo lay in a parallel to the falling row of dominos I saw in the red flashes behind each car. It was time to let him in. The only way to explain my feelings was by answering his original questions about where I came from.

"Domingo, my father is in prison."

He didn't look at me in shock, as I had half expected him to do. In fact, he didn't look at me at all, but rather kept his eyes steadily on the road. I continued, "He murdered someone. He's in for life — no parole."

"Truly?" Domingo asked with more pity than interest as if being in jail was not such a big deal.

"Yes. But that isn't what bothers me."

"*Non?*" he said, as his semi-interested eyebrow slowly jacked up into an arch. "What is it that bothers you, then?"

"It's…well it's the *way* it all happened. The reason that he murdered. When he went to prison, I was just a kid and didn't understand any of it. But today I began to see it."

Domingo perked up a little.

"He killed a stripper?"

"No, no. It was the men in the club. They reminded me of my father. By playing their game instead of being home with their wives. Those men today were trying to convince themselves their game was real, and they had no control over this. And my father was trying to convince me that his game hadn't been real — that he hadn't ever played."

I braced against the hard back of the seat as a memory came back to me.

"Jesus, I remember the last time I saw him. It was at the jail, and he was wearing a blue jumpsuit and his hair had been recently cut. We were in a room that felt too small for both of us. It was kind of like this traffic jam."

"What happened?" Domingo asked, flipping on the truck's headlights.

"Well, I was incredibly angry and the anger seemed to come from a part of me that I didn't know existed. I had never been mad at him before — ever. He told me to sit down, but I couldn't. This anger kept pumping into me, filling me up like air in a balloon, and I was getting bigger inside this tiny room. It was hard to breathe. My father kept telling me that he was innocent but it was all lies. He had never lied to me before but now everything he said was a lie. Each lie was another gust of air that filled me up until I was ready to burst.

"All I wanted was for him to stop. I felt as if I'd been held tightly in a dark constricting place for most of my life. I tried to tell him this, how I could never be sure of anything he had ever said to me, and how I never really knew him, but as I spoke, my rage tried to force its way out. It was like standing too close to a fire. My throat got dustier with each sentence, like I'd swallowed ashes, and I couldn't breathe right — I had too much air but, at the same time, I couldn't get enough. And he kept talking, but I couldn't listen to him anymore, telling me that he was innocent. So finally I did explode. I just burst — I don't even remember exactly what I said to him. You know, I once saw a car hit a fire hydrant on Arlington Street and the water shot out like a geyser. I was like that. The words just shot out of me and even though I was trying to say just one thing, the words were too jumbled, they came too fast."

"What were you trying to say?"

"I was...I was trying to tell him that he wasn't my father anymore. That I couldn't be sure if he ever had been."

Domingo's eyes creased like folding cloth. A moment passed, then he asked:

"But why do the men in the club remind you of all this?"

That answer stung my throat so that it was almost too painful to sigh.

"When I was inside the club, I felt an attraction. Along with feeling pathetic, I was also being pulled into something I couldn't control. Look, just like I don't care that my father is in jail, I don't care if men go to watch naked girls dance. That's just the small picture. It's not having control that scares me. For so long, I've been fucked up because my father couldn't control his urges. I don't want to lose any control I might have. But I'm afraid that's already happening to me."

Domingo kept looking forward and said nothing, but he must have been thinking about what I'd told him as he nearly missed the signs that pointed to the Cambridge/Somerville exit. He quickly started to cross into the right lane and only when he was halfway over the line did he remember to flick on his turn signal. Usually, horns would blare when anyone pulled this kind of maneuver, but strangely there was no protest from any of the other cars. We slipped into the lane and headed towards the exit. I wondered if the other drivers spared us their complaints because Domingo had, at the last moment, used his turn signal. Although this idea was very far-fetched, especially with Boston drivers, it seemed magical that no one behind us paid any attention. That such a small action should have such a large implication made me think about technicalities.

The shower had become my place for reflection. It had been so long since I'd had the luxury of daily bathing that I took full advantage of it. When Domingo and I returned from Playland, I headed for the shower to think.

Since I had started sharing Domingo's apartment, I'd gone through various stages of adaptation. Reaching for the soap, I remembered the first showers I'd taken there, and how ashamed I had felt for moving away from my own principles, away from my reasons for being on the street. Although I knew I had to play Vince's game, each pinprick of water had stung my face accusingly. I would greedily lather and rinse my body and then try to convince myself that turning the water temperature as hot as it would go could serve as a form of penance.

Over the next few days, confusion began showering along with me and a guilty giddiness took the place of shame. I knew this feeling — I'd felt it once in high school, when an underage friend and I had tried to buy a six-pack of beer. We were turned away with the warning that the next time the owner would call the police. Years later, when I was living on the street and was of legal age, I went into a liquor store in Kenmore Square to buy a bottle of cheap beer. The store was on a sub-basement level, so I had to walk down a few steps from the sidewalk to reach the doors. That same giddiness walked alongside me as I approached the store. Rationally, I knew I wasn't doing anything wrong, but I couldn't quite believe that it was legal for me to enter. Crossing the metal threshold of the shower gave me this same thrill. My stomach was randomly squeezed like a taboo-soaked sponge. The showers I took were quick, as if I might get caught. But as I began to feel cleaner, my apprehensions were distilled.

Now my showers had become luxurious. I began to use a washcloth instead of hastily scrubbing with my hands. I was exploring parts of my body I had almost forgotten existed. Every day, I found a new spot to clean — behind my ears, between my toes, the crevices of my elbows — and I would revel in my new morning ritual while each day trying to find a different part of my body to wash.

I had become too complacent. The showers were still luxuries, as I hadn't forgotten what life without them had been, but I was getting too used to them. And my initial shame, though somewhat faded, still clung to me. I discovered this shame wasn't just confined to the shower but had spread to other facets of my new life:

the mattress Vince dragged in for me to sleep on; the clothes he bought for me; the three meals I knew I would eat each day. My upside-down world was beginning to appeal to me and the desire to return to my former life was loosening its grip. My choices see-sawed, swinging to my former principles on one day, and returning to the possibility of accepting this new life the next. And the fulcrum on which these choices balanced was one of control.

But after confessing to Domingo, I was able to see my situation differently and realized that maybe I could have the best of both worlds. Vince had given me an opportunity that I hadn't immediately seen and, as the water rinsed the soap from my face, this became clear. Working for Vince allowed me to take my own revenge.

Perhaps I had been too young or too numb to understand it when I first landed on the street, but now I saw that this was really what I had been looking for. I had tried to anesthetize myself from society, blocking out as much as I could and only acknowledging its existence when necessary. The unknown transformation from pigeon to squab was an example of this. Stepping into the world had been like walking onto a stage — when I stepped out again, the transformation was my curtain, dropping to separate me from the eyes of the audience.

However, during the last few months I had slowly begun to *feel*. As each shower cleaned away a layer of dirt, it also scrubbed free some of my numbness. I saw that becoming a non-person had accomplished nothing, with the possible exception of making a few people wonder what had become of me. Occasionally, my name may have died on the lips of nostalgia, but other than that nothing had changed. My protest against society had been moot *and* mute.

But instead of losing control, I had actually been gaining it from the very society I had run from. Working for Vince and embracing his philosophy that nothing is the way it appears gave me the power to take revenge. Each time a member of my father's world ordered squab but in fact ate pigeon, he was savoring my retribution. And this would accomplish much — for me and everybody who had, somehow, been wrongly hurt. Vince's plan gave people who played harmful games a literal taste of their own medicine. And while it was illegal, when I weighed the scheme against the crimes committed by our "victims," I felt it was justifiable. It was just a technicality that I'd overlooked. I turned off the shower and stepped out. Toweling dry, I felt clean and refreshed. I wanted to feel like this forever.

Chapter Eight
Out of the Dust Pan and Into the Mire

In the following weeks, I began moving towards the fringe of the mainstream. Fortified with the new belief that I could help right some of society's wrongs, I began taking steps into the public fray. At first I was tentative, moving slowly like a child walking on a frozen lake. After a few weeks, however, I gained confidence and forced myself to venture into crowded public areas like Downtown Crossing during the daytime. By degrees, the numbness I'd felt for so long left me like the soul from a corpse, and each of my nerves seemed exposed and vulnerable. My senses were overloaded as if, for years, I'd been blind and deaf and then suddenly cured in the midst of a Mardi Gras parade.

But it gave me an important insight. I began listening to the businessmen's slick-deal cell-phone conversations; I noticed that the cops on horseback looked away from certain violations; I caught jewelry vendors cheating tourists by inflating prices on the spot. I could see I wasn't the only one who had been hurt and this strengthened my resolve.

And then, after a few months of my awakening, Vince turned my world around again. Only this time, the shift was in my favor.

One afternoon, Vince and I were walking down Summer Street together.

"This ain't so bad now, is it, Birdy?" he said.

"It's worse."

Vince laughed.

"You've been away too long. But you're starting to see what you've missed."

We continued towards Washington Street. Both sides of the long blocks were eclipsed by renovations which made the street look more like a war zone. Tractors and cement mixers were parked inside the hollowed-out shells of buildings; fluorescent orange arrows, like battle lines, covered the sidewalks in a schematic promise of a better future; in the distance, where the over-budget and prolonged highway construction known as the Big Dig was in full force, lay a graveyard filled with dinosaur-like cranes. Vince paused and turned around.

"Look at all these people. Every one of them — an opportunity."

I scanned the busy shopping plaza. Mothers tugged on the arms of crying children; teenagers yelled at their school friends; haughty adults skirted the drunks who were passed out on the cobblestones. No one seemed cognizant of the world around them, but Vince was able to take in everybody and lump them into the one category of Business Opportunities.

We burrowed through the ancient cement corridor of a side street. Its darkness and dusty odor was typical of these barely used throughways in the city. Forgotten except when proved useful, many of these roads are destined to become alleyways. The chances of finding other people in them were slim and, in another time and place, one could easily imagine war refugees hiding there. Ironically, this corridor opened up onto the bustling Tremont Street. Dark to light, deserted to over-populated, the transition was violent and swift. Like dregs in wine, Vince and I filtered through the crowds that flowed towards the shopping plaza.

We entered a small bar on Boylston Street and the world shifted back, from light to dark. Despite the vibrant crowds outside, the bar stood still. A timeless world within a world, its origins were as indecipherable as its patrons. Paneled walls held yellowing team photos of the Red Sox and Celtics while the autographed face of Carl Yastremski hung behind the bar, centered above the tops of dusty bottles with age-curled labels. In the corner sat an old television with a horizontal hold problem that Domingo would have coveted — each person on the screen was multiplied by three, and black and gray lines jumped across the picture like kids dodging puddles in a rainstorm.

I sat at a red vinyl booth. There was a large gash in it and most of its foam cushioning had bled from the hole. Vince walked up to the bar to order. The bartender was ancient with dull yellowish-white hair and thick black-framed glasses. He wiped his hands on a dingy apron and scowled. Vince had interrupted his viewing of a triplicate episode of *The Price Is Right* by ordering two Scotches. We were the only people in the place, except for an old man in the corner who could have been either dead or asleep. A smothered cigarette limply hung from his mouth and his head rested against the mirrored wall.

Vince came back with the drinks and slid in across from me.

"Cheers, Birdy," he said, raising his glass.

"What's the occasion?"

Vince sipped at his Scotch and then put the squat glass down. The ice cubes swirled like swimmers in a whirlpool, and Vince waited until their clinking stopped before answering.

"We're expanding."

"Really?"

"Yeah. We got a new contract."

Vince didn't appear to be overjoyed and drinking Dewars with me in a dive at lunchtime certainly wasn't his usual idea of a celebration.

"What kind of contract, Vince?"

He absentmindedly stirred the ice with his finger, reinvigorating the whirlpool.

"My associates have decided that it's time to work with some new people. We're going to be collaborating with a few other operations on a whole new venture. Basically, we're going through a merger."

I said nothing to fill his pause and he studied me with silent eyes. The sound of the ice against glass was the only thing we had in common. Finally, Vince drank again and when he put down the glass, he looked tired from the effort.

"Okay, here's the deal, Birdman. My associates gave me the chance to make a go of this business. I had to…pay them back for some help they gave me years ago. This was the only way I could do that."

"I thought you said this wasn't the Mob."

"Keep it down," he hissed with no change of expression. "I said the less you know, the better. But, it doesn't matter, at least not for you. Things aren't going to change too much on your end. There'll be some new people around — "

"I'm not so sure I want to work with 'new people', Vince."

Vince lit a cigarette and viciously snapped his lighter shut.

"Listen, Birdy, you ain't really got a say, so get used to it. Remember, you're the only one who's not anonymous."

His eyes flared and the tip of his cigarette reflected in them. He rubbed his temples.

"Look, the fact is, there's nothing for you to worry about. I'm the one whose neck is on the line."

"How so?"

Vince paused, momentarily caught between the crevices of a decision. Then he sighed.

"Remember when I told you I was in jail?"

"Yes."

"And I told you about Clem, the old guy who liked being in prison?"

"The guy who liked chicken dinners."

"Right. Well, Clem's real name is Clementino. He was high up in a Boston family, which was why people didn't mess with him. He's a lifer, but he had outside contacts — and still does — so, inside, he had nothing to lose and he'd kill you without thinking about it. But he had other ways of getting at you, too. A word from him and it would be your family or girlfriend. He's a serious guy — you don't screw with old Clem."

Vince looked over his shoulder, as if the old prisoner might have walked in the bar.

"So what does this have to do with us?"

"Well, like I told you, Clem liked me. One day, I got into a fight with another guy. He was just this lowlife who held a grudge against me — for two years! — because once I didn't give him a cigarette. Do you believe that? You hear about that kind of shit and might not believe it, but that's what prison does to you. It's a whole different world, Birdman. It's primal — for God's sake, imagine a cigarette being that important to a guy! Anyway, he was about to be released so he figured out a way to get back at me without being caught. A few nights before he was gonna walk out a free man, he ambushed me in the bathroom and broke my jaw. They had to wire it shut and I couldn't talk for six weeks. See, that was his plan. He thought that by the time I

121

could tell who did it, he'd be long gone. 'Course the dip shit shoulda broke my hands too. Clem came to see me in the infirmary the next morning and asked me to write down the guy's name. That night they found him hanging in his cell. It was reported as a suicide. Of course no one said anything about how he was able to hang himself after cutting off all his fingers."

"Jesus Christ."

"After that, Clem and I became even closer friends. I had no choice but I also had his protection while in prison. The guy he offed was a pal of a lot of the other cons, but they knew the score and no one came near me. So, when I was up for parole, Clem called me to his cell and made me understand that I would be expected to pay him back by helping his friends on the outside."

"So you joined them?"

"I got pulled in. Every so often I was approached by these guys — my 'associates'. They would have a special little job they needed done. Lots of different shit — roughing up people who owed money, small break-ins, that kind of thing. And then one day, when apparently I had proved myself, they told me about the network."

There was something he hadn't told me; I knew it just from the way his face twitched when he took another sip of Scotch. He lit another cigarette and inhaled as if it were a breath of air and I braced myself for the truth.

"As I told you, they set up a legitimate importing operation as a front for the food business. But *that's* always been a front for them to funnel drugs through."

"What!? I thought you said —"

"Come on — you didn't really think those guys would be into selling squirrels to Hong Kong, did'ja?"

I shrugged hopelessly.

"Christ, Birdy, I think living on the streets all this time has affected your brain. You're smart, but you're naïve. Well, hang on 'cause it gets better. It turned out that the food business worked better as a front than anyone had thought. The network was getting pretty rich smuggling drugs out of the country, and I was seeing a nice chunk of that. Then last week everything changed."

"What happened?"

"An operation out of Illinois went down. The Feds got a tip and busted that ring. Good thing for our safeguards. You see, besides screening people, the different operations have no communication between them. Everything's coordinated by the associates. So the cops think the operation they busted is just out of Chicago. Still, the network had plans to shut down for a while until things cooled off, but then Clem gave them a different word."

I took a sip and waited for the new direction.

"They've decided to increase the food supply operation."

"But you said that there's no real money in it."

Vince drew one last time on his cigarette before snuffing it out in the plastic ashtray.

"There's money, Birdy, but not in exporting. We're gonna be selling to prison cafeterias."

My glass fused to my hand.

"Prison...?"

"You'd never think it'd be big money, would ya?"

"No, not really...."

Vince lit another cigarette and the *wheeewww* sound he made dragging on it prefaced some astonishing figures.

"Well, in the state of Texas, there are roughly a hundred and fifty thousand people locked up. It costs the state two bucks a day per inmate to feed all those guys.

That's three hundred grand per day. Or almost one hundred and thirty million dollars a year. Tax free, of course."

"My God."

"Oh, yeah."

"But…how are we gonna pull it off. I mean, getting that much food is…."

"It ain't gonna be that much food right off the bat. We're starting with a smaller sized pen that holds about three thousand inmates. Once it starts taking off, then we start expanding. But no doubt, it's gonna be a fucking nightmare. And it's also gonna cut into my profits significantly, so you can see why I'm not so thrilled about it. I'm not going to be making as much as I did before, but the network stands to make a bundle more. As far as our work goes, even by joining forces with all these new people from around the country, it's gonna be insane trying to keep up with the supply, but there's nothing we can do about that. We're all stuck — you, me, Dommy, everybody."

Vince stared silently at me, his dark eyes watering from the cigarette smoke. I looked at the wavy TV. A contestant was jumping up and down, ecstatic at being picked. The bartender was still engrossed in the show — he hadn't moved since pouring our drinks. Neither had the sleeping drunk against the mirror. I looked back at Vince.

"So how is this going to work, Vince? I mean, how is the network going to sell the food to the prisons?"

"Think about it. The guys running this show are pretty heavy. Most of the top people are in jail. They lined up a number of prisons with boards of directors that could easily be swayed or who were already corrupt. And they've got people working for them who aren't exactly demanding company cars. So, when they did the numbers, they realized they could make a killing.

Of course the beautiful thing is, who's gonna know? Suppose a con gets sick from some bad meat — you think anyone's gonna give a shit?"

Vince threw the rest of his Scotch down but I savored mine, along with the thought of this new operation. This was going to target the very people I'd been after, those like my father, who had lied about the games they had played and left innocent people suffering in their wake. As I licked the slight burn of Scotch from my lips, I grinned at the recollection of the snow blanketing Park City, and what my father had once said about our snowjobs — this would be like shooting fish in a barrel.

———

I remembered how to smile. Though Vince became increasingly disgruntled about the merger, I worked harder to help facilitate its progress. I imagined my father and the countless, faceless game-players like him falsely relishing every rabbit I brought in; I grinned at the thought of their mouths watering over fried fish patties made from frog legs and the garbage seafood which normally wouldn't even be considered for bait.

My good mood seemed to spread to the vendors, as each time Domingo and I went for a pick-up, there was even more food than the time before. All the vendors were giving us more — Santos, the geese-catchers and even Joey.

"You guys are really bringing it in," I told him one night.

"Yeah, well the Places o' Plenty have been good to us. There's lot's of bunnies these here days," Joey said, pulling imaginary rabbits from his beard. "'Cept of course in Providence, but we can't do nothin' 'bout that, you know."

"Well, you've really increased the haul, Joey."

"You knows what they say — business is business and these critters are business, right?"

He assumed his fighter's stance, shadowboxing in a drunken bob-and-weave.

"Right."

Joey put down his fists as if he won an exhausting fight.

"So — 'cept for Providence — we ain't got no trouble, right-o?"

"No, why would there be any problems? Things are going great."

He backed away, then quickly dropped his head and lifted it like a shovel, taking me in with a long, scooping look.

"Hee hee, great. Good, things are great. See's I've got an extra man or three and we expanded the Places o' Plenty. Down in Canton we found a lot of new, good bunny holes."

"Well, keep up the good work. 'Cept in Providence."

He winked at me and I jumped into the truck. Joey patted the door and then, when Domingo started the engine, he backed away quickly as the flatbed came to life. We drove away from the trestle, leaving Joey in the shadows of his shelter.

A few nights later, Domingo and I had gone to New Bedford to pick up some clams, lobsters and other seafood. As one of our first regular vendors, Santos knew the ropes. Although Vince had predicted he might try to cheat us, Santos was always fair.

"You guys give me business I need. We all need it — my men they send it home to their families. You can always trust me."

And we did, along with all the vendors. Santos, who was trying to support his family; Joey, who'd been brutalized in the boot camps; the nomadic geese-catchers in constant search of decent living conditions — they were among the innocents who'd been hurt. And so I carried Vince's iron rod for show but never checked the balance of the scales. Santos and I had an unspoken understanding. As long as he played fair, I wasn't going to check up on him.

So when Domingo and I arrived at the dock and the boat wasn't in, my initial thought was that maybe he had pulled something. We waited in the shadows of a weather-scraped office on the pier for a half hour just in case he was late. But the boat never slipped up to the dock. Starting up the truck, we finally left the drowsing black tide behind us and headed back to Boston.

"What do you think happened to them, Domingo? It's not like Santos and his crew not to show up."

"I do not know, Birdman. But I do not like it. *Non*. Not at all."

We got our answer the next morning. Vince burst into the apartment with the *Boston Globe*.

"Did anyone see you two last night — at the dock!" he yelled, jerking us to consciousness.

"What's going on — ?"

"Dommy?"

"*Non*, no one saw us, Vince."

He let out a sigh like a reverse gasp he'd been holding in all night.

"What's the matter, Vince?"

"Did Santos show up last night?"

"No, I was going to tell you this morning. Dommy and I got to the dock and it was deserted. We waited about thirty minutes before we left. We didn't know what happened to him."

Vince showed us the small article in the *Globe*.

"This is what happened."

I read the story while Domingo looked over my shoulder. He only had to look at the picture, and then he focused on Vince, who was pacing in the kitchen.

"Vince, was anybody left alive?"

"No. I'm sorry, Dommy."

Domingo nodded and walked to the bathroom.

"The paper says they ran out of fuel, drifted and hit a reef. They'd have to be out there a long time to run out of fuel, Vince."

"Yeah."

"So, what do you think?"

"What do you mean, what do *I* think? I'm no fuckin' sailor. Obviously, they didn't fill up their tanks enough."

Vince turned away and lit a cigarette.

"They were sailors. They knew how much fuel they needed, Vince."

He turned around and blew a veil of smoke before his face.

"Then maybe they were trying to bring in more fish. I told you, these guys will try to cheat ya. Maybe they were trying to get me to buy even more from them."

"Would you have, Vince? Would you have bought more?"

He sat down at the Formica table, squinting through the smoke.

"What are you getting at, Birdy?"

I looked down at the cracks in the table. Over the past few months, the rivers in the Formica had been overflowing from use.

"I'm not getting at anything, Vince. It's just that you seem so...paranoid about the whole thing."

"Of course I'm paranoid, Birdy. I was worried that somebody might have seen you last night. That would blow our whole operation."

"Nobody saw us, Vince."

"Well, thank Christ. It's a good thing that there were no survivors, either. As far as the Coast Guard knows, Santos was out fishing legitimately and had an accident. So, we're completely out of it."

"Yes. That's a good thing, Vince."

He flicked his eyes on me.

"Hey, this shit happens. It's a tragedy, but it's part of the risk any fisherman takes. Ask Domingo."

"I will, Vince. Thanks for bringing us the news."

"Yeah. I'll see you later."

———

When Domingo heard Vince leave, he returned to the kitchen. Without a word, he walked to the refrigerator and pulled out the remaining three beers from a six-pack. Then he turned on the television and, as static washed over him, opened the first beer and guzzled it.

"Domingo."

He said nothing but just rocked to the soothing waves of the static.

"Dommy. I'm sorry."

But he kept rocking, staring straight ahead at the fuzzy lines.

———

Late that afternoon, I walked to the office. It was a cold day and the wind bit at my legs through my blue jeans. Dusk was beginning to fall earlier as we headed into late autumn. In the dimness, brown leaves danced in the gutter with a haunted rustle. I remembered these leaves when they had been born, when I first met Vince. I was chilled in that early summer heat, but now, despite the drop in temperature, I was reasonably warm. So much had occurred during their lifetime.

In my office, Vince was on the phone. He signaled for me to wait a moment, and I loitered around the factory. I saw Gloria. She was sluggishly packing boxes with trembling arms.

"Are you all right?"

She looked at me. Her eyes were like dying flowers.

"I'm great, Tweets."

"You sure?"

"Yeah...I'm great. I...I just missed the clinic today."

"What are you doing here, then?"

"I've been working a double. We need to get all this shit out."

I looked at the boxes piled on the pallets, all ready to be shipped out to the penitentiary in Texas.

"You need your methadone. I'm gonna call Domingo and have him take you to the clinic."

"No!" Her brittle fingers grabbed my arm. They were surprisingly strong, as if seized with *rigor mortis.* "No, don't do anything, Tweets. I'll be all right."

"You need the methadone, Gloria."

"It can wait. Please. We need to get this out and...and besides...I need the money."

The eyes of all her demons, present and past, stared me down.

"Please. I'm almost done. Anyway, the clinic's closed until the morning. I'll go then, I swear. Please, Tweets? Okay?"

"Okay, Gloria."

"Thank you. Please. Thank you."

I left her alone to finish her work. I wondered about the pain that must be racking her body. I could see its effect, but I had nothing to compare it to. She suffered in a different language from me, in a foreign existence.

When Vince waved to me, I entered the office and shut the door.

"Where've you been?" he asked, as I slipped past my reflection in the mirrored wall. He didn't look at me, but instead concentrated on crude tabulations he was making on a legal pad.

"With Domingo."

Vince stopped his calculating and glanced up at me.

"How is he?"

"Not great. He won't talk, won't do anything but watch the TV and rock."

"That's because he's a fisherman, Birdy. I guess it's sorta like being in the war and having your buddies shot down."

"Maybe."

"Just gimme a few minutes, would ya?"

I sat in front of the desk and, to kill time, I watched the workers through the window. Gloria wasn't the only one acting strangely. All the others were working fast and hard — contrary to their routine— sweating panic in shimmering drops. Charlie's concentration was so stringent that his eyes refused to blink, while Davio and Claude, the pair who manned the filling machine, urged it on with fervent encouragement instead of their usual joy.

Vince finally stopped writing. He looked up cautiously, as if a fluid move would burst the guilt-filled bubble he seemed to be trying to contain.

"What's wrong, Vince?"

He looked down at his pad again and sighed deeply; the top pages shuffled with the noise of a stalled propeller.

"Things aren't good."

He got up and walked to the window, watching the workers as he spoke.

"My associates aren't happy. We're not bringing in enough product."

"We're doing what we've always done."

"That's the problem. They expect more."

"But we're all working together, Vince. I thought that was the whole idea. To combine with other suppliers to bring more food in, collaboratively."

"Well now they've changed the rules."

"How can they — "

Vince turned and yelled:

"Because they're the fuckin' bosses, Birdy! They can do whatever they want because it's their fuckin' operation!"

Vince's forehead was like pumice. He took a handkerchief from his jacket pocket and wiped away the small pinpricks of glistening light that squeezed their way out of him.

"They're spreading the penitentiary plan throughout Texas and soon to Tennessee and Georgia. They've already made the deal and been paid so there's no going back. So now the pressure's on. They've told every supplier to increase by two hundred percent. And that's just for the first two weeks. After that it doubles."

"Jesus…"

"Yeah. And don't give me any more 'how are we gonna do that shit' because the answer is we got no choice. You don't say no, Birdy. Not to these guys."

"So, what's your plan?"

"First of all, we cut out anyone not pulling their weight."

I nodded towards the window.

"Like the guys outside?"

"Right. They've all been told. There're enough people we can get to replace them. Especially with winter coming — there'll be a lot of people in search of hot meals."

There was a pinch in my stomach.

"What else?"

"The vendors will have to start bringing in more. And anyone who can't keep up will also be cut. Tomorrow, I'll send Dommy out to let 'em all know. And we'll start lining up replacements right away. I can't afford to bring too many new people in — never mind spending the time to do the background checks — but we'll start."

"Jesus, Vince. Everyone's doing as much as they can."

"They're fuckin' bums, Birdy. A little extra work won't kill them."

His statement muted the room. Each moment of silence carried a scene with it — the day Vince first bought coffee for me; the day he told me about his jail time; the evening in Somerville when, instead of killing me, he offered me a place to sleep. But there were negative scenes too, interspersed vaguely amongst the silence. Translucent, as if viewed from underwater, they were visceral rather than visual and I could only just grasp their implications before they disappeared like snow melting on my tongue.

"Birdy, if we don't bring more to the table — and I mean quick — I'm a dead man. And that goes for you, too. You're in the middle of this right along with me, so don't think about trying to disappear. Because *if* my associates don't get you first — and that's a big if — the Feds'll be all over you like flies on dog shit."

"What are you talking about?"

"I'm saying that you're tied to this organization in ways you don't even know about. So don't think about running out. You won't get ten feet."

"Vince, I may not be anonymous to the vendors but — "

He chuckled.

"I'm gonna let you in on something. Just so you know." He opened the desk drawer and brought out a videotape. "We'll just call this your work contract."

He smiled at my consternation.

"That day you went to Playland. As soon as you stepped inside, the cameras were on ya. I got it all, right here. That Candy's quite a number, huh? If you had stuck around a while, she might have twisted that red hair of hers around your dick. And the chick Roxanne was checking you out, too, and not just when she was looking at the hard-on you were tryin' to hide. She snuck a good long look while you were walking down the hallway with Ritchie. So, Birdy, if I were you, I wouldn't even think about splitting. 'Cause when that happens, everyone in the organization gets a copy of this tape. You won't last a day."

My body started reacting under my clothes. Tremors rippled under my skin, pulling on muscles and bones in frenetic tugs-of-war. My lungs couldn't get enough air and my heart floated in the vacuum.

"Why, Vince? You didn't think you could trust me?"

He chuckled again but, this time, his throat was coated with steel wool; any emotion which may have been inside was scrubbed bare before it was released.

"Not forever, Birdman. You had to know that eventually the price of the meals would go up. And I needed to make sure you could always pay that price."

Chapter Nine
The Wasp Nest

M y father used to talk about classes: the lower, middle and upper, and then the subdivisions such as the lower-middle, the upper-lower, and so on. As a child, I would marvel as he described the status of "important men" and where they belonged in this intricate structure. Although I didn't fully understand the class concept, I was pretty sure it was difficult to move up in its ranks, and I based this assumption on a story my father and Mr. Peterson told each time they got together for dinner.

The story concerned their other college roommate, Harold Lexington Stingly III. Harold came from an "old money" New England family with "the bluest of blood running through their WASP veins." Better known as Stinger, Harold wasn't a very good student and, consequently, he wasn't living up to his family's expectations. Harold came from a long line of brilliant surgeons and was expected to continue that line. But though he tried, Stinger just wasn't cutting it and, in his sophomore year, found himself failing Biology.

To save his academic record, Stinger came up with a desperate plan. He decided he would try to date his professor, a rather unattractive middle-aged woman named Professor Dotings, in hopes that he would get a better grade. Of course, the guys all laughed at him, but Stinger wasn't dissuaded.

"Look, if I don't pass Biology I'll never get into med. school," Stinger said. "Going out with Professor Dotings for a few months isn't gonna kill me."

So he began his affair with the professor, and pretty soon they started meeting secretly after class in her small office that overlooked a leafy quad. They spent a lot of time "with the door closed," as my father would put it whenever I was within hearing distance. But despite the affair, at the end of the semester, Stinger was astonished to learn that he received an F for the class.

"I can't believe it!" he cried. "How could this happen!"

He confronted the professor and demanded an explanation.

"So you dated me just to receive a passing grade?" the professor asked Stinger, who had begun ranting as soon as he entered her office. Then Professor Dotings reportedly said: "Well, Mr. Stingly, let's just say your performance *in* class, even at its most dismal, never failed to outshine your performance *outside* of class."

Whenever my father or Mr. Peterson delivered this line, everyone would break into hysterics, and then they would chant:

> *Stinger stung her to rise in class*
> *But he stung himself and fell on his ass.*

When I heard this story as a child, I associated the line "rise in class" with moving upwards in life, up to the level of the "important men." Naturally, it had to be difficult to make this move if Stinger stung himself during the attempt. Furthermore, an image of what the class system looked like, based on Stinger's family background, formed in my mind. It was a wasp's nest — after all, where else would WASPS be found? I imagined Stinger's long, ruinous fall through this nest, arms and legs splayed and kicking, as he desperately clutched at layers which fell away like paper until he hit bottom.

As I grew older, I began to understand the class system much better but the image of the wasp nest stuck with me as a mental analogy. It always made sense to me; as I thought of people crawling their way to the top, I thought of the insects scurrying through the paper combs. And the notion of getting stung was fitting for someone who falls from his position. But after my talk with Vince, the wasp nest became more complex.

I left the office and took a walk. It was a late October day and the air was thick and cold. Before I realized it, the sun had disappeared. The afternoon was still supposed to be in full force, yet the sounds of homeward traffic and footsteps indicated that the day had swiftly lost itself somewhere between the second and minute hands. I looked around and saw two images — day and night scenes like a photograph and its negative — wherever my gaze focused. These images alternatively flashed behind my eyes, tricking my senses with each blink. Then in Union Square, I sat on a bench of wooden slats and paint-flecked wrought iron and took a deep breath of the chilled air.

Vince's comments about the workers were stabbing my mind. His words — *a little extra work won't kill them* — sliced through my image of the wasp nest to reveal even more layers: the fragile partitions, chambers, levels, and sections, each of which had a certain status attributed to them. But, more importantly, I began to think about the degree of subjectivity attached to the individual layers, and that's when I had my major catharsis.

I thought back to my wealthy childhood, and then followed my moves chronologically, to life on the street and then my work with Vince. I had experienced three aspects of the same world; I had traversed assorted sections within the wasp nest. Vince's image of me as a bum — because doubtless, he lumped me into that group — was just his perspective. But the idea of unique perspectives led to a vision of the world I'd never had; it was as if, until this point, I'd seen everything through squinting eyes.

Although the wasp nest was about status, status was about subjectivity. We all paste labels on those around us, but which labels are true? I thought about Vince's associates in prison. They were convicts looked down upon by society, but they also had more power than most people ever dreamt of. And while my father had been judged by a "jury of his peers," none of those twelve people would ever admit to being associated with him. He was like a financially ruined man ignored by his former friends. But who was he in jail? Was he looked at in the same light which our old neighbors had cast, or was he dismissed as a joke by more hardened prisoners?

And then I looked at myself. For ten years I'd isolated myself, moving invisibly through society like oxygen through water. I had been virtually unnoticed by all who saw me, ignored by anyone who was ensnared into giving me a glance of attention. But now I inhabited a completely different part of the wasp nest and I was not only recognizable, but significant.

I looked around, shaking my head in disbelief at my ignorance. The streetlights, which normally glowed like dull fluorescent paint stains now torched brilliantly, illuminating the crevices and potholes of the road as if it lay upon a finely detailed topographical map. Instead of tuneless blares, the car horns played sharp, rich melodies and harmonic counterpoints. And instead of just the smell of food, I could now pick out various menu items from the small take-out restaurants around me.

This was when I had finally understood that removing myself from society had been an impossible folly.

All the excuses and justifications I'd used to convince myself that I'd succeed now wilted, and as I sat on that bench and broke it all down, I saw that society holds a place for everyone, regardless of our role. If we exist, there is a label for us, and even though that label may be subjective, and may even change, we must accept it. There is no escape. The wasp nest encompasses us all.

The temperature had dropped, but oddly I didn't shiver. I decided to head for the liquor store. I was standing on a new threshold, one I hadn't known existed but that I realized I must cross. All of us who were relying on Vince were in danger and we needed to move to a safer place within the nest. I didn't need alcohol to do this, but I needed Domingo's help and I had a feeling I would need to loosen his tongue first. I knew why he was so upset about Santos and his crew. But he would have to get past that so we could make sure there wasn't another accident. Dommy and I had to make sure we didn't lose anybody else inside the wasp nest.

Domingo was still rocking inside the televised tidal waves. Looking about, I could see the twelve-pack of beer I'd bought was unnecessary except as a token gift — empty cans littered the floor like aluminum carpeting. Opening the cardboard box, I took out two bottles before putting the rest in the refrigerator. I had to rummage through a drawer filled with rusty utensils, tools and other domestic outcasts to find an opener. The bottles were icicles in my hands and each one opened without the *psst* sound of the cans which I'd grown accustomed to. Cutting up a lime, I thrust two wedges down the long, icy necks which settled and bobbed in the foamy tide like miniature shipwreck survivors. I handed a bottle to Domingo and he stared for a moment before accepting it.

"How are you?"

"It is my fault, Birdman. Santos and his crew. I am to blame."

"When did you tell them?"

Domingo didn't look surprised. He knew that eventually Vince and I would speak.

"Last week."

"So Vince lied to me about you telling the vendors tomorrow."

"*Non.* I just told Santos. He was a friend."

"Then why was Joey acting so strange when I last saw him — talking about all his new Places o' Plenty?"

"I do not know that, Birdman."

As I drank from the bottle of Corona, the lime bobbed to the surface and tried to escape through the neck.

"Dommy, we're going to have to stop it. All of it."

"You are crazy. We will never do it alive. Vince will kill us, or we will go to the jail and in the jail we will be killed. The jails are where the deals are happening — are you stupid? All the big men are in there. We will never do it and live."

"What makes you so sure we'll be caught?"

As he eyed me over his beer, the reflection of his blinking mocha eyelids treaded water inside the bottle.

"How do you think I am able to work here? Vince. He took care of my papers. He has them all. And you. You know about the videotape?"

"Yes."

"So put it from your mind. We keep on working, but we work harder."

I sipped at my beer, watching the tiny bubbles of foam that had gathered on Domingo's mustache pop and splatter gently on his lip.

"Do you want to go home to Aruba?"

He stared at me in contemplation.

"Do you?" I repeated.

"*Si*," he whispered. "In fact…in fact, Santos was going to help me get home. We were all going to escape together. But now, without Santos, there is no escape."

I handed him another beer.

"Let me tell you a story about escape."

———

At fifteen years old, I was at the age when most boys naturally begin to doubt their fathers. I wasn't immune to this teenage rebellion, as the world had rebelled on me. But all I wanted was peace again. I didn't want to "believe that woman," as my mother had referred to Gillatano. I wanted her to be the sleazy patient with an agenda, the bitter gold digger trying to discredit my father simply because she was beyond his help. The treatment he provided and her cancer were mutually exclusive — they had to be. As my mother had said, Gillatano was delusional and just out for revenge, and because her claims seemed so inconceivable, my mother had to be right.

But that was exactly why Gillatano blew up our house.

It was her symbolic gesture before she spoke out. My father had ruined her life so she would ruin his home. However, her real revenge was taken out on me. Gillatano showed me a side of my father that was so sickening, it forever changed the way I viewed him. Like spilling red wine upon a white carpet, Gillatano irrevocably stained his image.

However, until his trial, I was able to keep alive the fallacy that my father was innocent. The outrageous accusations and my overall shock made it easier for me to believe in him and it got to the point where I almost felt sorry for this woman. What she was saying couldn't possibly have been true. She was dying and desperate. Her mind was twisted; she wasn't thinking straight. It was impossible to concieve that my father could have ever committed those acts, and I conjured up excuses to support this. When I read the newspaper stories, I knew that the letters would eventually rearrange themselves as if in a bowl of alphabet soup. And somehow the local newscasters had been tampered with; I carefully listened to them and could easily tell the difference between their alien and real voices. The phony reporters spoke about my dad while the real ones told me when school was cancelled or whether the Celtics had won or lost. My mother and I were living at my aunt's house because our own home was being renovated — *not* rebuilt. And my Dad — my trusted, idolized father — was merely out of town at a long medical convention.

I nearly convinced myself. And then I went to his trial.

Because it was to be the last day of the trial, my mother allowed me to come. I saw my father for the first time in months and, as he was led into the court-room, my fantasy crumbled. Shackles bound his arms and ankles so that he moved with a staggered shuffle. His prison outfit whispered with rustling finger point-ing as he sat at one of two large brown tables that faced the judge. Gillatano sat next to the other table. This was the first time I'd seen her in person. She may have been pretty and vibrant at one time, but her wasted body was now strapped into a wheelchair. Her face was gray and her bones seemed anxious to puncture her tight skin. The skirt of her suit was short enough to allow the court to fully see her legs. Her left leg ended in a shoe that sat on the footrest on the wheelchair. But her right leg was interrupted by a patch of skin below the knee, and then a gap that was more noticeable than her flesh, which extended to the floor. The moment I saw that gap, I knew the power it held. The entire world, every member of society, could fit into its infinite space.

I felt as if I'd scrubbed a window clean only to look through and discover an entirely different room from the one I had always expected to find. Sitting inside that room was the man I had worshipped and adored, whose word I had taken to be unconditionally right and fair. And he was a complete imposter.

This broke past all boundaries of teenage rebellion and continued to the point of judgment, and at fifteen no son should ever have to judge his father. It seemed the equivalent of a parent having to choose one of his children to be put to death. But as the trial progressed, I not only judged my father, but began judging myself. How could I have been so blind — especially after the story came to light — as to put so much faith in him? So much evidence had mounted against him and, as I thought about all the developments in the case over the previous months, Gillatano's story didn't seem so implausible. Still I stuck by him and now, as I looked at myself, I hated what I saw.

The majority of the evidence having already been heard, the prosecution called Gillatano to tell her story "in her own words." As Gillatano was sworn in, I watched how each of my parents regarded her. My mother was stiff next to me and stared with hatred, although not so much at the woman in the wheelchair as at her severed leg. My Dad looked at Gillatano in two ways. When he stared into her eyes, his look was unforgiving and arrogant. But his glance frequently landed on her stump and, when it did, his eyes became moist and his gaze appeared to stroke the end of her leg.

The lead attorney, a tall, clean-shaven man named Constantine, approached her. His thick black hair was cropped just above his ears and he wore a wide, gold wedding band. As he questioned Gillatano, Constantine paced slowly from one side of the room to the other, as though suspended on a pendulum. While he walked, I noticed his habit of twisting his ring as he listened to his client.

"Mrs. Gillatano," Constantine began, "please tell the court when your affair with Dr. Franklin started."

"Soon after he treated my leg — for the fracture."

She had a voice like syrup poured over gravel and I imagined how enticing she probably had been.

"A *severe* compound fracture, correct?"

"Yes. I broke it skiing."

"And that was?"

"Six years ago."

"Six years ago. Aside from that, how would you describe your health?"

"I was in perfect condition."

"You had regular check-ups…all routine testing and screenings?"

"Yes. Faithfully."

Constantine moved to the wall opposite the jury box, creating a triangle between himself, Gillatano and the jurors.

"Mrs. Gillatano, when you first visited Dr. Franklin, what was his diagnosis of your leg?"

"That the leg had been broken in five places. The tibia was nearly entirely crushed and part of my femur would have to be reconstructed with artificial bone and pins. He said that to reconstruct my leg, I would need to have a series of operations."

"I see. And over how long a period of time were these operations spread out?"

"About two years. There was quite a bit of therapy between operations, which he oversaw."

"So, how often did you see Dr. Franklin?"

"You mean before — ?" she looked at Constantine with disgust.

"Yes, before the affair started."

"Many times...I couldn't tell you precisely."

Constantine continued his swinging walk but brought his hands together so that the fingertips touched. His wedding band shone and he looked as if he were praying.

"But enough to get to know one another pretty well?"

"Yes."

Her eyes dropped.

"So, sometime during this time frame when he 'oversaw' your therapy, you and the doctor began to see each other..."

"Socially."

Constantine stopped in front of Gillatano, his body dead like a mime, but his head cocked in mock surprise.

"Socially. Would you please tell the court how your social interaction with Dr. Franklin evolved?"

Gillatano glanced at my father as though she would spit on him. Then she looked straight ahead, over all of us, at a big iron medallion mounted on the rear wall of the courtroom.

"Dr. Franklin routinely visited me in the hospital, and we got to know each other quite well. One day, he confided in me that he was unhappy in his marriage and, in the time I had been under his care, he had fallen in love with me. Dr. Franklin was...very kind and gentle. He was also extremely charming and had the ability to ease my mind tremendously."

"Your husband wasn't able to 'ease your mind' at all?"

"No, Mr. Constantine, I am widowed."

"Aah, I'm terribly sorry, Mrs. Gillatano."

"My husband died at a very early age. I've been alone for more than ten years."

"Then would it be safe to say that because you were alone during this trying time, you welcomed Dr. Franklin's advances?"

"At first I told him that I couldn't have an affair with a married man. But he was persistent. He said the love had gone out of his marriage long ago. He told me he wanted to take care of me."

"To take care of you. Hmm," Constantine mused and walked towards the jury. "And so the affair started," he stated and then turned to face Gillatano.

"We were together for a year."

"Were you happy?"

"Very. I fell in love with him. Until — "

Constantine cocked an eyebrow.

"Until?"

Gillatano eyes began to melt. Her voice became slow and numb, as if she were remembering a bad dream.

"After what was to be the last operation, I developed a pain in my leg. Robert examined me and told me there was nothing to worry about. But when the pain grew worse, Robert did a series of tests and discovered there was an infection. He explained to me that there was always a risk of this."

"And in your case, how severe was the infection?"

"Robert told me the leg would have to be amputated. Below the knee."

"Can you describe your reaction when Dr. Franklin broke this news?"

She choked back a sob.

"I was devastated, of course. I thought my life was over. Not only was I losing my leg but I thought I would lose Robert, too."

"The thought of losing Dr. Franklin was just as devastating as losing your leg?"

"Yes, I told you, I was in love with him."

"Yet, you didn't lose Dr. Franklin, did you?"

"No. No, I didn't. Robert...explained everything. How he would still be with me. How he was in love with me and this wouldn't get in the way of us."

"From the sound of it, I would think Dr. Franklin must have been deeply in love with you."

"I thought so, too."

"But something changed your mind," Constantine suggested, walking towards her with steps that were timed to each word so that he looked to be dancing to his speech. When he reached her, he asked, "What was it?"

Gillatano hung her head while her thin, pointy shoulders shrugged rapidly, like menacing spears. Constantine's eyes never left her. Finally she raised her head, which was shaking with her sobs. Her tears shone dully against her gray skin like candlelight behind wax paper.

"Mrs. Gillatano?" Constantine backed away from the witness box, slowly, as if we were watching it all on TV with the camera zooming in on Gillatano. At least two minutes passed and the echo of Gillatano's sobs seemed stitched to the air. Constantine waited until the sound finally frayed and fell away, and then posed his next question.

"Mrs. Gillatano, would you please tell the court what an acrotomophile is?"

A murmur, like thunder miles away, wafted through the room. The strange word paralyzed Gillatano. Her tears had stopped, although their tracks remained on her face like candle wax hardened in mid-drip. With a stolid face, she stared through my father and answered in a steel monotone.

"An acrotomophile is a person who is sexually aroused by an amputee."

The room shrank. Only Gillatano's voice fit and she continued in a voice that sounded like a compressed scream that would burst the courtroom apart.

"More specifically, an acrotomophile is aroused by an amputee's stump."

Constantine, who appeared more surprised than anyone, prompted her for clarification. "Are you saying that Dr. Franklin derives sexual gratification from women who are amputees?"

"That's correct. He told me later, of course — after the operation — that he preferred me like this. He said there are many people like him — devotees is the common term — who want to engage in relationships with amputees."

"But surely a — devotee — wouldn't find an attractive potential mate and then sever her limbs?"

"Of course not. Devotees look for people who are already amputees."

"In the same way that other men might prefer blonde or tall women...?"

"Exactly."

"But Dr. Franklin was different." Constantine turned to address the room, and his voice relieved the suffocating pressure. "He was a surgeon who found himself in a position of power that he horribly abused. Through a carefully orchestrated series of needless medical procedures, the doctor planned first to take Mrs. Gillatano's leg and then her life. Mrs. Gillatano, please tell us how the infection really came about."

"During the last operation, Robert had infected my leg by injecting a strain of bacteria."

"When he told you about the infection, did you seek another opinion?"

"No. I trusted him completely. It never occurred to me that — "

"That he was planning your eventual death."

Gillatano's eyes froze on my father.

"That's right. A few months after the amputation, I began experiencing more pain. At first it was in my leg, but very quickly it spread to other parts of my body. Robert took me to see an oncologist."

"And that's when you were diagnosed with cancer."

"It was everywhere. It had traveled through my bone tissue."

"But again, it originated with Dr. Franklin. He had again infected you, while he had amputated your leg, only this time he injected cancerous cells knowing that within time the cells would metastasize. And this," Constantine turned to the jury, "ladies and gentleman, was the final stage of Dr. Franklin's horrific plan."

Gillatano's emotions cracked her iron composure, and she began to cry again. Constantine paused only long enough for Gillatano's first sobs to be heard. Then he summed up the charges.

"During this trial, we have shown you the evidence that Dr. Franklin coldly calculated every detail of his plan — a plan which his status as a doctor allowed him to carry through. For a few selfish months of sexual pleasure, Dr. Franklin was willing to sacrifice an inno-cent woman's life. He carefully plotted the murder of his lover in order to hide the affair from his family and colleagues, thinking that when his trusting mistress died, his horrible secret would die along with her."

When he ended his speech, Constantine looked over at Gillatano. She was still weeping and, as she did, the stump of her leg shook. I noticed my father watching it, his face like stone except for his eyes that followed the baton-like motion with a look of betrayed disbelief. I thought about the degree of damage contained in the gap he had created. And I wondered if he shared my thoughts.

Domingo's face was pale.

"How many people have you told this?"

"No one, except you."

"Why do you tell me?"

"Because, Domingo, you once asked me where I am from. So now you know. And by knowing it, you can understand why I became involved with Vince. It wasn't for the money. As far as I'm concerned, I wish my father had cut off Gillatano's leg just for money. It would have made it easier, in a way."

"How, easier? A leg is a leg."

"Yes, but if he had only done it for the money, I would have been able to get over it — eventually. There's no emotion attached to money. It's a cold substance and it only serves one purpose. Money is like the static on your TV."

"How do you mean?"

"Well, the static gets you something — it buys you a kind of happiness, but the thing is, Domingo, you could be happy without the static. If you had never been dragged off Aruba, you would never have needed the static but you *would* have needed or wanted happiness. You would have desired it and you would have found something else in place of the static to give it to you. The happiness — not the money — is what's important."

I waited as Domingo took a long draught from his bottle and wipe the foam from his lips. Then, when he lay back against the wall, I continued:

"My father committed a horrible crime because the result made him happy. It would have been simpler on me if he'd done if for the money. I could have said my father was a crook and eventually let it go. But it was more complicated than that. I could never understand the way he went about getting his happiness."

"He was crazy, Birdman. Sick in the head."

"No, he wasn't. At least not because he was a devotee. You see, there's nothing wrong with *what* made him happy. It's like that lawyer said — some guys get turned on by blondes or tall women and others by amputees. But doing what he did — that's something I can never forgive him for. His actions and lies were what really tore my family apart. It ruined my relationship with him and it nearly ruined me. I couldn't bear the thought of living in the same world with him, and so that's why I ran. But I didn't understand. I couldn't feel anything. The statues I slept under were more alive than I was. As time went on I thought I had escaped his world, but I now know it's all the same world — there're just different parts to it. And now...."

"Now you're with Vince."

I gazed above Domingo at the cracked plaster of the wall before looking back at him.

"Yes. And, little by little, my head cleared until I thought the operation would be a perfect way to get revenge on my father and all the people like him. But I can see that it doesn't matter. Revenge is even more worthless than money. In the end it buys you nothing."

"*Si*, Birdman. But you are in the revenge business."

"I was, but not anymore. Look, I'm not defending my father — for too many years I hated him for lying to me. But really, he was lying to himself and I just got in the way. He gave off a different appearance — he was playing a game — and that's what hurt. That's why I

151

ran and wouldn't allow anything in. It was like bandaging a wound so tightly that the air can't get in to heal it. But you see, Dommy, that's what we're doing here. This whole operation is only hurting people, and most of all it's hurting us. Everyone who works for Vince, including the vendors — like Santos — are getting hurt and it has to stop. We've got to stop it. Because in the end a pigeon is a squab. It just depends on how you look at it."

Chapter Ten
Of Mice and Moles

Vince immediately began to get rid of people who weren't "pulling their weight." New hands that worked quicker began to push the familiar ones from the conveyor belts. Claude and Davio were the first to be squeezed out. Vince called them into my office, and the rest of us watched the door close behind them, knowing we'd seen the last of the pair.

Closed-door meetings became frequent occurrences. They always took place in my office. Vince would ask me to leave and show in whoever was waiting outside. Most of these people were men I'd never seen before. Some were interviewees, driven in secret to the plant by Domingo for Vince's rapidly overturning work force. He had been right — there were a lot of people who wanted the work and he made sure he siphoned every drop of productivity from each one before replacing them. It got to the point where one new face would show up and two old ones would be erased. Meanwhile a paranoid silence grew in the plant. These new workers were looked on with the fearful hate of union scabs. They possessed all the elements of the informant about them, and everyone was afraid to speak, lest they too be called into the office.

Other meetings were conducted with slick men in dark suits and tight neckties like nooses. These were Vince's associates. They barely looked at any of the workers, whose eyes would rise and fall as if transmitting warning codes to one another. Yet they didn't act

Andrew K. Stone

as if they were worried about keeping too low a profile. With each glance, shrug and chuckle, they threw around their unaccountable status like kids skipping stones.

After one of these meetings ended, Vince called me in.

"Sit down."

I took a seat in front of him and stole a quick look toward the window. Some of the workers exchanged cautious glances.

"Have a cigarette," he offered. I lifted one of his thin foreign cigarettes from the silver case. He lit it for me, then lit his own and dropped the lighter into the inner pocket of his blazer. The label on the jacket lining flashed at me like a badge.

With a sigh, Vince sprayed the air with heavy-scented tobacco smoke. It floated and bobbed gently, as if riding water currents.

"Birdy, the changes we've made have helped us some, but not enough."

"How bad is it?"

"Not so bad that we can't get out of it. But I'm going to have to reassign you."

With the information I had on him, I knew Vince wasn't going to fire me, but still I panicked. Images of that first night in Union Square popped into my head, and I imagined him taking me somewhere equally as deserted to permanently get me out of the way. But when Vince saw the look on my face, he laughed.

"Jesus, Birdman. I mean I'm giving you a new job."

"Oh," I exhaled. "What is it, Vince?"

"Those guys who just left — they're from the head office. We were talking about the overall operation. Now, the good news is, everyone's been having trouble meeting the product quotas. So they're changing things a little."

I grunted and waited.

Vince continued. "Here's the deal. We're going to rotate the product lines. We'll still keep the geese going — because there's enough guys around the country catching them, as well as ducks and swans and other birds — to be able to satisfy the fowl quota."

"Seafood?"

"That's always gonna be a big market — especially for us. We keep it."

I drew in the heavy smoke, thought a moment, and then let it out in a hesitant breath.

"What about the meat lines?"

Vince sat back in the chair. He looked bigger, yet more comfortable.

"No more rabbits, squirrels, chipmunks — none of that."

"So you're going to get rid of Joey and his guys?"

"No. I'm reassigning them, too. And you're going to supervise them — and as many other guys as we can get."

"To do what?"

With a banner of smoke, Vince announced the new plan.

"To catch rats."

I nearly gagged.

"Jesus!"

Vince exhaled a placid cloud of smoke.

"Get used to it, Birdy. Those are the instructions."

"But Vince, that's going too far."

"Too far?!" He leaned towards me. "When are you gonna get it, Birdy? Those guys are running the show now. We have no say in this — other than 'yes' to their orders."

"But the State Pen we're supplying — I mean, the big guys are in there."

Vince chuckled condescendingly.

"And you don't think they'll eat rat meat?" He pushed himself back in the chair. "Listen. If this all works out, do you have any idea how much money it's gonna make for them? Think about it. They're building a nationwide network. The pen in Texas was the prototype and it worked. Now, with the new prisons they're adding, there's even more money up for grabs. You think these guys are gonna pass up that kind of an opportunity? Ya gotta do the math, Birdy. The food we're supplying is free to us and the labor cost is almost nothing — homeless people who are happy to earn a few bucks a day with meals included. The heavies in the Pen would eat their grandmothers for the kind of dough they're gonna rake in."

It seemed as if Vince had been connected to a volume control which had been turned up for only one sentence.

"Wait a minute, Vince," I said. "Is that what you're paying these people?"

"Sure."

"A couple of dollars and… 'meals'? Jesus. And on top of that, you're working them until they can't keep up and then shoving them out."

Vince leaned even closer to me. I could faintly smell yesterday's cologne.

"You listen to me. These people are grateful. They've got easy work, shelter while they're doing it and security. You have any idea how many bums there are in this city? I'd think you would, seeing as you've been one for so goddamned long. You'd also know that almost any one of them would be happy to have a situation like this. So don't talk to me like I should be handing out charity."

"No, I wouldn't do that, Vince. After all, you're no Samaritan."

———

"I gotta idea and it might maybe be good. It could work, maybe, but I don't know."

Domingo and I had gone out to see Joey in his ramshackle hut. With its insulation and partitions and electricity, it was much more livable than anything I'd ever had on the streets. But since I'd grown so accustomed to the apartment, I looked at Joey's place as a sort of tree house. It was difficult to imagine sleeping there.

We sat on milk crates stolen from a downtown convenience store, while Joey was contemplating how to achieve the new plan of catching rats. Of course, for his safety, we only told Joey that we were switching product lines. Like the other vendors, Joey didn't know anything about the operation. He just gave us the product and we paid him — that was the extent of our relationship. But the Boston part of the operation was going to be piloting the rat plan for the rest of the country. Its success was contingent on us and Vince didn't know how to go about making it all work.

"They're not giving us any methods, Birdy," Vince had complained. "They're not telling us how to get the rats — they want to see if it can be done, and they want us to figure out a way. Of course, that means they don't know how to do it, either. If they did, they'd tell us. So, our orders are to figure it out."

I had suggested talking with Joey.

"The lunatic from Georgia?"

"He's resourceful, Vince. He may be able to help."

"I don't know."

"Do you have any other plans?"

"I got a couple things in mind."

"Good, so maybe we'll have a few options to pick from. The more the better, right? Think globally."

"All right. Just be careful what you say to him."

"Of course."

As Joey contemplated the problem, he kept swatting at his back and hopping around as if the rodents were crawling over his body. Claws seemed to be pricking him while whiskers teased with every twitch. I wondered if, on some level, this inspired him to find a solution.

"We can't trap the little critters like we do them bunnies," he said, hopping on one foot. "Trapping's only good in the Places o' Plenty."

"And we can't poison them, Joey."

"Why can't we?" Domingo asked.

"Because people have to eat them — so they would also eat the poison, and get sick or die. They've got to be clean."

"Hee hee, clean rats, rats clean — no never, ever, hee hee."

"So, what do you think, Joey? What's the best way to do this? And remember, it can't cost us any money."

As I leaned back on the milk crate, my head brushed up against the hanging light bulb fed by the illegally siphoned electricity. Our shadows began to sway under the light, growing larger and then smaller like spirits trying to decide whether to rise from the dead.

"Look at the couple two shadows on the wall. What do they make ya think about?"

"Black ghosts," said Domingo.

"Yes, good, good!" Joey clapped his hands. "'Cause that's what them critters are gonna be when get through with them!"

"You have an idea? Then tell it to Birdman and me," urged Domingo.

Joey twirled around a few times and gently swatted the light so that the shadows grew big and blended together on the wall.

"This is my idea. And it's a good 'un. We'll catch more critters than we ever did in the Places o' Plenty."

Domingo stared impatiently at me.

"Joey," I said, "why don't you sit down and explain the plan?"

For a second he froze, like performance artists I'd seen in Harvard Square who, for hours on end, pose absolutely still. Then he moved between Domingo and me, squeezing onto a third black milk crate.

"We electrifry them!" he whispered, with a look around as if the place were bugged.

"What does this mean?" Domingo asked.

"Joey, do you mean electrocute them?"

"Yes, yes, yes!" he clapped happily.

"That is crazy. How will we electrocute the rats?"

"Domino doesn't know, hee hee! You don't know about what I can do, do you Domino?" Joey said, slapping his left shoulder blade. "Ya see, ya only needs a half dozen or seven wires and bango! Ya got electric critters!"

Domingo stared at Joey until the small man looked at the shadows on the wall and picked at his beard. Then Joey looked back and shouted at Domingo:

"I know all about electrifrying! I can electrifry anything just like I did my house, here."

"Joey's been stealing electricity from Amtrack and powering this whole place, Domingo. That's how he got the light and his freezer. But Joey, how are you going to get the rats?"

Joey pulled on his nose and looked at us expectantly, as if he had already given his explanation and was waiting for our feedback. His eyes twinkled deeply in the hanging light, like far-off headlights. Then his expression jumped, he leapt off the milk crate and explained the procedure. After he finished, Domingo and I walked back to the truck.

"He is a strange little man," Domingo said. "But I believe him. I believe he will make this work."

Boston doesn't have a rat "problem" but the city does have its share of the rodents. They lurk in dumpsters, alleyways and even in some buildings. In fact, a number of years ago, there was a nightclub in Kenmore Square called the Rathskellar, but known as the Rat; the name wasn't just a fond abbreviation. Soon after my arrival in the city, I spent a night at the club. I had met another homeless man who used to sweep the sidewalk in front of the bar in exchange for an occasional meal. One night he convinced a bouncer to let us stay there, so after the last band had played and the bartenders had pushed all the leather-clad kids out, we entered the deserted bar. The bands performed downstairs, and as we walked into the darkness that seemed to be still reverberating with the music that had played earlier, I heard what sounded like scratching inside the walls.

"What is this, an Edgar Allen Poe story?" I asked my friend. He said nothing, and we walked to the back of the room and lay down on the solid stage, which was covered with duct tape, broken guitar strings and a few crumpled sheets of paper with the names of songs that the bands had played that night. For the first time since I'd been sleeping on the streets, my back relaxed. Still, the scratching in the walls made falling asleep difficult. Then I heard metallic clicks above me, like the sound of high-heel shoes on manhole covers. The noise was quick and sizzling, like static electricity.

"What is that?"

My friend turned toward me and said: "Rats. They're running on the lighting grid above the stage. And they're burrowing in the walls."

"You're kidding!"

"That's why they call this place the Rat. During the day, humans get it, but at night, the rats come out."

"Jesus!"

"They won't hurt you. They're afraid of you. Go to sleep."

For a long time I listened to the clicking until, finally, my sleepiness chased the rats away. In the morning, the bouncer came back and let us out. I looked up to the metal pipes and rods above the stage and shivered. The bouncer laughed.

"Did dey keep youse up?" he asked, the words churning from his mouth like clumps of tar.

"No, it was fine. Thank you."

"Tank youse. Now da brooms are in dat closet. Sweep it up down here and den scram."

I didn't know we were going to be put to work, although it was fair for a good night's sleep and I didn't mind. But as I swept in corners and in the darker areas of the room, I couldn't help shuddering whenever the bristles touched a pile of rat droppings or a small chunk of gnawed-on wood.

The one place to find the largest population of rats was underground in the subway stations. Since the Big Dig highway construction had begun rerouting waterways and unearthing old sewers, the rats had been driven from their homes to the already-infested stations.

They were mainly visible at night; my homeless friend had been right in that rats are afraid of humans. There weren't many scurrying during the day, but after the trains stopped running, around one in the morning, they came out *en masse*. And so, a few nights later,

Joey, Domingo and I met at the mouth of the Kenmore Station and walked the tracks all the way to Park Street. We had a flashlight, which we kept dark as we walked as quietly as we could. Whenever we heard a squeaking panic in front of us, Domingo aimed the light and caught dozens of rats tearing off in every direction. They ran frantically, as if they had exploded into a bizarre rat mitosis. When we reached Park Street Station, we knew our supply was almost unlimited.

"I bet we saw three or four hundred," I said to Domingo, who nodded slowly but kept quiet.

"This will be easier than trapping bunnies! This is the new Place o' Plenty!" Joey said and danced around one of the tiled pillars on the platform as if it were a totem pole. Each time he circled it, Joey would slap it as if to keep count.

"How will we catch them?" Domingo asked.

"Hee hee, that's simpler than easy!" Joey said. "I've already got it worked out. I thought about it for a day or three," he whispered and nodded rapidly. "I know it all!"

"Tell us what your plan is."

"Well, we need to get..." and Joey thought for a minute, standing on one foot like a lawn flamingo. Then he brought his foot down, as if on cue, and started talking, "ten or twelve feet of metal nets. Then we put the nets over the tracks and connect some wires to the power supply. Then, we wait until a bunch of critters come in the net, and we hit the switch and zap! Fried ratties!"

Joey danced around the cement pillar again, singing "fried ratties" over and over. I glanced at Domingo.

"God, that's disgusting."

Joey stopped and looked at me with disappointment.

"No, it's not. It's quick and fast. And we'll have ropes on each corner of the nets, so we just have to pull 'em up and empty 'em into sacks!"

Domingo was pulling on his mustache.

"What do you think?" I asked him.

"I think it would work, Birdman. If we have enough men, we could cover many stations each night. It would bring in enough for Vince. He would be happy."

"But...?" I was expecting him to continue.

"Nothing. He would be happy."

———

But Domingo wasn't happy. I had told him we would find a way to stop the operation and, although he knew that in the long run stopping was best for us all, his eyes were still narrowed on the immediate future.

"We'll just work harder," was all he said when I promised we would eventually end it all. "It doesn't matter."

"It does matter, Dommy. We'll do it. And not just for ourselves. For everyone. Gloria, Joey, everyone. We just need to figure out a way."

He threw a half-full beer can over his shoulder. It hit the wall with a crack, and bled over the plaster and floor.

"Even if you find a way out, Birdman, what is everyone going to do? Now, at least they make some money. What about when you stop it?"

"They can go to shelters, hospitals..."

"Aah. Bullshit! You know it is, Birdman. I do not see Gloria in a shelter. I see Gloria on the street again, selling her body for the needle."

"Look, Dommy. What we're doing isn't helping any of us. Yeah, Gloria gets a little money, but she's the one who gets herself to the clinic now. Okay, so Vince helped her get started. Vince helped her get clean. But she has to stay clean by herself. Besides, the way Vince is bringing people in and then throwing them out, it's a tease. Most of them have never worked, but Vince gives them a job. He gives them hope. Then he takes it away from them. Everyone is better off working somewhere else, doing something legitimate."

"*Si*? And what of you, Birdman? What will you do, if you get out alive?"

He stared my eyes down and pinned them to the floor.

"I don't know," I admitted. "I haven't thought of that."

"You have not thought of it yet you are planning on stopping everything. But at least you have got a head start on everyone who does not know your plan. I tell you, Birdman, you should not interfere."

"Yeah? And what about Santos? If we had stopped this earlier, he'd still be alive. You'd probably be back in Aruba right now."

Domingo's glance ricocheted off opposing walls, desperate to deflect my challenge. He walked to the refrigerator and opened another beer. Then he walked back and looked up at me, his eyes dissolving like sugar cubes in coffee.

"Birdman, I have been gone so long…my wife…my wife may not have waited for me. She was not that…that kind of woman. *Si*, I want to go home. But, like you, I do not know what I will find there."

"Dommy. Whatever it is, it will be better than this."

"Perhaps," he said silently. "Perhaps."

Chapter Eleven
Going Underground

Vince loved the plan.

"You know, I was thinking of getting rid of that lunatic. Send him right back to his Places of Plenty. But I guess I was wrong about him. Who'd have thought?"

The first night's shipment of rats had come in. Joey and his crew had run a test, caught over one hundred rats and skinned them all within a few hours. Vince watched two men he had hired — one a former butcher ruined by alcoholism, and the other a Vietnam Vet who, for reasons I didn't ask about, was good with a knife — filet the bodies and get them ready for the grinder.

I watched the butcher, appropriately named Butch, put the bodies into the machine. The entire process made me nauseous and the only way I could keep my stomach settled was by thinking of the rats as product. Vince stood beside me, smiling, but his teeth weren't as white as his face, and I was glad to see that this new venture had gotten to him, as well. It lent Vince a bit of vulnerability. The grinder crunched and whirled and my head and stomach fought — product versus rat. But a few seconds later, as the strands of gray meat churned out and were collected into a stainless steel pan, I breathed easier. My head had won. Butch smiled and the Vet nodded approvingly at the unrecognizable mass of meat. In a few seconds, the status of the rats had been shifted; they had traversed their own wasp nest and they now belonged to the class of product.

"I bet they taste just like chicken." Vince's irony was lost on Butch and the Vet, so he started walking toward the office, and asked me over his shoulder, "So how many guys did it take to get these babies in?"

"Joey had five men at Park Street. It took about three hours to catch and prepare them."

"Fuckin' brilliant!" Vince opened the door and took over my desk. He sat down with a notepad and began calculating out loud. "Okay, if we build it up to, say, five crews a night, all moving from station to station — double the manpower at Park to work the Red line and the Green line — and hit, let's see, Kenmore, Porter Square, Downtown Crossing and South Station, we should be able to bring in a pretty big haul. I'd bet we could easily get four hundred pounds a night. They would be happy with that."

"We'll never meet that kind of quota. We don't have enough people."

Vince looked up.

"We got the people right here. We'll have them go out at night and catch the rats, then come back in the day and package them up."

"Jesus, you'll have them working around the clock."

Vince was restrained like an attack dog on a leash. He growled softly:

"If they want to eat, they'll do it."

"But you can't have them working those kind of hours. Look at it this way — a few weeks of it, and people will start to drop. It'll hurt your production."

"Birdy, if we make this work, then rats become a nationwide product line for the network. That will make my associates very happy. So, we're gonna make this work, see? 'Cause this is my gold ticket, and your job is to put that gold ticket in my hands."

Vince put his pencil to his lips.

"Anyone who doesn't pull his weight is on the street, got it? There's always someone else to take their place."

He bit into the eraser, decapitating the pencil. His eyes never left me as he spit the eraser into the corner of the room, where it rolled under a filing cabinet and ceased to exist.

———

I left the office and found Gloria shaking violently as she loaded boxes of iced product onto wooden pallets. I walked to her workstation.

"How long's it been?"

"I missed yesterday," she said without stopping her work. "And then this morning."

"Gloria..," I sighed.

"Listen, I can deal. When I get some time, I'll go back to the fucking clinic, okay?"

"You don't have the time. You've got to go now, Gloria."

She put a box down. The veins in her thin arms quivered like fault lines.

"Shit! You don't have no idea, do you? If I don't work, I'm out on my ass again."

"That won't happen. I won't let it."

Gloria coughed up a laugh.

"Yeah, right. Some pull you have. Vince's right-hand fucking man. Shit! Tweets, I thought you were different. But I've seen the way you and Vince have been meeting behind them closed doors. Funny thing is, you're no different from the rest of us. If I don't do the job, I get shit-canned. And the same goes for you."

"Look, no one's going to fire you, Gloria. But you can't keep working like this — if you don't get your methadone, you're not going to be able to work at all."

"I'll take the chance."

"Gloria — "

"Look!" she slammed a box down. "You have no fucking idea what it's like out there! So just leave me alone."

"What are you talking about?"

She whispered fiercely, the bright red veins crossing her irises as if her eyes were made of cracked glass.

"I'm talking about living on the street. Not having enough money for a piece of bread. Blowing businessmen in a toilet for a coupla bucks but, before you can get a bed for the night, the smack starts running through your mind. Then when it starts running through your body and you're feeling fine, you're really fucked because the shelters are either full or won't take you 'cause you're strung out. That's what I'm talking about."

A few boxes had backed up on the line and she started working even faster. I tried to help, but she pushed me away. I never considered that Vince might not have told the other workers that I'd been homeless too. I wondered if he thought it might give me more authority with them.

"Gloria, there are places —"

"Yeah. They're lots of places. But I ain't going to any of them."

"You could get help, Gloria."

"There's no help."

"You're wrong. You're wrong about it all. There is help if you really want it." Then I whispered. "And I do know what it's like, Gloria. I've been out there for ten years."

She stopped shaking.

"What?"

"While you were shooting up on Boylston Street, I was catching pigeons and selling them to restaurants. That's how Vince found me."

"No shit, Tweets."

"So, I know what you're talking about, Gloria. I may not have gone through exactly what you have, but you haven't lived my life, either."

Gloria started to tremble again.

"But that's just it. When we look the same, we're really different, and when we look different, we're the same. And right now I see a guy who's got a much better chance of keeping his bread than me. Maybe that's because I haven't had the chance to live your life."

She continued packing the boxes, her slight frame shaking from the twisting pain that seared throughout her body. She was right. She wasn't so different from me. And she wasn't that similar, either.

It was a different world underground. At night, the labyrinth of tunnels and stations of the T seemed like an archeological dig.

Because the T traveled both above and below ground, we could enter its tunnels at a variety of places. Despite our flashlights, the damp corridors grew darker as though we were wearing sunglasses with lenses that dimmed with the light. With every step, we lost some definition while a pervading sense of timelessness was amplified, making our progress hypnotically slow. It was difficult to breathe as each successive gulp became murkier. The air in the tunnels was heavy with stale fumes, urine and sewage, and sometimes I felt as if I was trying to breathe with a mouth full of dirt. But then, like the flicker of a match, we'd see a station in the distance, and the air would become lighter and the oxygen would pour through our heads while our lungs tripped over one another, trying to equalize the flow. Finally, the dim light would burst in the distance and, as we approached the wide-open space of the next station, time would recalibrate and the trance of the tunnel would be broken.

Between Joey's men, the people Vince pulled from the factory, and the geese-catchers, we had about forty people. As the geese had migrated south for the winter, the mill-dwellers migrated to Boston to assist with the new venture. As crusty as always with their vitriolic sense of competition, they spurred the other workers on towards trying to catch as much product as possible. And after a few nights to get the kinks out of the system, we were meeting Vince's goal.

Dommy and Joey helped me with the supervision. We soon learned that the first haul of rats would send any other rodents into hiding for the night. They weren't like the geese — the warriors in our product line which fought back. The rats were more of the hunter and gatherer class. Interested primarily in filling their stomachs, they knew that, when provoked, the best action was to retreat.

However, we overcame this by staggering the work along each station. By setting up shifts — a few men at various stations along a line — we developed an effective system for our hunt. While one group would be electrocuting and gathering up the product, a second group would be laying down nets at the next station. The first group would pack the product on ice and move to the third station while the second group was waiting for enough product to gather on the nets. The electrocuting experience was always the same. On the signal, Joey would hit a makeshift power box and there would be a crackling, vibrating hum and then a wet popping sound. It would end with a disquieting and awe-filled silence. Then, as the vinegar-sharp stench arose, the workers' stupor over the execution would be broken, feet would start to shuffle and the nets would swiftly be pulled up. The bodies would quickly be hidden from view. They were only rats, but their mass murders affected everyone the same way.

"It's disgusting...sick," said Gloria one night, as she stood next to me on the subway platform. "It's like a rat Holocaust." Gloria was no longer quaking. I had talked with Domingo and he made sure she got to the methadone clinic. He started picking her up each morning, early, and driving her to the clinic. Until we could figure out a way to stop the operation, this was the least we could do for her. Gloria was adamant about working as much as she could. If anyone — even Vince — told her to take a break, she'd just work harder. "I can't afford a break," I overheard her say to another worker one day. "Takin' a break means dying here."

But despite Gloria's determination to fill every possible moment with work, Vince finally realized that he couldn't force people to work the number of hours he had originally planned on. After a few weeks of watching the workers drift in after a night in the subway, their limbs moving slower as if their muscles were turning to glue, he called me in to the office.

"Okay, Birdy," he said, leaning back in my squeaky chair. "You made your point. I'm starting to get diminishing returns out of the labor force."

I shrugged.

"They're working hard, Vince."

"I'm not arguing with that. Shit, they're working too hard. They come in here like fuckin' zombies."

He lit a cigarette, then held the silver case towards me.

"No, thanks. I'm...cutting back."

"No shit? What, becoming a health freak?" He laughed, blowing a mocking plume of smoke past my right ear.

"It's just that, down in the subway the air's hard to breathe. My lungs need a break."

"Huh. I'll have to check it out one night. I wouldn't want any of my employees trying to sue me for unhealthy work conditions."

I could barely force a tight grin.

"Birdy, I've gotta tell ya. I'm happy. And my associates are pleased, too. But we're killing these people and eventually that's gonna kill business. So I've got this new schedule worked up."

He passed a sheet of paper across the desk at me.

"From now on, everyone works a twelve-hour day, then takes twelve hours off. This way, we can rotate people around. Some will work the afternoons here in the plant, then go underground. Others will start in the subway and then come here."

"It's better than what we're doing now, Vince, but I don't think it's enough time off."

"What are you talking about?"

"You're still squeezing a lot out of these people. They'll barely have time to sleep and get dressed before they've got to get back to work."

Smoke spurted from his mouth as he yelled.

"Birdy, it's not like these people have heavy social calendars. They're fuckin' homeless!"

"They're still people."

"Oh, Christ. Lemme ask you something. What kind of schedule were you on before I found you? Do you remember? When you were sleeping on the sidewalks and in dog shit in the Common — did you have a lot of outside commitments?"

My eyes scraped the tops of my shoes and I said nothing.

"I'm giving these people a chance to make more money than they would by begging or sweeping sidewalks. They'll be glad to get this new schedule. So go post it. It's effective immediately."

———

When I told Gloria about the schedule change, she panicked. I thought she might hyperventilate, so I took her to a corner in the room and had her sit.

"Relax, Gloria. Just breathe."

But she bled a quick flow of words.

"You can't do this, Tweets...I need to work, I need it. Tell Vince, he'll understand, tell him, please don't cut me off, you can't cut me off."

"Gloria, you've still got your job — and the money will work out to be about the same — "

"It's not the money."

She sneezed, then brought a wilted tissue from her pocket and wiped her nose.

"Well, what is it?"

She sneezed again, but this time she didn't bother with the tissue.

"What will I do when I'm not working? I need to keep busy."

"Gloria, I told you, there are plenty of things you can do — and places to go. You're not tied here."

But she just rubbed her hands together, vigorously cleaning an invisible stain from her palms.

"I'm not tied. Shit, it's starting to get colder outside. Yeah, the holidays are coming — people start to feel guilty so they give you some more change instead of just ignoring you. You know that score, don'cha? But that's just a few weeks and then it's all over. I'm out

173

freezing my ass off 'cause there ain't nothing I can do. So stop bullshitting me. I'm staying. I'm gonna keep on working. I'll talk to Vince — he knows the deal with me. Keep your schedule for the others. But I work the same as always."

———

We started the new schedule that night. Half the manpower worked from one in the morning to four-thirty underground, then the catch was taken back to Somerville where the shift worked until early afternoon. About twelve-thirty, Domingo arrived with a fresh batch of workers who spent their twelve hours packaging the meat. At one in the morning, it all started again, with Domingo picking up the workers from the night before and dropping them at the subway entrances before driving to Somerville to retrieve the day shift.

With so many new people working for him, Vince was even more concerned about secrecy. He could no longer house everyone who worked for him, especially with the high turnover. So he designated a few stops around town where Domingo would pick up and drop off the workers. He also bought a new cover for the truck that was completely solid and had two doors in the back. This way, no one could see out as Domingo drove to and from the factory.

"Even if half these bums are retards, I'm not taking no chances," Vince stated. "No one's gonna find our location."

After a few weeks, productivity increased to an all-time high. It seemed that there was no end to the rats. The workers were more alert, too, as they were all on a stable schedule — by working consistent shifts, their bodies quickly adapted to the routine.

The only one who didn't seem to adapt was Gloria. Vince wouldn't change the schedule for her, and on some days she was euphoric while other days she was jumpy. She also seemed to have a perpetual cold; her nose and eyes ran while she constantly sneezed. Every time Dommy came to pick her up at the end of the day, a peculiar dread crept from behind her like someone pulling her hair. Her eyes grew wide and her mouth twisted into a frown. Lines sunk into her face as if by erosion. Gloria would walk slowly to the truck and always enter last, as if being trundled away to her execution. Her eyes would be the last things I'd see — always peering out until the doors shut them from view.

The day Gloria didn't show up for work shouldn't have surprised me at all, but maybe I just didn't want to believe it would ever really happen.

I searched for Domingo to ask about her. His head was buried in the engine of the truck, like a giant's face peering down into a tiny city. When he emerged, I asked if he had taken Gloria to the methadone clinic that morning.

"*Non*, Birdman. Vince told me to stop that."

"Stop? Why?"

"Because he says she is off the stuff and has no more need for the clinic."

"That's ridiculous!"

"Still, that is what Vince told me, Birdman." Domingo slammed the hood shut. "But I do not know where she is now. She was not at the pick-up place."

The answer reached us by the next morning's *Herald*. Vince didn't even knock on the apartment door. He just walked in on Domingo and me as we were having coffee, and put the newspaper down.

"We're suspending operations for the next few days. Not in the plant, but in the subway."

"What is the matter, Vince?" asked Domingo.

"Gloria O.D.'ed last night. They found her on the Green Line with the needle still stuck in her arm."

"Jesus Christ." I grabbed the paper. There was a short, two-paragraph article about the unidentified woman discovered by a passenger late the night before. The man who had found her body said he had seen her board the Red Line at Harvard Square, and heard her muttering something about finding the crew. Apparently she changed trains at Park Street, and sometime between then and the end of the line, out in Riverside, she had shot up and died. An autopsy was scheduled for later that day.

"The cops'll be asking questions. So for the next week, no one goes down in the subway. This'll blow over soon enough and then we'll get back to work."

"Vince, why did you tell Dommy to stop taking her to the clinic? She was in recovery — she needed her meth."

"She was a big girl. She knew how to get there. Besides, Dommy needs his sleep."

"Jesus, Vince. You killed her."

Silence hung from the end of my sentence, freezing time. Then, slowly, Vince responded.

"Excuse me? I didn't quite get that."

"You heard me," I said quietly.

He stood up and walked around the table. "Birdman, you shouldn't make false accusations like that. Gloria was a smack addict. And I was the one who tried to help her get clean. But I couldn't baby-sit her twenty-four hours a day. What she did in her off hours was out of my control."

"Which is why she wanted to work more. So she wouldn't have so many off hours."

"I wouldn't know about that, Birdman."

"Sure you would, Vince. She told me she was going to talk to you. She said you wouldn't force her to work the new schedule. But you said no, didn't you?"

"Now listen here." Vince moved closer to me, dwarfing the river-cut table between us. His tone turned defensive and he spoke accusingly. "You were the one who wanted shorter fuckin' hours for everyone. And I agreed with *you*. So don't try to pin this shit on me. It's not my fault that Gloria scored and then offed herself. As far as I knew, she was fine — Dommy had taken her to the clinic up until we started on the new schedule. When we began that, she had plenty of time in the morning to get herself down to the clinic herself. So don't be goin' around saying I killed her. That's not exactly the kind of thing you'd want people to hear — for your own safety, Birdman."

Then, as if nothing had happened, Vince focused his attention on Domingo and gave instructions in a voice as emotionless as if he were dictating a grocery list.

"Dommy, when you go to pick up the subway crew tonight, tell them that all work has been cancelled for one week. If anyone asks why, tell them we're waiting on a new order to come in. Give everybody this," and Vince handed Dommy a manila envelope. "There's four hundred bucks — give 'em each a twenty and tell them that next week we'll start working again."

He walked out, slamming the door behind him. Domingo picked up the paper but dropped it immediately, as if he had expected to see the article retract itself.

"So I should have taken her to the clinic, still?"

"It's not your fault, Dommy. She had been going through withdrawal — when she was at work, did you ever notice how she shook and sneezed?"

"*Si.*"

"Those are the symptoms. She told me she had missed a few days of her methadone but I guess the work helped keep her mind off it all. When the new schedule came out, she had more time to herself and she probably started buying again. And last night, she bought too much."

"And she was looking for us, Birdman. On the train, she was looking for the crew."

"Yes."

Domingo stood up. The winter sunlight bit at his face through the cracked window.

"Another one dead."

"Yes," I repeated. I looked at the paper again. As I read, the words bubbled and disintegrated through my tears.

Chapter Twelve
Dancer Around the Truth

A few nights later it began to snow. Like soggy cotton, it showered down on the cars which slowly paraded their way through the grayish-white street. An hour after it had started, the snow had accumulated quickly and filled in the roads like marrow.

Domingo and I dragged our mattresses into the kitchen. It was so cold that we had started to sleep in front of the stove; unbeknownst to Vince, we turned it on full and opened the door to heat the room. A few weeks earlier, we had covered the windows with discarded sheets of plastic from the packaging department of the plant. The plastic billowed like balloons each time the wind howled at them, but they held fast and kept us somewhat protected from the biting gusts.

As we still weren't going underground, and the forecast had predicted that the snow would be too heavy to drive through, Vince had called off work for the whole day. Dommy had made it to the package store before they locked up, and had brought home a case of beer. We sat in front of the stove, each with a can of Budweiser, and for the first time in months, existed outside the present moment. The storm muted the city and the only sound was the rushing, hypnotic wind. Time drowsed, and I would have fallen asleep with it, but the warmth from the stove tugged me into a suspended consciousness just outside the realm of seconds and minutes.

"So, Birdman," Dommy said with some of the beer's froth filling in his mustache, "do you have any idea what to do?"

I looked at him.

"About stopping the operation?"

"*Si.*"

"Are you agreeing that it has to stop?"

He drank again.

"*Si,* Birdman. It is time."

Now that Domingo supported stopping the operation, his original arguments jabbed at my conscience. I nodded and began to speculate about his life in Aruba. What had it been like and what would change when — or if — he made it back there? I couldn't promise him that stopping the operation would guarantee he would get back home, and I wondered if he and the others would be better off working. Although I held Vince responsible for Gloria's death, and even the deaths of Santos and his crew, did I really have the right to choose for everybody else? The people Vince employed had nothing else to keep them going and, while my gut feeling told me that stopping Vince would be best for everyone, I couldn't help thinking of all the people who were warm and protected from this storm because of the operation. I imagined them all out of work — shivering under benches, curled up on grates, wrapped in tattered blankets and torn newspapers. I heard their moans above the wind, and felt their hands as they reached out to grasp my shoulder....

"Ssh," Dommy warned, his hand on my arm as he woke me from my drunken dream. "Listen."

There was a soft knocking at the door, muffled by the storm.

"Vince?" asked Dommy, who started to turn off the oven.

"He wouldn't knock. He's got a key."

I walked to the door and looked out the peephole. Wet flakes had plugged up the glass so all I saw were magnified crystals. I shouted, "Who is it?"

The knocking stopped and a frantic voice cried, "Roxanne."

Domingo and I exchanged glances. Then the voice said: "From Playland."

"The strip club?" I asked Domingo. He nodded with a wide-eyed expression, as if this were the worst possible omen or a dream come true.

"Hang on!" I yelled and, after making sure there was no evidence of our work in sight, I opened the door. Standing there was the girl I'd met in the strip joint, the one who had been totally nude in the dressing room. She now wore an old flannel coat and faded blue jeans with water stains on each knee; I imagined she had fallen in the snow. Her soaked hair was caught up in a net of ice. Behind this veil, her eyes cried mascara.

"I'm Roxanne — do you remember me?"

I barely recognized her as the pretty stripper from Playland.

"Sort of. How did you find — ?"

"I have some information for you."

"What kind of information?"

The muted scraping of a snowplow startled her and she leapt forward as if the truck had pushed her aside.

"Please!" she said, looking behind her. The air was dense with snow, as if the sky was disintegrating and falling upon us. Translucent grays and whites painted the world, but Roxanne acted as if she were as visible as graffiti on a white wall.

"What information are you talking about?"

Her thin fingers clutched my arm so hard that I felt their jagged bones through her gloves.

"It's about the videotape," she whispered over the screaming storm.

Domingo had come to the door in time to hear this. When they saw each other, time briefly suspended in a moment of suspicion.

"Listen," Roxanne said, restarting the clock, "I brought a copy with me. I'll show you. But you have to let me in, please. They'll kill me."

Domingo and I hesitated. Vince had always been strict about having no visitors and, if this were a trick, we would be the ones in danger.

"I'm sorry. I don't know what you're — "

"Tweets." Her eyelashes were frozen open. I stared back and she nodded. "Gloria was my sister."

"Take off your coat and come into the kitchen."

She followed me, her canvas sneakers squishing as she walked, oozing melted snow and sludge onto the linoleum. Domingo hung her coat over a chair in front of the oven.

"If you want to, take off your shoes and socks. I will get you some heavy socks to wear."

"Thanks...thank you," Roxanne said, and began to unlace her sneakers as she shivered in her wet jeans and an old plaid shirt. Domingo came back with a heap of clothes.

"I brought you a dry shirt and a robe, too, if you want to let all your clothes dry."

"That would be great. Thanks. Is there a..."

Her sentence trailed off shyly.

"Oh, you can change in the bathroom. Right over there."

"Good. Thanks. Really."

Roxanne walked towards the bathroom with Dommy's clothes.

"What is this, Birdman? Gloria's sister? Do you think it is true?"

I shrugged, listening to the squishing noises of the stripper peeling off her clothes. I couldn't help equating the bathroom door with the curtain at the back of Playland's stage. However, as Roxanne emerged, all thoughts of Playland had vanished. Offstage she still danced, although pale and beaten, in a different room within the wasp nest.

Dommy's clothes swallowed her. One of his shirtsleeves hung below her hand, and this sight ignited a memory of Gillatano. Roxanne walked to the kitchen and sat in front of the open oven. Her jacket had begun to slowly dry, and the flakes of snow that had covered it dissolved into puddles on the floor. This simple transformation robbed the storm of some of its power.

"So. Gloria was your sister?" Domingo said, breaking a tense silence.

"Yeah."

"I am sorry about Gloria. She was a good woman."

"She was a fucked-up smack addict," Roxanne spat. But then in a jagged turn of emotions, she crumbled and began to sob. "I'm sorry. I shouldn't have said that. She was good, she really was. She just never had a chance."

Roxanne held her face in her hands, and her damp hair hung in clumps like a shredded curtain. I glanced at Domingo and read his hand signals of twisted uncertainty: should he hold her? Should he pet her? Instead, he turned up the temperature of the oven.

"Did you and Gloria grow up in Boston?" I asked. Nothing I could say would be right. We were held in a limbo, bound by Roxanne's tears, and the most I could hope for was to talk her through those tears.

"Roslindale," she sniffed. "At least for the first few years. We moved around a lot — Dorchester, Boston, Roxbury, Mattapan."

"Why did you move so much?"

"The D.S.S. Department of Social Services. We were taken away from our parents — for abuse. I barely remember it but Gloria was old enough...I have images...unclear memories.... But Gloria could have told you the entire story. Shit, she did that when she was five years old. She told the judge about how our old man raped us."

"Jesus."

The room became uncomfortably warm but Roxanne's tears and emotions slowly dried up. Her face flattened with a detached paleness and she began to speak in a gray monotone. But she seemed conscious of this shift, as if she had to remove herself from her own story in order to tell it.

"The D.S.S. had a hard time finding a group home that would keep us together. 'Cause we were sisters, the court thought we should stay together. But there never seemed to be enough beds, or when a group home decided to take us, it would lose its funds or some shit like that. But we kept close anyway. We stayed in touch and saw each other whenever we could. For a while Gloria had a foster parent who would bring her over to visit me. We weren't exactly your typical family, but who is?"

Roxanne's laugh slid weakly from her lips.

"Anyway, we got older and I started to strip. And I made good money — at sixteen I was bringing in five or six hundred a week."

"Sixteen?" I asked.

"If you look the part, no one's gonna ask. Gloria wanted to know where I was getting the money and I told her. I told her she should do it, but her memories of what our father did were too strong — she couldn't ever feel safe stripping. I don't think she ever felt safe, period. She used to talk about being robbed. How her whole life had been stolen by our father. I was lucky — I didn't remember any of it, except those fuzzy memories I sometimes get — but not Gloria. She was haunted by it all. And she found the only way to escape was with dope. The only time she felt good was when she was high."

Finally I found words that would fit, although I was reluctant to ask.

"Did you help her?" I said. "I mean…did you help her with the buys?"

She struggled to justify her explanation.

"Look, I knew it wasn't good for her, but…it was the only thing that ever made her smile. I thought…I thought it wouldn't hurt her. I mean, that she would never get hooked. But I was a kid — what did I know? It wasn't like I had goddamned parents to advise me. I just wanted to do something to make my sister happy."

"So Gloria was taking the heroin for a long time?" Domingo asked.

"Long enough so she could tolerate it and live normal if she was high. That's when I knew how bad it was, and when I tried to get her to stop. I told her I wouldn't give her any more cash unless she got into rehab. But she didn't and, for a long time, I lost touch with her. I didn't know she was on the street. I looked for her, but couldn't find her until she got involved with Vince. See, he's friends with Ritchie, the manager of Playland. I overheard them talking one night — Vince was bragging about a girl who blew him for fifty bucks. From the description, I knew he was talking about Gloria."

Roxanne looked at us with eyes of cement. Domingo got up to bring out some beers, walking heavy and slow, as if his feet were plowing through the floor as Roxanne's had plowed through the snow.

"So you found her again?"

"Yeah, Tweets. I found her. And she told me all about the work she'd been doing. About how she finally got into rehab and about you. How kind you were to her. Thank you for helping my sister." Her eyes slightly softened.

"You're welcome. I always liked Gloria."

"She didn't deserve to die. Not like that. When I found out...I had to come here. I was hoping that...that you could do something."

"Like what?"

"Stop it, somehow. Stop the whole goddamned thing. Before others..."

Domingo handed me a beer, his eyes urging caution.

"And you brought the videotape?" he asked, putting a beer in her hand.

"Yeah."

"But what good will it do, Roxanne?" I asked. "They have copies."

She smiled now.

"Of course they do. But you haven't seen it, have you?"

"No. Why?"

Roxanne sipped her beer and chuckled at some inner comic relief to her own tragedy.

"Let me explain how it works — the cameras in Playland. There are three — one pointed at the stage, one in the corridor that you walked up to get to the main room, and one in the corner of the room. They all give the club security, see? The stage camera does two things. It keeps an eye on the dancers to make sure we don't pull any shit with the customers — you never know who's gonna come in looking for sex or drugs, and the club don't want any of us cutting any kind of deal unless they're in on it. It's how they protect themselves. The camera is also there in case a customer gets out of control. Once…once this guy fell for one of the dancers — a really good friend of mine named Cheetah. She led him on — you know for the tips — but when she told him she had a boyfriend, he got so angry, he climbed onstage, grabbed her and beat the hell out of her. Almost killed her. She's still in a coma, today. With the stage camera, the police would have been able to catch the guy while knowing that Cheetah didn't provoke him."

She paused a moment and stared at the stove. A few moments later, she looked up.

"The other two cameras are also for the club's safety," she continued. "The room camera gets a picture of the whole joint and the hallway camera shows anyone walking in and out the back. And again, it keeps the girls honest, if you know what I mean."

"Great. So three cameras picked me up."

"Not really, Tweets. You got a VCR?"

Domingo gestured to the TV. Roxanne reached into her coat pocket and took out a plastic video case. She handed it to me.

"Play it."

I put the tape in the machine and pushed play. Even though I could hear the tape rolling, I thought the VCR had broken. The picture was black, with slight gradations of light and dark as the camera panned the room. Shadows, like ice skaters at night, skirted across the screen, accompanied by a soundtrack of Roxanne, who was giggling next to us.

"I don't get it."

"What is this a picture of?"

"This is a picture of Tweets that day at Playland."

"What — ?"

"Remember when you asked Ritchie about the masking tape we wear on our nipples? Well, masking tape can hide more than a little tit."

"So, you taped up the lenses?" I smiled.

"All three. That morning before anybody had showed up. See, Tweets, I'm like an assistant manager for Ritchie. That bastard trusts me to open up — I've never let him down until this, although God knows he deserves it."

Domingo was watching the tape and smiling grimly.

"What's the matter, Dommy?"

"This is good for us. But not for her," he pointed to Roxanne.

"Don't worry about me. I knew you were coming that day, so I taped up the cameras, then turned them on — part of my job is turning them on. Afterwards, I took the tape off — no one saw me, 'cause I came back that night to close. Ritchie had an appointment. He didn't find out until the next day. But the thing is, there's always something wrong with those cameras. I've been telling him for years to replace 'em. The reason the cops didn't catch the guy who beat up Cheetah was because the cameras weren't working that night — a short in the system knocked them out and that's how he escaped. So, when Ritchie asked me about the tapes, I played dumb. He didn't let on what the problem was — he just asked if I noticed anything weird with the cameras. I told him I had no idea — when I switched them on, they were working. But I also told him to check the system and, sure enough, he found a bad fuse. That rig is so old, you can screw it up by breathing on it wrong."

"But Roxanne," I began, unconvinced. "Vince has a copy. He told me my every move. He's *had* to have seen it."

"He's bluffing, Tweets. When Ritchie found out that the cameras went down, he called Vince. They were on the phone a long time — knowing Vince, he asked Ritchie about every thing you did and said, from the minute you walked in. He's bluffing. Because it's the only thing he's got on you."

"But...why did you tape up the cameras in the first place? When I came to Playland, Gloria was cleaning up, making money — she was okay."

A sad smile crawled along Roxanne's face.

"I know Vince. And I knew my sister. I had to keep her clean and safe. From what she told me, I knew you would be able to help me do that. So I had to keep you safe, too. Unfortunately, I was too late. But listen. Gloria told me everything. She was tighter with Vince than you might have known about. He paid her extra every time he wanted a little action. In return, he did help her try to clean up. But cutting her hours killed her, and that bastard knew it would. She was frightened of the time alone — the hours spent thinking about getting high. She would have worked twenty-four seven if she could have, just to keep her mind off the withdrawal. But he abandoned her. Even you tried to reason with her — she told me — but you didn't know, Tweets. You didn't know what she was going through, not really. Not like Vince knew.

"He's actually a little afraid of you, ya know. Out of all his people, you're the one who knows the most. And now you know this. I hope you can use it, Tweets. I hope you can use it to give that bastard Vince what he deserves."

After much cajoling from Domingo and me, Roxanne stayed the night at the apartment. The storm had begun to wane and the progress of the snowplows was more visible as dark swaths began pushing their way up through the whiteness. The sky was now crystal black and full, and the streetlights regained their dominance over the night, sparkling like flags of victory. Initially Roxanne had been afraid of staying, for fear that Vince may show up, but she decided to sleep through her fear, knowing that Domingo would drive her home in the morning.

After she lay down, Dommy and I whispered by the stove.

"What do you think?" I asked.

"I believe her. But...what does she want us to do? And how did she know that we want to do something anyway?"

"That's what's worrying me."

"*Si*. And me. You did not tell anyone about wanting to stop, Birdman?"

"No. I just promised the vendors we'd make sure they'd be all right. We'd see that they were taken care of. But we haven't even been able to keep that promise. What about you?"

"I spoke to no one."

"So, nobody knows what we want to do, but Roxanne shows up with the one thing that's been getting in our way of doing anything." I sipped at my beer. "How are you so sure that she's telling the truth?"

Domingo answered, chewing his lip between sentences.

"The day we went to Playland...Vince told me that you had never been to a strip bar before. He said he wanted to make sure you got in to see the place. To see the girls. But he did not sound sincere about it. The way he spoke, I knew there was another reason for it, although until I heard about the videotape, I did not know what it was." He nodded to Roxanne, sighing in a dream on the mattress. "Then she told the story about the man who attacked her friend, and I knew the camera part was true. I knew how they were bad cameras and were never working right and the man who beat up the girl was not caught because of it."

"How did you know that?"

Dommy's lips were nearly bleeding where he'd been biting them. His words picked up their pain from their rawness as he admitted:

"Because that man was Santos. We were there that night, together."

"What?"

"It is true. We used to go there often. I first went as a messenger for Vince. Then one night, I told Santos about it and we drove together. He met the dancer, just like she said. And when she turned him down, he went crazy. That was the last time I went there — until you and I went together. We were sitting in front of the stage and when she came on, he jumped up and grabbed her. If not for the bouncers, he would have killed her. I helped pull them off, and we ran out. We were lucky to escape. And luckier that the police never found us. But that is why he wanted to go home. They were still after him. He was smart enough not to tell her what he did or where he lived, because he was here illegally. He never told anybody — he knew how to lie. Still, his plan was to make enough money to get home. And take me, too."

There was a part of the story which wasn't quite right, and I asked Dommy, choosing my words cautiously, like a blind man crossing an unfamiliar street.

"Dommy, if you were there that night, Roxanne would have recognized you. She would have known that Santos was the one who almost killed her friend and you helped him escape. You're an accomplice, Dommy — as soon as she saw you tonight, she would have left and turned you in."

"*Si*. You are right, Birdman. And she did recognize me. I saw it in her face as soon as she came inside. But, you see, that is how I know we can trust her. Tonight she took the clothes from my back to stay warm. She would not have done it if Gloria were alive. She would have left here and called the police — you are right about that. But getting revenge for Gloria's death is more important. It is like people say in this country — blood is thicker than water."

Outside, the snowplow scraped along the street again. Pinkish-gray light tentatively poked through the window and as I looked out over the white, jagged humps outlining the black streets, I'd wondered how many times the world had been reborn during the night, and during my stay in that apartment.

Chapter Thirteen
Without Blinders On

Roxanne's story finally swayed me. Like status, fairness is also subjective. But while we can change our own status, some aspects of life are irrevocable. I thought about the degrees of fairness in the lives of Roxanne and Gloria and what could never be altered, and I realized that it wasn't my job to control anyone's destiny; however, I couldn't sit back while another took over that same control and did irreversible harm. And while I knew even the idea of harm is subjective, after experiencing the hurt my father caused, I had no choice but to try to help everyone involved with Vince. I could no longer argue with myself about this.

But not having a plan terrified me. It made it easy to image the worst consequences and I had to face facts — this fear played a large role in why I'd been hesitating to figure a way out. Before Roxanne's visit, there had been too many reasons to delay putting a stop to the operation, but now each had been peeled away, bringing the future closer than it ever had been. I found it frighteningly empty of any reassurance. I couldn't even use my "if versus when" rationale because both were now moot. We *were* going forward and there would be a cost. I did have one saving grace, however, and that was the wisdom of a man I hadn't seen in years, but who came to me now as a reminiscence.

He was an old sobered-up homeless man named Thomas who lived inside an overpass near the BU bridge. The bridge crosses the Charles River between

Commonwealth Ave. and Memorial Drive, in Cambridge. On the Cambridge side it spills out to a rotary that helps to neutralize the traffic congestion. The rotary lies like an asphalt roulette wheel below the gray cement pylons and rusted girders. Inside the graffiti-decorated overpass was a crawlspace about three feet high, and this was where Thomas lived. Above his cement ceiling ran Memorial Drive, and great red sheets of metal, which seemed to be unsuccessfully smoothened by hammers, made up his floor.

I had found him accidentally. It was my first or second winter on the streets, and I'd learned that it wasn't uncommon for homeless people to live in bridges and trestles. These shelters are inconspicuous and easy to get into. I used to look out from various bridges and watch people passing a few feet underneath me. Young couples holding hands; kids spraying-painting their names on the walls; old women stopping to rest with their metal shopping carts — no one ever even thought to look up even though they could have heard my breathing if they really listened. In those rafters, I was contentedly divorced from the world.

Bridges also provide the homeless with a measure of protection, and not just from the weather. An early sign — which I chose to ignore — that my "freedom" from society wasn't entirely complete, was my vulnerability to it. The security of a locked door can never be underestimated. While many homeless people have been killed in their bridges by addicts looking for a few bucks, criminals who'd realized their actions had been witnessed, and even other homeless people looking for a better living space, they still regard their shelters with a sense of territorialism. Bridge dwellers will defend their makeshift homes. It's not difficult to get inside a bridge, but the climbing can be a bit of a struggle and the effort isn't a silent one. Once finally inside, the chances of being challenged by an occupant are great.

So when I climbed inside Thomas's bridge, I was surprised to find him sitting up as if he were expecting me. A few lighted candles were stuck into old bottles and lava-like streams of colored wax ran down the glass. Thomas was draped in rags of discarded coats and sleeping bags. His patchy beard was brittle like steel wool and his skin was cut deeply by age. The only thing about him that seemed alive were his eyes. They were watery and yellow, like dripping custard, but they held a resigned peace.

A heavy rumble sounded from above.

"It's all right - just the traffic," said Thomas softly. "Come in."

I was cautious; he might have had a knife in his coats. But he rose, as much as the low ceiling allowed him, and made room for me on a small makeshift bench opposite him. As he did so, his coats fell open and I could see he didn't have any weapons. Another car passed, and then another. With each one, I instinctively ducked, thinking this must be what living through an air raid was like. Thomas was used to it, though, and didn't move. He simply smiled and introduced himself.

"If you're looking for a place to stay, you can stay here. But I've got no money, no food, no drink. I just want to tell you that up front."

I nodded and thanked him. Behind him, taped on the cement wall, was a piece of paper, bubbled with moisture. In the dimness, it looked like an old grocery list.

"You're very young," he stated. He didn't say anything more and I got the feeling that if I wanted to explain myself, the choice was mine. I just nodded again as he stared at me, taking in my youth. When he spoke again, it was with a confessional, rather than authoritative tone; perhaps he thought my youth wouldn't allow me to judge him.

"I've been out here fifteen years. I once had a home, good job, family. Like everybody else," he smiled, ironically. "It was booze, of course. In the beginning, I had no motivation to quit until, little by little, I lost everything. And then I saw how so much loss draws the future closer, making the emptiness you live in timeless. See, I was living in the present and the future, because nothing was going to change for me unless I regained some part of my past. So I started going to AA meetings — see this," and he pointed to the curling paper taped to the wall. "The twelve steps. You know them?"

"I've heard a little about them."

This time he nodded.

"They're the steps toward recovery. They're like pledges you make to get your life back in order. It took me a long while. I thought if I went to a few meetings I could put everything straight again. But there are some things you can only straighten so far. Like a pipe cleaner. You bend it but you can never get it perfectly straight again. It took me a long time to understand that.

"When it did sink in, I started to really read through the steps. There's one that tells you to take responsibility for your actions. At the time, I didn't fully know what that meant, but now I've figured it out so that I've been able to make some much-needed changes."

"So what did you regain?"

"Power over my life. I know that it isn't going to ever get my pipe cleaner existence perfectly straight again. But it's given me hope."

He blew out the candle and I heard him rustling around as he settled into sleep. I lay there with the cars rumbling over me, and thought about Thomas's story. I had grasped the simplicity of its significance. He didn't need to confess, nor was he was trying to give me sage advice. Thomas just needed to talk. It was almost as if he were reassuring himself. I wondered why was he still on the street and how much straighter he thought he could mold his life. Perhaps these were the questions he needed answers to and, in lieu of the bartender, he spoke to total strangers in hopes of figuring it all out for himself.

But Thomas's story also gave me an answer that would help me in the coming days. The loss of all the reasons for not stopping the operation had fused my present and future, but the idea of taking responsibility allowed me to separate them. In the present, I would have the control to concentrate on stopping Vince one step at a time and, in the future, I would have to contend with the consequences of those steps. But this helped me to go forward in the same way that my thoughts of the transformation from pigeon to squab allowed me to justify my life. I would be able to look away from the consequences while in the present. It was true that this proved detrimental while I was on the street, but in the next few days, I'd have to confront ghosts of the past, present and future. This was my only chance of making it through.

"The only way we will be able to stop is to get rid of Vince."

Domingo uttered these words effortlessly, like dropping scraps of paper on the ground.

"Get rid of —? You mean kill him?"

"If that's the only way...*si*."

Killing Vince hadn't even entered my mind. I had been trying to come up with a solution that wouldn't get *us* killed. But for me to kill — it was impossible. I searched Domingo's face for an alternative, but he gave me none. He just sat by the stove, drinking his beer.

"Dommy...I can't. You know that. After my father..."

"I thought you said you did not mind that your father killed. It was the reason your father killed that bothered you."

"Yes. He killed because he didn't have any control over his selfishness."

"So this is different. This is not selfish. This is the opposite."

"But we still lose control."

Domingo was beginning to get exasperated.

"How?"

"By playing his type of game. Vince would kill us for selfish reasons. By doing the same, we wouldn't be better off. Killing is the game that Vince's people — and people like my father — play. I just can't do that, Dommy."

He stood up and suddenly towered over me, as if he had sprouted from the floor and was continuing to grow.

"Birdman. I am tired of you changing sides! First you want to stop this, then you do not. Are you blind? Stop talking about games! You are the only one playing a game. It does not matter to me about your father. I do not care. I care only that two people are dead — two people who were friends and died needlessly. That is where the selfishness is! If you cannot do this, then leave. You are free now, Birdman. There is no videotape of you. So if you do not want to help, walk away! Leave!"

"Dommy..."

He spat dryly on the floor and crossed the living room for his coat. At the front door, he turned to face me.

"If you do not want to help me, Birdman, I will shut it all down without you. But you better leave here tonight."

––––––––––

The sound of the door slamming rang about the apartment. It seemed that it would reverberate forever, bouncing off of the sparse furnishings and slamming back in my face, as if everything in the apartment represented the conflicting emotions and thoughts that, since the day I'd met Vince, had collided in my head. In this game of aural pinball, I tried to collect all these emotions in order to make sense of them. But, although the room was nearly bare, there was enough clutter to prevent a single decisive thought. The room couldn't be tidied up; my feelings couldn't be put into simple order.

I needed to get outside. The cold air would help me to think, so I strapped on my small bag and left the apartment. The wind cut through my trousers like razors and my face stung from the blast. Hardened mounds of snow lined Somerville Ave. where the plows had heaped them. A small pathway had been shoveled on the sidewalk, but every few paces I had to sidestep the patches of ice that spread like jelly fish over the cement.

I had been heading away from the plant, into Davis Square. As I walked, the neighborhood became more residential with two- and three-family houses lining the street. Porch lights glowed like captured fireflies.

The muted crunch of tires on snow came from behind me and headlights reflected off the snow, brightening the night like stars on earth. As the sound grew louder, I instinctively stepped away from the road. That's when I felt the stinging crack against my face.

The houses quickly turned on their sides. Heavy clouds of my breath bled from my mouth in flashes of disorientation as the black pavement and white mounds of snow jumbled together like pieces of a puzzle dumped from its box. And then it all stopped as I hit the ground.

For a moment, I lay stunned in a snow bank, not sure of what had happened. I heard a rustling in some nearby bushes, a high-pitched voice that yelled, "shit, let's get out of here!" and then boots stamping in the snow as if an army were retreating.

My face burned wetly where the snowball had hit me. As I lay there, slightly warmed from the insulation of the snow bank, distant parallels burned inside my memory. A man on skis, lying in the snow. A doctor hovering over him, pretending to help. A young boy who didn't understand.

The snowjobs of my youth had just been for laughs. They had seemed harmless. But now, I was the victim of a snowjob and saw its effect from another point of view. With winking glints, the icicle daggers that clung to the drainpipes tore open old wounds:

My father should have known better, but what about me? Why hadn't I thought of the effect of the snowjobs before?

And then the night sky, pinned above me by the stars, was whipped away like a magician's cape to provide the answers.

Because I had been frozen at fifteen years old.

I had the same stunned disbelief one feels when discovering the secret and ease behind an illusionist's miracle. I hadn't been able to separate the good from the bad because my emotional growth had been stunted. My every thought, judgment, or action was based on black and white justification and I hadn't developed the skills to grasp a truer concept of society.

I lay in the snow and thought about the act of killing. Being hit in the face had left me vulnerable, knocking me into a realm where I could think from the point of view of a victim. For the first time I put myself in Gillatano's position and found that, to a degree, I could identify with her. In a basic way, I could understand what she must have felt at the hands of my father and his abuse of power. But as I looked from Gillatano's perspective, I was also able to view my father in a new light. The reverse vantage point I'd be granted helped me to delve deeper, and I was able to filter the control aspect from the actual crime. My father had killed. Death is not subjective and there is no technicality about that.

I spent the next few hours wandering. I needed to think and the frigid air continued to keep my head fresh. The night trudged on as I walked aimlessly in a frozen river of anonymous footsteps. Near daybreak, I finally decided to go to the plant. I could stay there for a few hours while I tried to figure out what to do. Since Vince had suspended all work, the place would be deserted and, if anyone did show up, I would just say that I'd lost my key to the apartment and that Dommy had gone out.

I had never seen the plant so lifeless. The machines all stood quiet, like architect's models. When I turned on the fluorescents, I heard how loud they actually buzzed. In comparison to what I was used to in that room, it was deafening, and I turned them off and found a small flashlight which Davio had used to look inside the filler when something had gotten stuck. With the flashlight, I made my way to the office and closed the door behind me.

When I finally sat, I realized how cold I was. My teeth chattered as my wet clothes defrosted and seared my skin. I undressed, hanging my trousers and shirt over a radiator, which I turned up by unscrewing the ancient metal valve on the bottom of the iron grillwork.

I settled back down behind the desk. The radiator tubes echoed with brittle crackling and *pings* as the heat flowed through them, and the soft hiss of steam steadily rose in volume with an approaching sigh. One of Vince's notebooks was on the table and I glanced at it. It was an employee list, with the names of all the people who worked for him filling two sheets of paper. Like relentlessly flashing neon signs, each name rekindled my thoughts from my night's wandering. All these people would be unemployed again and back on the streets with no means of support. But then I made a mental list of Santos's crew and Gloria and held it up against the names in front of me. I finally had to push the notebook aside. The dead would always outweigh the living. Death is a robbery of life, a larceny with no degrees.

The radiator began to spittle as my clothes dried, and the increasing warmth in the room seeped into my body and filled me with a heavy drowsiness. I put my head on the desk and slept so deeply that even dreams couldn't penetrate my mind. I only awakened at the sound of keys in the front door.

On instinct, I jumped up. Grabbing my now-dry clothes from the radiator, I looked around for a place to hide. I heard Vince speaking to someone — a voice vaguely familiar — in a tone that was too loud in the silent plant.

"So he showed up at the club again?"

"Yeah, Vince. And they were talking."

"Shit. Let's go in the office and you can fill me in."

Footsteps approached. Like a doorknocker, my hearted thumped against my chest. I scrambled into the bathroom and shut the door. The darkness of the small room provided a comfort of secrecy that clashed with the fear of sudden exposure. I heard the office door open and the scuffling of chairs.

"Okay, so what's the deal?"

The other man began to speak and I realized it was Ritchie, the manager of Playland.

"He came in alone and sat in the back. He bought Roxanne a drink."

"Did she recognize him?"

"I'm sure she did — she was Cheetah's best friend, and she was there the night it went down."

"And you got nothing from her?"

"I think she was playing dumb. But I didn't want to say too much to her, ya know?"

"Good thinking. But we gotta assume she knows something. They talked?"

"On and off, all night."

I heard the metallic scraping of Vince's lighter and the long suction that drew in smoke and contemplation.

"If Roxanne and Domingo recognized each other — which is the likely case — then something's up. Domingo's not stupid. He wouldn't go down there unless he was trying to pull something."

"Do you think the other one's in on it?"

"The Birdman? I wouldn't know. But we're not taking any chances."

"So, we off them both?"

Again, another inhalation.

"We kill the three of them."

"Roxanne, too? Vince, you're crazy. We can't — we'd never get away with that!"

"We have to, Ritchie. Clem's thinking of shutting us down."

Ritchie's voice became subdued, as if it were being filtered through cotton.

"You're shitting me."

"I got the word yesterday. He thinks it's getting too risky."

"Jesus, Vince, if this whole thing goes down...."

"It ain't gonna happen. But we need the three of them out of the way. Then, we show Clem that things are smooth and we'll be all right."

"But, Roxanne...."

"Ritchie! She knows too much. We'll just have to play it right. Given the circumstances, Clem will ask questions but he'll never find out."

I could hear Ritchie's chair rocking back and forth, in nervous, squeaky jerks. Then I heard him speak again. His voice was shattered.

"Okay. So, you got a plan?"

"Domingo's easy. He's an illegal alien, so right there is an excuse for his disappearance."

"They won't buy that — they can easily check on his deportation. And when nothing comes back from the I.N.S. — "

"There'll be a record of it. We get another busboy from Sid. The busboy gets shipped out under Domingo's name. We've pulled that scam dozens of times, Ritchie. C'mon — you know that."

"Okay. So what about the homeless one?"

Vince sighed.

"He's more of a problem. We can't have another on-the-job accident — too suspicious. It'll have to be just a question of another poor homeless person freezing to death."

"And Roxanne?"

"We'll have to be creative. But that's what our whole business is about."

Chapter Fourteen
To Tell the Truth

I waited thirty minutes after Vince and Ritchie had left before I dared to move. When I finally crawled out of the plant, the late-morning sun reflected from every direction and concentrated in my eyes. The temperature was well below freezing, however, and the few cars on the street drove slowly, weighed down by gray stalactites of sludge and ice hanging from their chasses.

I started to run back to the apartment, slipping along the way a number of times until I fell on a snow-covered patch of ice. My knee slammed into the cement with a splintering crack, and the pain crashed throughout me until I blacked out. I don't know how long I was unconscious, but when I finally came to, I pushed myself up and, as the cold air chipped away at my disorientation, I hobbled towards the apartment.

The door was open, and I cautiously peeked inside. Domingo wasn't there and, except for its sparse furnishings, the room was empty. All of Domingo's belongings had been cleared out; even his gaff had been taken. The television stood in the corner, silent.

I sat at the kitchen table and tried to think. He had gone to Playland the night before, but he had left before me and he certainly hadn't cleared out his things then. I banged my fist on the table.

"Shit!" My voice echoed around the empty room. In a fury, I ran to the door and back to the far corner of the room. "Shit!"

I slumped to the floor, holding my head in my hands, and rubbing my scalp to release the pressure that was throbbing against my temples.

Outside came the noise of rats. It was the quick scurrying sound I'd heard the night I slept in the bar, claws clicking on metal. But as the sound came closer, the denseness in tone changed and I realized it was the noise of footsteps; someone was running, trying to stay balanced on the icy sidewalk. I bolted upright, looking in vain for a place to hide in the vacuum of the apartment. I flattened against the wall and squeezed my eyes tight. As I gritted my teeth, the door to the apartment blasted open.

"Tweets!"

My breath caught in my throat and realigned after a deep gasp. I looked up to find Roxanne there, dressed in a miniskirt and halter with a scuffed, brown leather jacket thrown around her.

"Tweets! They've got Domingo!"

"Who — where?"

Her words came quickly, almost too fast for her mouth to keep up.

"Vince and Ritchie. Domingo came to the club last night to tell me he was going to help stop the operation. But he had too many drinks and I let him sleep in the office, 'cause I was closing up and opening this morning. But as I was pulling up, I saw Ritchie's car already there."

I stood up.

"How do you know they got Dommy?"

"I drove around back, and hid behind some old dumpsters. I saw Ritchie and Vince dragging Domingo out. They had some metal rod to his back — it looked like a knife."

"His gaff."

"What?"

"It was Domingo's fisherman's gaff. Do you know where they might have taken him?"

"I tried to follow, but got lost in the city traffic."

"So they headed back to town?"

"Yeah." Roxanne trembled and looked out the door. "So, what do we do? They must know about me, too. Maybe even you."

"They do. You've got a car?"

"Yes."

"Good. Let's go. We'll head to the North End."

———————

I hadn't been to Sid's restaurant since the day I sold him the pigeon that had made Vince ill. It was one of the tiny trattoria-like restaurants off of Hanover Street, which runs through the heart of the North End. My parents used to love the North End and every month or so, they would drive up to this Italian section of Boston and have dinner.

The neighborhood was ready for Christmas, with wreaths on doors, trees and holiday figurines in the shop windows, and lights strung across the street which slept in a maze of camouflage-like netting during the day but would awaken at night as colorful angels, Santas and reindeer. People disregarded the cold as they walked the labyrinth of cobblestone sidewalks and entered various multi-colored coffee houses, butcher shops and markets. Holiday smiles rested above woolen scarves and underneath fur-lined hats of the shoppers, while delivery boys called out to one another in loud joking voices. A man in a black Salvation Army uniform rang a bell, choreographing the holiday spirit as the street danced to his constant jingling.

Roxanne cruised up and down Hanover until she finally found a meter a few blocks from Sid's. I used the time in the car to explain some of what I had overheard.

"But Tweets, why would they be at the restaurant? They could get the busboy from this Sid guy anytime."

"Yes, but they won't touch Domingo in the daytime. Plus, they'll want to find out where we are. He'll have information about both of us. My guess is they're keeping him here until night."

"But what can we do?"

I opened the door.

"For one thing, we can see if I'm right."

I got out and started walking. I heard Roxanne's heels clicking behind me and I slowed so she could catch up. We walked side by side up Hanover until we came nearer to the small side street where Sid's restaurant was. We didn't speak and I walked at a steady pace. When we reached Sid's street, Roxanne turned right, then hesitated as I passed the street. I stopped and turned around to face her. Roxanne's face flushed with a cautious mix of fear and vengeance.

"They're after you, too," I said quietly.

She stood at the corner of the street that she shouldn't have known, poised as if she would run. But she stood her ground, heels firmly set between the ice-crusted stones of the pavement.

"You can't bullshit me, Tweets. Vince just wants you and Domingo."

"You're wrong. I heard them."

"You heard them!" And she exhaled a short laugh. "You really think Vince is gonna kill me? You really think he'll kill Clem's granddaughter?"

Everything around me went silent; even the bell seemed to stop. I tried to register what I'd just heard.

"What?"

"That's right. Clementino. He's my grandfather."

"You're bluffing."

"Tweets, my grandfather has been in prison for most of my life — you wanna know why? I told you how my father raped me and Gloria. When my grandfather found out, he sent some of his men over to take care of him. They tied my mother up to watch. Clem wanted to give her a lesson about marrying the wrong type of guy. From what I've been told, it lasted all night — way past the point when my old man was begging for them to kill him. They started with cigarette burns, then moved on to knives — you get the picture. Finally, in the early morning, they shot him in the head with a sawed-off shotgun. It was tough luck because my mother was also hit. She had broken free and tried to run to my father just as Clem's guys fired. So, that's why Clem is a lifer and how Gloria and me ended up being bounced around in group homes. But he always watched out for us, as much as he could, and when we were older, he helped us get work."

"So Vince didn't meet Gloria in the Boylston Street T station?"

"Shit no," Roxanne laughed, again. "Clem hooked them up together, just as he hooked me up with Ritchie at Playland."

"But Vince killed Gloria."

"No, heroin killed Gloria. Just like Domingo almost killed Cheetah."

"So, that's why you're doing this."

She turned towards the restaurant for a moment, and when she faced me again, her eyes were moist.

"Cheetah was the only real friend I ever had. And because of your Spic friend, she's laying like a fuckin' vegetable...."

A few tears squeezed their way out of her eyes. The cold made her paunchy cheeks look like tiny red throw pillows. When she felt the wetness, she brushed the tears away, erasing her emotion with her tattered glove.

"Roxanne, it wasn't Domingo's fault. He was just trying to help his friend."

"While mine was getting hurt."

"He pulled Santos off. Yes, they got away, but the point is Domingo wasn't trying to hurt Cheetah. But now Vince wants all of us — including you."

"That's crazy, Tweets! He wouldn't dare."

"He would. Because he's worried about the operation."

"So am I. Because it helps out people like Gloria, people who don't have any other chance. But you want to stop it all. You think I don't know how you feel about it? You think word hasn't gotten around? When I deliver you to Vince, he'll take care of you and Domingo. So, the operation will be saved and I'll get my revenge on that bastard for what he did to Cheetah."

"Well, your plan backfired 'cause Vince is after you, now."

"Look, don't bullshit me, Tweets. They'd never touch me."

"They would. Clem's planning on pulling the plug and Vince and Ritchie know that if the business goes, they go. Think about it, Roxanne! If that happens, Vince will have failed Clem."

"Big deal."

"How many other opportunities are there for Vince? The only place he's gonna find work is from Clem's enemies. People who would kill for the information Vince can give them."

My words were slowly beginning to register.

"That'll mean crossing Clem," I continued. "Before Vince even gets out of the door, he'll be a dead man. Roxanne, your grandfather will send the same type of guys that killed your parents after Vince and Ritchie."

"No…no…."

"Listen to me! Vince's plan is already set. Domingo, me — and you. Because you know too much. And you know how he's going to cover it all up?" I bent down and picked up a handful of snow. "Next spring, your body will be found in a snow bank. They'll pin it on a guy from the club — some random guy who hangs out there. And no one — including Clem — will ever know."

"I…I don't believe you." And she started running down the side street towards Sid's. I followed and grabbed her arm. She slipped on the sidewalk and twisted her ankle as she crumpled to the pavement. She gave out a long, squelched cry as I held her down and I whispered fiercely into her ear.

"Roxanne, you've got to believe me. Look, at first I only wanted to stop this whole thing so no one else would get hurt. But now, my life is at risk. If it weren't, you think I'd be here now? Like you said, Vince doesn't have anything on me — the tape's blank, I could disappear. But I know too much. Roxanne — *think!* Ritchie saw you and Domingo at the club last night. I overheard him talking to Vince — telling him about how you and Domingo spoke on and off all night, how Ritchie asked you about him but you played dumb. They've got no choice, Roxanne. You know too much, too. They'll take their chances and kill you because if they don't, Clem will definitely kill them. Is your revenge so important that you'll sacrifice your life?"

She stopped struggling and lay quiet. A few people had stopped to look. When she noticed them she rose, pretending to let me help her.

"My ankle!" she wailed to me. "Honey, help me to the car. They should shovel these sidewalks better. We should sue these bastards."

Roxanne leaned on my shoulder and limped back towards Hanover Street. The crowd that had gathered began to disperse, quickly forgetting the interruption as they once again synched up to the chiming Salvation Army bell.

To remove any further attention from ourselves, Roxanne and I returned to the car and left the North End with the intention of parking further away and walking back to Sid's. To further convince her of Vince's plan, I filled her in on the entire conversation I had overheard.

"Jesus. They'll never get away with it," she said.

"But they have to try. They've got no choice."

She chewed her lip and drove past the Fleet Center, then took a left in the tangle of construction and headed for Government Center. Finally she looked at me.

"Is it true that your father is in jail for cutting off some woman's leg?"

The shock of the question, the words, the emotionless tone sent me reeling back to the days before I ran to the streets. I could only just stare at Roxanne while I struggled back towards the present. She smiled tightly.

"After the shit I went through as a kid — that's nothing."

"It nearly destroyed me."

"I guess that's what makes us all different. What it takes to screw us up."

"That's one thing, at least," I agreed. I knew I had to be honest with her to solidify her trust. I also knew she wasn't going to let the subject go.

"Domingo told me he got turned on by chicks with one leg. I've met a lot of guys with sick kinks, but that's the top."

"He wasn't sick. There are plenty of people who find amputees attractive. But what my father *did* was sick. Just like what your father *did* was sick."

A layer of hatred smeared her face.

"You don't think my old man was sick because screwing kids turned him on? You just think it's sick that he *did* it?"

I thought carefully about how to answer, taking in a long breath to buy time.

"I don't think we can help the way we are."

"So my father couldn't help raping his two babies?"

"I didn't say that, Roxanne. If you want to know what *I* think, yes, your father was sick. But it's not unreasonable to think that there would be — and probably are — other people out there who *wouldn't* think that. Other pedophiles, for instance. But then again, you read it all the time — child molesters who say they know they're sick and if they get a chance, they'll do it again. All I'm saying is there are varying degrees of what we'll accept as abnormal. And I think *that's* what makes us different."

"So there could be people out there who would think what your old man did was a great idea — a bunch of slime balls sitting around saying, 'why didn't I think of that?'"

I puffed out a breath.

"Yeah. There could be."

"But you don't feel that way, Tweets, do ya? You hide it all behind a fucking technicality. He couldn't help who he was — what bullshit! You know what I think? I think you can't admit your father was fucked up. I think that's the real reason you ran away. You couldn't look yourself in the face and say 'my father is a sick fuck.' So you took the easy way out, Tweets. You let your father off the hook by making an excuse for what he *did*. And then you ran away because you didn't have the guts to face up to who your father was."

She careened around the Haymarket T station and headed back up towards Cambridge Street.

"I couldn't accept that my father abused his power. Just like your father did. They both took advantage. Stealing other peoples' lives. Maybe you're right — I didn't have the guts to live around people like my father. So what does that prove?"

Roxanne's lips twisted to a tired smirk. Stopping at a red light, she looked at me and shook her head.

"You thought that running away from him would keep you clean, somehow. Clean from all the garbage and shit we have to live with every day. All those people whose filth we have to deal with every minute of our lives. And maybe you really did think you could do this but maybe you also thought you could get back at your old man by showing him how he messed up your life, too."

I was looking at her, incredulously. She laughed and then the light turned green and we took a right, putting us back on Causeway Street.

"Do you think you invented rebellion?" she went on. "I just can't get over how long you kept it up. Jesus, if you really thought you were punishing him by sleeping on sidewalks for ten years, then *you're* the one who's sick."

"I wasn't trying to punish him."

"Come on — you were being so high and mighty by leaving his world. But you couldn't get away from the filth because you were sleeping in it every night. Didn't that ever cross your mind?"

"No," I whispered, my eyes blinking back the stinging moisture. "Not until very recently."

"'Course not. Because you were fooling yourself the whole time — it was all a part of the excuse you made for your old man. Except it was a pretty big technicality."

We turned onto North Washington Street, then entered the Charlestown Naval Yard and pulled up along the curb. In the distance, the U.S.S. Constitution sat in the dense, bluish water. A lone seagull, like a piece of plaster falling from the concrete-gray sky, circled the ship, looking for a place to rest.

"There are degrees to what people will accept as normal, too, Tweets."

Roxanne turned off the car and got out. But I sat there, watching the seagull as it flew in its endless searching spiral.

It was early afternoon when we made it back to the North End. It took about twenty-five minutes to walk there, and our plan emerged in puffs of frosty breath.

"We're not going in?" Roxanne asked.

"No, we'll just see if Vince's car is here."

"So how will that help Domingo? You don't even know if he'll be in there."

"I'm assuming he'll be there."

"Assume shit. Look, you used to sell pigeons to Sid." Again I looked at her incredulously. "Domingo told me," she explained. "Anyway, you know how tricky these guys are. We've got to know for sure."

"And how will we do that?"

"We ask."

I'd heard this same tone in the voices of weary liquor storeowners telling college kids they were closed. I stopped walking and faced her.

"Ask who? Roxanne — you know how small Sid's place is. It's not that easy."

"None of this is easy. Like you said, we're all on Vince's hit list, so we're all gonna have to take some chances to save our necks. So, I'll tell you what. You just go around back to the delivery door. But don't ring the bell. Knock three times. Two soft, one loud."

"You're kidding."

Roxanne grabbed my arm.

"Listen, Tweets, I still don't completely trust you. Sorry, but this whole story sounds too crazy — they may be after you, but I still can't believe they're really after me. So prove it. Prove that if I went to the door, I might get grabbed. That knock I gave you is a little code I've got with one of the waiters. When I'm... entertaining, this guy makes sure it all looks legit and, to thank him, I turn a few favors for him. You knock like I told you and he'll answer the door to try to warn me about Vince — if there's anything to be warned about. When I see that, I'll know."

Her bottom lip trembled but her teeth weren't chattering; she wasn't cold and I could see that her reluctance to go to the door held more fear than she let on. She didn't *completely* trust me, but doing as she asked would prove I was her ally.

"Okay," I agreed, and we started walking again. As we turned down Sid's street, I pointed to a faded green trash dumpster, decorated with graffiti, No Parking signs and gouges in the paint. "You can hide behind there."

"You got it, Tweets."

The muscles in my legs melted with each step I took. A trail of food scraps led from the dumpster to the door, and from inside the green trash container came a bitter smell like fermented vomit. The iron door itself was sealed tightly, as if it were painted onto the red bricks of the wall. The small black button encircled by a brass plate hadn't changed since the last time I'd visited Sid's, but as I reached the door I ignored the button for Roxanne's knock.

For a few minutes, nothing happened. I looked back towards the dumpster and saw Roxanne's face peering out. She nodded for me to stay put. Then I heard a soft scuffling inside: tentative footsteps that stopped with caution every few steps before coming closer.

The lock turned slowly, as if the person on the other side was trying to muffle the sound. The door was opened by a thin, slightly stooped man, who looked surprised to see me.

"Wha —?"

"I'm a friend of Roxanne's."

His eyes furled in suspicion.

"A friend of who?"

"Roxanne — from Playland. I'm also a friend of Antonio — the cook's assistant. I used to sell pigeons to Sid — now Vince is after us."

The man looked me over as if I were crazy. A moment crawled by as he glanced back into the kitchen and then stepped outside. He closed the door behind him and approached me, carrying a long paring knife. As he walked, tiny cubes of onion fell from it like a miniature version of the snowstorm.

"Where is Roxanne?"

"She's safe. She and I are looking for our friend. An Aruban man named Domingo. Vince and Ritchie are after all three of us. Is Domingo inside?"

The man hesitated, and pumped his fingers around the knife handle as he decided whether to answer.

"Where is Roxanne? How do I know she's safe?" he said, raising his knife toward my throat. The blade

Andrew K. Stone

grazed the bottom of my chin when I heard two short hollow bangs and one long one. The man looked past my shoulder toward the dumpster, smiled and nodded. Then he lowered the knife.

"Your friend is inside."

"Is he all right?"

"He is. For now."

My eyebrows lifted.

"They're going to take him out after dark. They've been asking him questions."

"About us? Roxanne and me?"

"Yes."

"That's what I thought. Do you know where they're going to take him?"

"Park Street station. Three in the morning."

"Thank you."

He nodded and, after smiling over my shoulder, re-entered the restaurant, shutting out the sun behind him.

————

"Okay," Roxanne said once we reached her car.

"So you believe me?"

She'd been silent on the long trudge back to the Naval Yard. As we dodged patches of ice and the occasional small glaciers that had been heaped onto the sidewalks by the city's snowplows, I tried to read her expression. But with the exception of infrequent twitches like responses to an inner dialogue, she was rigid. Now at the car, Roxanne sighed with exhausted resignation.

"I guess I'm lucky to have lasted this long. I've always known the game, Tweets. As much as Clem loves me, it's always been business first. Clem wouldn't want anything to happen to me, but this is the world he lives in. It's funny, though. I used to fantasize that this day would never come. That no matter what, my grandfather would always protect me. But I always knew that was a stupid dream."

"I wouldn't say it's stupid."

She smiled wryly.

"No, I guess you wouldn't."

We got in the car. The early winter sun was setting while the moon was rising. As a child, I always thought of this as a staring contest between the two. I'd wonder if the moon would ever lose and, if it did, would the sun win the night and continue to shine.

"Where are we going?" I asked, as she headed towards the highway.

"My place."

"Why? We don't have time. We need to come up with a plan."

"We'll have time. They won't move until after midnight. If Carmine said three AM, then they'll probably leave the restaurant after it closes — about two-thirty — to get to Park Street and get rid of Domingo."

"Okay, but we still need a plan."

As she glanced out the window to merge onto the expressway, Roxanne caught my eye.

"I know. And I've got an idea."

————

It took nearly an hour and a half to get to Roxanne's apartment. She lived in Lynn which, during non-rush hours, was usually less than thirty minutes from the city. We crawled over the ancient Tobin Bridge. The bridge's struts resembled hardened licorice and beyond them the buildings were in various stages of sleep. Lights flickered in windows like the eyes of drowsy children. The lull of the slowly moving car and the hesitant, haunting darkness worked on my own eyes, and I drifted off after what had been a long, sleepless night.

My eyes shot open when I felt a hand on my shoulder.

"It's all right, Tweets. We're here."

We were parked in front of a scarred tenement that appeared dark and ruinous under the concentrated stare of the headlights. Even in the black night, the building was coated in extra darkness.

"There was a fire here a few years ago," Roxanne explained, pointing out charred marks on the walls as we walked to the front door. "They never found the kids who did it."

"What makes you think kids did it?"

"Because that's what kids around here do. It doesn't really matter. No one lives here any more, anyway. Except for the owner, a little old man named Ernie, and he's down in Florida for the winter. I've got the building pretty much to myself, and I don't own it, so I don't care what it looks like."

As Roxanne was opening the front door, I noticed the air had become denser as if it might start to snow again. We walked up a drafty flight of stairs to a plywood door with the number seven painted on it in with one sloping, careless brushstroke. As she unlocked the door, the warmth from inside teased me, and I had to hold back from running from the icy hallway.

The apartment seemed a trip through the looking glass. Comfortable and bright, it didn't belong to the world outside its door. Roxanne had a flair for decorating — a plush sofa sat against a cream-colored wall. A glass-covered coffee table with oversized books on it stood between the sofa and a large entertainment center, with a television, stereo system and a few rows of CD's. The floors were hardwood, and probably original to the building, but had been polished so that they resembled an ice rink.

Roxanne went into the kitchen to get us some coffee. She returned to find me holding a small framed black-and-white photo. The woman in the picture had a beehive hairdo like the women I'd seen in old photographs of my mother and her friends. The man had a sour smile and thin mustache. The couple each held a child on their laps.

"My parents." Roxanne said and handed me a mug. "Hope you don't mind instant."

"No, it's great."

I gulped half of the coffee down, barely feeling it scald my throat.

"Do you think it's strange that I have that photograph?"

"No. Why?"

"Gloria always hated it. She wanted me to destroy it, so when she came by I would hide it. I couldn't get rid of it — I don't know why. Maybe just because they were my parents."

I nodded and sipped at the coffee, now. It was bitter but it still tasted wonderful. As I drank, I realized that despite how far I had been pulled into this world, I never lost my gratitude for any food. Taste wasn't even an afterthought. As if I had been drowning, only to come up for air in the most putrid fumes, I ate whatever and whenever I could. There are some things, regardless of the circumstances, you don't forget. For me, hunger was one of these.

I handed the picture back to Roxanne and explored the room in more detail. The furniture, appliances and artwork all looked new.

"A lot of this was given to me by...admirers. Clem bought the rest."

I nodded, and she crossed to the sofa and motioned for me to sit in an overstuffed chair in the corner.

"So. What's your idea?

She stretched back in the sofa, relaxing every part of her body except her eyes; they were tensed and unwavering as she watched my face.

"I can't tell you. Not right now."

"What the hell are you talking about?"

"Tweets, don't worry. I know what I'm doing."

"Hold on, Roxanne. First of all, we're in this together — you, me and Domingo. Secondly, after everything that's happened today, do you really expect me to just let you take over without knowing your plan? No offense, but I still don't completely trust *you*."

Roxanne reached out and took my hand. The feeling of her soft fingers was a new experience for me. I'd never been touched by a woman before, having spent my street years without any affection whatsoever. But now a fire that couldn't burn hot enough was seeping up my forearm and spiking through my head, giving life to this part of me which had lain dormant. Much more than sexual, Roxanne's hand held a nurturing reassurance that I'd been denied — or had denied myself of — my entire adult life. All my anxiety flooded to my palm and poured out of my fingers. Roxanne smiled.

"Tweets, you're going to have to trust me. You asked me to do the same and I did — now it's your turn. I believe you, Tweets, everything you've told me. Of course I had to watch myself at the beginning, but come on, don't forget my background. I always have to be careful who I get mixed up with. It's the only way for me to survive. But don't worry. By tomorrow morning, this whole thing will be over. We're going to save Domingo and ourselves. You're going to have to let me handle it, though — at least right now, this first part."

"Roxanne — "

"Look, we both know that Domingo's safe until to-night. There's nothing you can do but there are a few things I can do to help us out."

"Like what?"

"Like call on some friends."

"Jesus, are you crazy? We can't bring anyone else in this."

"Tweets, don't worry." She drew out the sentence, swirling her fingers around my hand with each syllable. "You're gonna have to be ready for tonight. Why don't you lie here on the sofa — get some sleep."

"You're crazy! I can't sleep."

"Try to. There's nothing else you can do before to-night. And, believe me, Domingo's fine. You'll see. He may be a little beat up, but Vince won't take the chance of doing anything more than questioning him at the restaurant. So you sleep for a while. I'll be back soon. Then we'll all be safe."

As she released my hand, I realized how exhausted I was and my body, now almost anxiety-free from her touch, shifted limply into the cushion of the chair.

"It'll be more comfortable on the sofa," Roxanne said, putting on her coat.

But I couldn't move. Between the warmth of my hand and the burning want of rest, my eyes shut heavily. For the next few hours, only the dark arena of dream-less sleep existed.

Chapter Fifteen
Mission: Control

W aking in Roxanne's apartment was another new experience. There was no sound of scuffing feet upon the sidewalk, or the persuasive voice of a cop telling me to move along; nor was there the alarm clock in the Somerville apartment or the slam of the door as Vince entered, unannounced. For the first time that I could remember, I woke as peacefully as I had fallen asleep. My eyes flickered opened and, during the moment or two that I spent reflecting upon where I was, a warmth spread throughout me as if my soul was becoming tangible.

The room was dark, and long shadows crouched on the walls and behind the furniture. In a drowsy haze, I turned toward the entertainment center to see if there was a clock. The cable television box showed the time in vibrating red numbers; in my waking fog, I wondered if too much electricity was being pumped into them, forcing the natural flow of time. The numbers read ten-thirty, but before I could fall into sleep again, the time registered like a flashlight in my eyes, and I jerked awake.

"Roxanne!" I called, jumping out of the chair.

Her name bounced in hollowness throughout the apartment. I reached for the floor lamp next to me and turned it on. Nothing had changed since I'd fallen asleep. Walking through the apartment, I hoped to find her in the kitchen or perhaps the bathroom, but the rooms were all empty. The clock on the microwave oven confirmed the time on the cable box. Roxanne had been gone more than four hours.

I began to panic. If Roxanne had been caught, I'd be stranded in Lynn without a way to help. I looked at the clock again. There were only a few hours until Vince and Ritchie would take Dommy from the restaurant, and I had no way of getting back to Boston.

Then I remembered the commuter train which ran to North Station. If it were still running and if I could find some money for a ticket, I might have a chance. I began to rummage in kitchen drawers and I found a train schedule and a few dollars. As I was unfolding the crease-weary schedule, the phone rang.

I froze. The phone rang three more times before I heard a series of clicks and the shadow of Roxanne's voice in the other room: "I can't take your call — leave a message." Then another few clicks and a man began speaking. Each word pierced a hole through my stomach:

"Roxy, it's Carmine — you there? Listen. The restaurant started getting busy so Sid told Vince to take the Spanish guy away. I don't know where they went but you gotta watch out. Somebody saw you in the street today and tipped them off. I heard them talking as they were leaving. They're gonna be waiting for you at Park Street tonight. Roxy, are you there? Roxy?"

Carmine paused, waiting for Roxanne to pick up. Finally he hung up with a definitive click. His message replayed in my head, building in loud echoes until the word 'Roxy' crashed between my ears.

"Fuck."

The message had drained the feeling from me and it took a few minutes to recover. When I realized I held the train schedule in my hands, I quickly spread it out on the table and traced my fingers over the purple lines until I found a stop in Lynn. Then, turning the map over, I found the address of the station and the timetable — the last train left for Boston at eleven-thirty-four.

In an instant I was aware of the ticking, humming and pulsing of every clock in the apartment. I looked up at the microwave. Ten-forty.

From the schedule I learned a one-way ticket would cost two seventy-five, and I would be able to save time buying the ticket on the train. I quickly counted the money in my hand — thirteen dollars. I had no idea where or how far the station was, but if I could find a taxi, I might make it. I put on my jacket and ran out the door.

My hopes of getting a cab were squelched as soon as I was outside. A new storm had kicked up, more violent than the one two evenings earlier. The sky screamed as snow bled uncontrollably from the night. I couldn't see more than a few feet in front of me, and every breath I took was suffocating. My heart was beating as if to escape the cell of my ribcage. I'd known many nights like this. Nights when the shelters were overcrowded and men and women froze to death on the streets; when it was so cold, it didn't matter if the temperature dropped further. Nights which lasted forever.

My plan for escaping back to Boston shifted from the nearly impossible to the unimaginable. Each step of it — finding a cab, getting to the commuter rail on time, getting to the subway — was, in itself, practically insurmountable. I'd have to force myself to think only in the moment. Any worries about what would come next would only barrage me with the overall hopelessness I was faced with.

And so I ran, careening blindly down Roxanne's street. There was an intersection with a larger road and a few cars slithered cautiously through the onslaught. Looking both ways, all I could see were soften neon signs that spelled out "Liquor" and "Pizza" in blurry hazes. The wind was blowing whorls of white tornadoes up and down the nearly deserted road.

I ran into the pizza place.

"We're closed."

"Can you tell me where the train station is? The commuter line."

Even on this frigid night, the burly man behind the counter sweated through his food-splattered apron. Above his head hung a menu board of plastic letters and numbers; in the middle of this board was a caricature of a happy pizza maker who winked while forming an "OK" signal with his fingers.

"Two, two an' a haf miles down."

"Which way? What direction?"

"For Chrissake, there's a storm! They ain't gonna be no trains running."

"No?"

"Whatta ya stupid or somethin'? Ah, check it out for yerself. Out the door, bang a louey."

I raced out the door, my wet shoes squeaking on the linoleum, and took a left. The wind tried to knock me down while the snow held me up. Every so often, I'd turn my head to search for the translucent beams of a car. I wished I had owned a watch, and as I battled through the streets, I would look up for glowing time and temperature signs. Whenever I did, the snow would slice into my coat and under my shirt, burning at my throat like frozen matches.

Then, through the swirling gusts, I heard a low growling noise. It grew louder as it approached, and provided an anchor amongst the chaos. Turning, I saw a hazy glow approach me. The light started as a fuzzy circle that slowly diverged into two swaths that tried to cut through the night. I waved my hands to signal what

I hoped was a taxi, but as the lights approached, I saw they were too high to be coming from a car. The noise modulated into a familiar gravelly sound and then I heard the horn blast. I tried to jump out of the way and fell against the sidewalk as the blade from the snow-plow just missed my legs.

My back was pelted by a hailstorm of rock salt. When I looked up, I saw the plow had cleared at least six inches of snow from the road. The street remained black for a moment until white pimples dotted it. Within seconds, its complexion had completely blanched.

I stood up and starting to run after the snowplow, which I knew I wouldn't overtake but had made my path a little easier to navigate. I couldn't afford to waste any more time, as I was fighting two clocks. While each footstep brought me closer to the train station, I was also outrunning the storm; the faster I ran, the clearer the road would be. As I looked ahead at the quickly disappearing pathway the plow had carved out, I sprinted as best I could.

To my right, a tall ghost peered out at me. It was a clock on the sidewalk with Roman numerals carved into its glowing face like a jack-o'-lantern. It grinned eleven o'clock.

"Shit!" I yelled into the wind, and pushed myself faster. The snow was winning the race, surpassing me in blinding, wet sheets. As it fell, it gathered about my feet like newly poured cement, weighing down every step.

Then I heard the grating again.

I didn't think about it. I didn't have time to, and if I had, I wouldn't have dared going through with it. I stopped running, pulling air in and out of my lungs. The truck approached me, and I saw that the plow was nearly as tall as me and the snow curled under its me-tallic tooth like a breaking wave. From behind the truck, I could just hear the feeder as it scattered the pellets of rock salt.

The truck roared past me and I jumped. I tried to keep out of the wake of the breaking snow, and managed to grab onto a rough metal beam along the side of the plow. The truck dragged me down the street, my feet drowning in the snow that was jettisoned behind the large iron tooth.

I gave myself a few moments to catch my breath, and then I pulled myself upwards. My arms burned as my muscles tore to shreds, but I slowly made my way to the top and rolled myself into the payload of the truck, collapsing into the coarse, stinging salt.

Apparently, the driver hadn't realized what I'd done as the plow continued making it way down the street. I ventured to pop my head above the side of the payload, remembering to be careful; I'd once seen some kids stopped by the police for skateboarding while hanging onto the bumpers of busses, and I figured what I had done must have been just as illegal.

But I needed to look for the commuter rail. I strained through the salt which burned my eyes and the snow and wind that reduced me to tears, trying to make sense of the street as it passed by in dizzying waves. I was crouched down so that my chin was just below the heavy metal side of the payload, and while the storm was exploding above my head, I tried to focus on any signs of the station. I was fairly certain the trains wouldn't be running. I'd woken up to many storms like this, and it wasn't uncommon to find the city in an icy gridlock of commuters who were fighting through the streets in their cars.

And now my mind was following the same route. I felt in my pocket for the money I'd found at Roxanne's. I had no idea how much a cab ride would cost, or even what my chances of finding a taxi were. But I knew that any available taxis would be hanging around the commuter station, just as they parked out in front of South Station and the Back Bay stop, hoping to pick up those who were stranded. So I watched for the glowing rectangles on the taxis' roofs that I hoped would appear in the distance. Below me, occasional chunks of ice flew up in the air, ricocheted off of lampposts or parked cars and slammed into the side of the truck with dull cracks. Finally I saw the darkened station. It was a shadow of a building behind the streetlamps. I got ready to jump from the truck, and concentrated on leaping far out and towards the back, away from the curved tooth of the plow. That's was all I allowed myself to think about.

I landed on my side, and rolled a few times toward the sidewalk. Each turn ignited pain in a different part of my body. My left elbow howled from where it had hit the asphalt, my stomach was punctured by my small bag of belongings, still strapped around my waist, my legs sizzled as the skin was pulled from them. Finally I stopped and lay raw against the curb. When I was able to get up, I limped towards the station.

A few cabs idled in front and I saw passengers walking from the platform, wrapping scarves around their necks and pulling on gloves. I quickened my pace, only to see the train pull away. I couldn't believe they were still running.

"That was the last one," a thin man in a long leather coat said. "Just missed it." He hid his face behind his collar and headed towards the taxis.

The cabs were filling with passengers. Muted by the wind, the slamming doors sounded like stacks of magazines being tossed to the pavement from a delivery truck. One by one the taxis drove off, their tires crunching through the snow as if padded with cotton.

Most of the taxis were local Lynn cars, but I found a Boston cab and opened the back door.

"Where ya going?"

"Back to Boston."

The cabby, who'd been reading the sports section of *The Herald*, put the paper down and turned to look at me. He was an old man in a brown flannel jacket and a Greek sailor's cap with a frayed braid. Under the cap, his gray hair dangled in greasy clumps like tattered curtains. His face was a mass of liver spots, overly chapped lips and sparse yellow teeth that jutted loosely from plump, tobacco-ravished gums.

"Ya kidding me?"

"No," I said, afraid he'd turn me down. "Will you take me?"

"Yeah," he answered, settling into his seat and pushing down the lever on the meter. "'Course I'll take ya — I've been waiting for a fare to get back home. Didn't expect to find anyone."

He pulled into the street and slowly made his way in the direction of the snowplow. The only evidence that the street had been cleared were the mounds of snow piled against the sidewalks. The cabby drove slowly as his wipers whipped across his windshield in a frenzied attempt to clear the view. The radio was on low, but it was mostly static which crackled from under the heavy breath of the defroster. The only other noise in the car was the meter, which winked with an incremental fluttering.

"Where you heading in town?"

I thought a moment. The safest way to get to the Park Street was where the T went underground just after the hospital subway stop.

"Mass. General," I answered.

"Hope you're not sick or nuthin'. The roads are a mess — highway's not too bad, but traffic's jammed."

"I'm fine. Thanks," I said, settling into the vinyl seat. My joints began to relax as the warm air from the heater started to filter through their hard numbness. The meter clicked again and, without looking at me, the cabbie said:

"I had a fare to Lynn — I wasn't going to drive the guy. Didn't think it was safe, but the storm hadn't really started and I figured we might outrun it. We hit Lynn when it started coming down heavy. I had to wait over two hours for it to blow over — and this is blown over compared to what it was. I never thought I'd find anyone needing to go back. Your fare'll help, but I'm still pretty much busted for the day."

I didn't answer, but watched as he slowly turned onto what seemed to be a main street. It was clearer than the previous streets, although the snow was still pouring from the sky. I saw what looked like an abandoned black trestle above us. The buildings appeared to lean in towards the street, adding a claustrophobic lethargy to the journey.

Again the meter clicked and I knew what I would have to do. The price had already blinked its way over three dollars and we hadn't even gotten through Lynn yet. In the comfort and warmth of the cab, it was difficult not to think about how the ride would end, and I strained not to stagger too far ahead in time. I tried to keep my mind blank, but the meter continually cheated me, upping the ante in my mind. It was a pulse, unwavering and consistent, and each click which raised the price also raised an inescapable awareness.

233

I slipped back in time. The snow streaking across the taxi's windshield dissolved into the snow I had streaked through on the slopes in Utah. The pulse of the meter was the pulse of adrenaline I'd felt as I honed in on my target during a snowjob. I would gauge the timing of it all — I saw the fat man with the stupid hat getting larger and larger as I whizzed towards him. Not yet...he looked up...not yet...he slipped and slid, trying to get out of the way...not *yeeeet*...I was yards from him, then feet, then — *swish* — I turned with perfect precision. Another millisecond and I would have collided with the fat man, but I controlled it all. As I saw my father rushing to the man who was struggling in the snow, the meter released me from the past, and I returned with reeling revulsion to the back seat of the taxi. My cascade to the past triggered a new catharsis, and as it sunk in, I was sickened and astounded.

It was I who had the power of Tom Brokaw.

I looked at the old man's face in the rear-view mirror. His gray eyes strained over the steering wheel, watching the road slowly disappear under the hood of the car. His jaw was tense, and the stubble on his chin and cheeks stuck straight out, as if every fiber of him was dedicated to driving the car. The meter blinked again. Seven and a half dollars. His livelihood, adding up by degrees before my eyes.

I could justify what I had to do, but that didn't mean he would able to do the same. What would he think, this man who was struggling to get us both home and who would be robbed for the effort? Even if I told him that the lives of three people were at stake, would he care? There were degrees of every larceny.

Finally I saw the frosted lights of the highway. We fought our way towards the onramp, the green signs acting as guides. Again the meter winked and I thought about the triangle between myself, Gillatano and my father. I wondered how my father justified what he did to Gillatano. What were his thoughts as he planned it, what went through his mind — that which he could speak to no one — just before he cut into her flesh? I tried to imagine the operating room: the anesthesiologist and nurses, all unwittingly assisting; the glare from the stainless steel lights which shone down and glinted off various medical machinery; the tubes, syringes, bandages. I could see everything except the face of my father as he reached for the scalpel. I couldn't even imagine his expression or the thoughts pounding in his head.

He must have been able to justify his actions to himself, at least, but whose judgment counted most? I looked one last time at the old cabby in the rear-view mirror. Every pair of eyes holds a different point of view, but for each of us, these differences hold equal weight. When I'd been hit with the snowball, I was able to identify with a victim; now I was thinking of myself in terms of the perpetrator. The cab skidded up the ramp to the highway and I thought about how we navigate the wasp nest. We must step lightly, as the floors are paper-thin and forged of subjectivity.

It took nearly two and a half hours to get back to Boston. Many cars on the Tobin Bridge stood mute, with engines shut off to save gas as the passengers huddled in blankets and coats, blowing on their curled, trembling hands. We had been stopped next to a car in which a young couple, out of exhibitionism or an effort to keep warm, made love; the girl was sitting on the man's lap, facing him as she pumped up and down. Other cars had skidded into one another, and people stood hunched in shadowy groups, inspecting damages.

235

By the time we arrived at Government Center, I had stopped looking at the meter. I couldn't face it; I couldn't face the amount — the degree — of what was to be my first larceny of the evening.

The cab inched its way across Cambridge Street, seemingly held back by a fresh onslaught of snow. The storm had caught another wind and, by the time we were passing Faneuil Hall, the night was completely painted in a thick splattering of white.

I heard the cabby mumble, "Oh Jesus," and I shifted my glance from the side window to his view in the front. Slow-motion red blurs swirled deliberately in front of us, fishtailing in swaths that crisscrossed the street. Finally there was the inevitable collision, softened by the caresses of the snow. The cabby carefully pumped his brake and turned the wheel into the skid that the taxi had begun. But he was experienced and was able to keep the car in his lane while slowing to an agonizing crawl.

I'd been waiting for this type of moment. I knew that escaping the cab would be easy. I wouldn't even be hurt jumping from it, and would only run the risk of being caught by the police. The old man wouldn't chase me.

Just after he righted the cab from the skid, I had eased my fingers around the cold door handle and pulled it towards me. But then he gave me a look of understanding which, for a moment, held me paralyzed in the seat. His eyes were watery, but his tears weren't from crying or from the cold. He was merely drowning. He had the eyes of so many other elderly people I'd watched in the streets. Eyes that had seen too much, that were full of wisdom, sadness and resignation. Eyes that looked from the opposite vantage point of the eyes of children. I stared back for a moment, feeling a sudden surge that made me both hate and want to sob for him. But he defused me by simply turning away. And then I was free. Free to be the Perpetrator.

Chapter Sixteen
The Degrees of Larceny

E ven though the cabby wasn't going to follow me, I couldn't bear the thought of him watching me. The look he gave me, and the way in which his head had slowly turned away in disapproving acquiescence, had smeared my conscience. So instead of heading straight down Cambridge Street, I turned right and ran down the steps that led to City Hall.

Boston's City Hall is an architectural nightmare. There's no cohesion to it; it is a building both unfinished and overbuilt. With its disjointed open spaces, windows stuck on like incomplete thoughts, and the layered roof that can't decide when to end, it sits on its plaza of sprawling red bricks and contemplates what might be added next. It was only recently that I understood why it had always given me a sense of comfort. This confused building which housed people to run the confused city provided me with a feeling of natural alliance. But as I passed it now, I resented the confusion and the lack of decision-making that seemed to go into its design. While I was being forced to make choices, I resented its luxury of ambivalence.

Once I made it by City Hall, I fought my way back up towards Cambridge Street. I passed a small building, all but invisible except for one beacon — a sign on its roof that flashed the time and temperature. Its lighted dots were blurred by the storm that seemed intent on erasing every aspect of the night. But I could make out that it was two-fifteen. A few minutes later, I reached the hospital.

The gate to the subway was broken open, its metal frame twisted and dangling as if it had been pulled down by a mob. I ran up the stairs leading to the subway turnstiles. A few men slept inside, their snores blanketed by soggy wheezing. They were rolled in cardboard and old flannel clothes, tattered and colorless. One was lucky enough to have a hat, which was ripping at the seams from being overstretched. I knew that feeling, that almost religious experience, in which the skin is anointed by the cloth that touches it.

Jumping over the turnstile, I turned right and ran up to the platform that headed inbound to Park Street. Snow covered the cement and lashed the faces on the billboard ads. It clung to the paper cheeks, and then slowly dripped down like white tears. I trudged over to the edge of a three-foot drop where the tracks lay and realized that if the trains had run tonight, they probably had stopped well before twelve-thirty. The tracks were covered completely.

Lowering myself into the white trench, I held onto the edge of the platform and began to follow the tracks towards the black hole that would lead to Park Street. The trench acted like a wind tunnel. Heavy gusts danced between its walls, picking up momentum in wild, white spirals. My fingers cramped as I fought to maintain my grip and my progress towards the tunnel was excruciating as the fury of the storm heightened and stunned every nerve in my body.

There was no way to judge how long it took me to traverse those few hundred feet. Time stumbled around me, caught up in a wild dance of antagonistic partners: light and dark, sound and silence, cold and stinging numbness. The storm had become a tyrannical orchestra and nothing could escape its sway.

But reaching the tunnel was like entering a room adjacent to the dance. The snow had spilled over the threshold and the wind was subdued, as if heard from behind a closed door. I sat inside the subway tunnel, achingly cold but thankful for this new shelter. Still, I only allowed myself a few minutes to rest, as it would take me at least a half hour to reach Park Street. I didn't think of what I would find there or what I would do. I only thought about each footstep, methodically pulling me forward.

Inching my way through the tunnel was like walking on the bottom of the ocean. I waded through the cold darkness, holding onto the right wall like a coral reef. Gusts of wind bit into me from behind and propelled me into the expanding blackness. As the tunnel became even darker, my senses evaporated. The air frosted my lungs. All the odors of the subway were frozen around me and I wondered if I would begin to smell them as I drew nearer to the flickering lantern lights I'd find at Park Street.

The familiar glowing in the distance caught me by surprise. Setting my concentration on each footstep had put me under a spell that was only broken by the light and murmurs carried on wind currents through the tunnel. Like the moans of ghosts, the voices were indistinguishable and haunted, but as the light brightened, the voices became clearer and when I reached the end of the tunnel, I saw a small group at the far end of the platform, huddled together around a lantern.

"Get another light down here!" yelled Vince. His words ricocheted off the tiled walls in sonic booms. Then, a second glow floated down from the ceiling.

When my eyes adjusted, I saw Ritchie, holding a lantern as he made his way down the stairs.

Ritchie's light was brighter and lit up the faces in the group. Domingo and Roxanne were standing together, their eyes on the black ice revolver Vince pointed at them.

"You shouldn't have come back, Roxanne," Vince said. "You should have run. Far away."

"Yeah, and if I had, Clem would have knocked you off for sure."

Vince sneered.

"Since when do you care about my welfare?"

"I don't," she said. "But it won't matter now. Not when Clem catches up with you."

"You got it all figured out. Except Clem ain't ever gonna know what happened to you. Face it, Roxy. Your kind of work is almost as dangerous as mine. And Clem knows that." Vince turned to Domingo. "Sorry it had to come to this, Dommy. But I never thought you'd try to screw me."

"Vince, Birdman knows everything. Roxanne is right — you will not get away with this."

Vince smirked and looked at his watch.

"Birdy is dead. Carmine went to pick him up at Roxanne's a few hours ago but guess what? Roxanne's apartment had another fire. Sorry, baby — you really ought to have moved to a safer neighborhood. All those fuckin' pyros running around. In the morning, the fire department will find him — an unidentified man in the ruins."

"You bastard!" Roxanne yelled. Vince turned on her and slapped her across the face. Her head snapped to the side and then back again as if it were on a spring.

"Ritchie, bring her over against that column. We'll do Domingo first."

As Ritchie struggled with Roxanne, the lantern swayed, casting long beams and shadows around the walls and ceiling of the station. Vince still held the revolver, but I could just make out his other hand, fumbling in his pocket. Because there were only two lanterns, the station was darker than I'd ever seen it at night. But the darkness hid more than I had counted on. There was a tap on my shoulder and fingers flew to my mouth to stifle my surprise. I tasted the acidic grime which tattooed the skin covering my mouth.

"Don't worry, Birdy, no sirree," a voice whispered. "We're gonna have us some real electrofried ratties!"

I stopped struggling and the hand dropped from my mouth.

"Joey! What are you doing here?"

"Roxanne told me."

"How did she - ?"

"Later, later. Me and the boys set the trap. The nets! Hee hee, they're all on the tracks. All we gotta do is get Vince and Ritchie over the side! Then it's all over."

"What?"

"We got enough juice — siphoned a little extra, yes we did. Now, no time — we've gotta get those two over the edge. The rest of the boys are hiding there," he said, pointing straight ahead to the inbound tunnel. "When I give 'em the signal, we'll all rush em!"

"No, no, Joey. You can't do that. It's too dangerous. By the time we get to them, they'll kill Dommy and Roxanne."

Puzzled, Joey tugged at his beard.

"They'll kill Dommy and Roxanne," he muttered over and over in various singsong inflections until he found a satisfying refrain.

"Joey!" I whispered. I must have yanked the needle from the turntable in his mind because he looked at me as if he'd lost the song forever. "We've got to do something quick."

"The juice is on — we're all set, all set we are. But now...well, how are you going to get them onto the tracks?"

"I don't know. I can't..."

Vince spoke again, his voice echoing throughout the station, and he sparked an idea.

"You see, all of you have to be done differently," he said to Dommy and Roxanne. "We've planned your deaths according to your individual lifestyles. It's a little treat from us to show how sorry we are about all of this. And it'll cut down on the suspicion when they find your bodies. It's kind of ironic for Birdman — you know, I first met him sleeping on a park bench." He chuckled. "The guy who never had a decent place to sleep, dying in a nice, comfortable apartment. Roxy, it'll be appropriate when they find you strangled by some poor bastard whose money you stuffed down your bush but never gave the time of day to. Domingo, my friend, we've got a special way to relive your past. You cheated death the first time, but not now. Usually, it'd be ladies first, but this will be like a present from Roxanne to Cheetah."

Domingo's eyes widened as he watched Vince draw his hand from his pocket. He moved backwards, slightly.

"Don't fight it, Dommy."

Vince raised his arm slowly. I could just make out Domingo's gaff in Vince's hand. I remember its rusted, blunt end from that first night when Domingo had tried to stab me. Domingo took another step backwards, helpless. Vince repeated, "Don't fight it," and walked towards him.

I had kept my mind in the present to avoid this moment and the decisions I would be forced to make, but now the past flooded through me and my body detached itself from my conscience to work independently. Perhaps this is what is meant by temporary insanity. Vince's speech had brought together the elements that allowed my detachment and blocked out any conflicting thoughts I might have felt.

I reached down into my sack and, as my hand brought out my slingshot, I thought about the day I had first met Vince. I remembered how incredulous he was about my weapon, as I pulled some small rocks from the sack. However, as I loaded the rock into the leather pouch, it was my afternoon conversation with Roxanne that came to my mind. Vince's mention of Cheetah conjured up the question I'd asked her — *is your revenge so important that you'll sacrifice your life?* My words revolved around my head, gaining volume and momentum like screaming children on a merry-go-round.

Vince had Domingo up against a column as Ritchie held onto Roxanne. He was still raising the gaff, slowly, as if to torture Domingo with thought of what was to inevitably come. I aimed at Vince's forehead — with enough force the rock would send him reeling backwards onto the tracks.

And then everything paused. For a moment, I went black and a split second later I found myself in two places at once. I let the rock fly and all the sound within the station was sucked inside itself. The only noise was the crack of the rock against Vince's head. But in the other place, a loud familiar speech was being recited in my mind.

Vince's eyes widened in surprise as he dropped the gaff and tumbled backwards onto the tracks. Snapping yellow sparks shot from the trench while, in the other place, I remained suspended.

In the confusion, I saw Domingo grab the gaff and lunge at Ritchie. Dommy stabbed him square in the chest

245

so hard that, within an eye blink, Ritchie's shirt changed from white to crimson. He staggering against the column and dropped to the cement floor.

Joey's men jumped out from the tracks and ran to Dommy and Roxanne. A few last sparks flew up from where Vince had fallen and Joey repeatedly slapped me on the back, yelling, "hee, hee!" But I barely felt or heard him; I was miles and years away from Joey and the subway station. I was still in the second place, that prison room, visiting my father for the last time. Like the snow outside, our final conversation showered into my mind and began to accumulate. But unlike the storm, I was able to navigate our discussion and, for the first time, grasp its meaning with clarity.

Chapter Seventeem
Disappearing Into View

"So, fill me in."

We were squeezed into Joey's shelter under the Amtrack bridge. Roxanne was sitting on an old milk crate and Domingo was opposite her, pouring hot coffee from an old tin pot. It was after daybreak and the storm had ended, giving way to the ironic blue sky and bright sunshine that typified so many mornings that followed blizzards. After disposing of Vince's and Ritchie's bodies in two separate snow banks, we had regrouped at Joey's to figure out the next steps. For all the uncertainties we faced, the fact that we were still in danger was the only surety we had.

"Roxanne, what happened to you? And Joey — how did you know what was going on?"

Roxanne sipped her coffee and then answered:

"Well, Tweets, after I left you at my apartment, I came here. I knew Joey would be able to help."

"That's true, hee, hee," Joey said, clapping his hands three times fast.

"But how...?"

"You weren't the only one Gloria told me about, Tweets. Joey and me are old friends. He once saved Gloria from O.D.ing. Found her in the streets, already strung out and trying to shoot one last needle. Joey grabbed the needle away from her, didn't ya, Joey?"

"Yeah. I don't like...don't like needles at all. Not at all because I know they're no good."

"Joey was shot full of some bad shit when he was living down South in that prison camp. But that's all over now, Joey," Roxanne added, when she saw him become agitated. "He fought with Gloria — actually held her down — until she gave him my number. To thank him, I hooked him up with Vince — got him and his gang some work."

Joey giggled in the corner, and repeated in a mumbling but bright voice, "hooked me up."

"Joey and me became good friends. Because he was working with Gloria, he kept an eye on her for me and let me know how things were going for her and with the operation. One night, she told Joey about the talk you had with her about it all being illegal. She was scared that you might try to blow the whistle on things. If that happened, she'd have ended up back on the street, so I hinted to her that she should get Vince to take out a little insurance on you."

"Wait a minute — you mean the videotape? That was your idea?"

"Of course. It was my way of watching after Gloria."

"But you taped up the cameras."

"Right. Like I told you at the apartment, I was also watching Vince. When Gloria told me about the merger, I spread the word to Joey to start bringing in more product. I knew how Vince could turn and I needed to cover all my bases."

I shook my head, trying to rearrange all the angles into a cohesive order.

"Sorry, Tweets, but I had to look after my sister, you know."

"You did a pretty thorough job. But what about tonight? How did you get caught by Vince? And why didn't Joey get caught?"

"Joey and his guys were already at Park Street way before Vince and Ritchie brought us there. They thought you were killed in the fire. But I knew better."

"How?"

"You got Carmine's message, didn't you?"

"Yeah."

Roxanne smiled, satisfied.

"See, I knew that I had to let Vince catch me. His whole plan was to get rid of all of us at the same time, and to make it work — so there'd be no leaks — he had to act quick. Domingo and you weren't that much of a problem, because you weren't really known by the 'associates.' But of course I was, and I could have gotten word to Clem. So I went back to Sid's and talked to Carmine. Vince was getting nervous about where you and me were, Tweets, so I let Carmine bring me in — he told them he caught me out back, looking for Domingo. After a little of Vince's 'persuasion,' I admitted that you were at my place, and that's how he came up with the fire plan. It was his way to buy some time, get rid of you, and take the suspicion off of him, all at the same time. It would all look perfect — a frustrated guy from the club follows me home. We struggle, a candle gets knocked over and the place goes up. But there's only one body — yours, which can't be identified 'cause of the fire and 'cause you don't have any ID anyway. So the cops think you're the guy who stalked me. But my disappearance is a mystery until Ritchie tells the cops that he saw the stalker at the strip club, and the guy had a buddy. Now the police think two guys came to my place, and the one who made it out took me with him. Then they find me in the spring — strangled. Of course, the second guy is never found, but that wouldn't matter to Vince and Ritchie. Eventually, the case would be closed. Simple, but it would have gotten you and me out of the way with no questions asked by Clem. It was even better than their original plan."

"So, what about Carmine's phone call?"

"I told him to do that — to make sure you got out of the apartment."

"Why didn't you just call yourself?"

Roxanne laughed.

"You said yourself you didn't completely trust me. Would you really have come back if I called?"

"Of course I would have."

She laughed again.

"Come on, I left you there asleep. I can only imagine what would have happened to you if I had made that call. You probably would have taken off and left us."

She had a point, and I was stung by it. I wouldn't have abandoned them, but I didn't completely trust her. If she *had* called, I would have been suspicious. Dommy caught my eye and reassured me that I was right to question her. But still she had taken a big chance.

"I had no choice," she said. "Look, they would have caught up with me eventually."

She sipped her coffee and I looked around the circle of faces, all hunched together against the cold.

"What about Dommy? How were Vince and Ritchie going to cover his murder up?"

"Simple. You know Vince had exporting connections. They smuggle his body onto one of their boats and have the captain dump him way out — too far to wash ashore. Domigo would have been shark food."

Dommy shuddered at this. As I took a sip of coffee, I realized that Vince had all the angles covered. The plan would have worked. But there was one question I needed to ask, one aspect about the entire evening I still didn't understand.

"Dommy, what were you going to do if I hadn't been able to get there? You knew that Joey's gang wouldn't have been able to get to you in time."

Domingo looked at me for a long time before answering.

"Birdman, once I asked you where you came from and you did not answer me. Then, after a time, you told me. If you had never told me, I would have been worried. But because you did, I knew you would be there."

———

Joey and his crew started packing up their belongings. It wasn't safe to stay under the bridge any longer. Vince had known where Joey lived and, doubtless, he kept records. We knew it wouldn't be long until someone found out what had happened and started looking for us. We all had to decide where to go. Everyone agreed that staying in Boston was out of the question as time now became a game of chicken; the longer we stayed, the greater our chances of being caught. But despite this, I had an unsettling urge to remain.

"Birdman, you are crazy," Domingo said when I told him. "You will end up dead."

"Yes, but…"

"But what? There is no but."

All around us, Joey's men were running about. The footsteps drummed along the plywood flooring as they prepared their retreat. Some were shoving their belongings into paper bags while others were rolling clothes into bundles. It didn't matter how they carried their lives out of the bridge; it only matter that they escaped. Domingo sat down on an old plastic milk crate. I looked into his almond eyes.

"All night long — while I was making my way back from Roxanne's apartment — I didn't think of it. I

251

couldn't, Domingo. I couldn't think about what I would do, what I knew — deep down — that I would have to do. I had to focus on the present, focus on getting to the subway. If I had let my mind go ahead — even for a few moments into the future — I don't think I would have been able to make it."

"But you did."

"Yes. I made it. And I killed Vince."

"Birdman, we all killed Vince. To save our own lives. We all did — and we had to do it."

"Yes, but here's the problem. In doing so, did I give up or did I have control?"

"Jesus, Birdman! You and your control. What does it matter?"

"It matters because while I was aiming at Vince's head...I was talking to my father."

Domingo peered into my eyes.

"What do you mean?"

"The conversation we had in the prison. Remember I told you about the last time I saw my father? In that room in the prison, when I blew up at him?"

"*Si.*"

"Well, it all came back to me and I remembered that I didn't blow up at him. Not at first, at least. First he tried to explain himself and I must have blocked out what he said because it all came back as I was aiming at Vince."

"What did your father say?"

I drew in a long breath and closed my eyes. It was all there, like a script laid out in front of me. I began to recite to Dommy:

"He said, 'Colin, maybe you're too young to under-stand this, but I'm going to try to make you realize it anyway. Because I owe you that.'

"'To the world, I'm sick. I know that, son. I know what they think about me. And sometimes I even wonder if I am but...when I think that way, I realize that we all have something inside of us that makes us unique, makes us human. These things may not be considered normal by most people. But there comes a time when we have to let them out. If we're going to be true to ourselves and live our lives to the fullest, we can't deny who we are.'

"'Colin, I know what you're thinking. I took it all too far. And you're right — I did. But this thing inside of me has been fighting to be released for years. I never meant to hurt you and your mother. I always hoped I could ignore this thing, and for a long time I was able to. But finally it became too much. It was stronger than I was. And then an opportunity presented itself.'

"'I know I was wrong and I deserve to be in here. When I'm eligible for parole, I'll see to it that I don't receive it. I'll stay here until the day I die, Colin, I swear to you. I made an oath before any of this happened — before I ever met her. I told myself that if this thing ever overtook me, I would live with the consequences. And I intend to do that.'

"'But you must know that I tried to fight it. The day she came to me, I began to fight. I had many opportunities to do something like this in the past, but I was able to resist. Yes, it was always too dangerous before. Yes, in this case, I thought Gillatano would be dead and I would go free. But freedom — that's complicated, son. I may have gotten away with it, but I would have had to live myself. Still, if I never did it, I would have denied myself a part of who I am, and that's another kind of prison. The thing is, I wish I could have met somebody else. Somebody who...I could have had an affair with, somebody who was already an amputee. At the worst, I wouldn't have resorted to.... At the worst, it would have ruined my relationship with your mother.

253

But I would have been completely free. Unfortunately I never did meet anyone else. And this thing inside me became stronger. It took over and I lost control. So now I intend to take responsibility for my actions.'"

It was at that moment that I had thought back to Thomas and his twelve steps. At that moment, a calm spread over me and steadied my hand as I had taken aim with the slingshot. I thought about him again as I opened my eyes. Domingo was still peering in at me. I breathed deeply again.

"That's when I really blew up at my father, Dommy. That's how it really happened. He tried to explain himself first, but I couldn't bear to listen. So *I* lost control. I started yelling at him. That string of words — I can still hear each syllable. Everything I said to him was unleashed again in the subway, except I heard the words in a slow, calm voice. And they made me understand. As I pulled back the slingshot, those words made me realize...."

"What, Birdman?"

"Dommy, I used to think that the worse thing in this world is when a boy discovers his father is wrong. But in the subway, I found out that it's even worse when a father admits his faults and his son can't accept them."

Domingo nodded.

"Roxanne told me I've been trying to punish my dad by living on the street. She was right. I didn't have any control over what I was doing because I didn't know better. I was a fifteen-year-old boy. I know that running away was pointless, but what confuses me is that I still believe in my reasons for doing it. I've thought hard about this, Dommy — I've thought about it from all the angles. I don't want to be like my father. I understand why he did what he did. And I can forgive him and even accept him for being human. But, I don't ever want to give in to some force inside me that will allow me to destroy something or someone. And that's what I did last night."

Domingo took another sip of coffee and then put the tin cup down and blew warmth into his rolled palms.

"Birdman. When I was being pulled into the sea by that fish, I had no control. The force inside of the fish was stronger than me because I was being pulled out of my own world and into the fish's world. A fish's world is water. Whenever I pulled a fish onto land, *I* was stronger because the land is my world and the fish has no control there. And so when I was pulled into the water, I had no control. You too, Birdman, were pulled into a world that wasn't your own — Vince's world. So, it is not a question of giving up or gaining control. You never had any to begin with, just as I never had any while I was in the water. The whole time you were in Vince's world, you were fighting to survive, from the day you met him until last night."

I sighed a puffy, translucent cloud that quickly evaporated in front of Domingo's clear eyes. But the clarity of what he said seemed to appear from within my breath and hung in the air for a long time. He had brought a new perspective to the wasp's nest, a new layer that I hadn't yet seen. But I was afraid to trust it. I remembered the subjectivity of perspectives.

"Dommy, I can accept what you're saying. But what about the next time? How can I ever be sure that I won't lose my control in the future — when I'm in my world?"

Dommy held out his hands and turned them over to show me the tangled scars on his palms.

"These," he nodded towards his hands, "are my reminder of the fish pulling me. Everyone on the island knows not to go into the undertow, but I did not pay attention. Now, each time I look at my hands, I can feel the pain of the gaff tearing away my skin. That pain reminds me to stay in my world. I was lucky, and now I have these hands to remind me that the next time I might not be lucky. You need the same kind of pain to remind you. Something that will always keep you in your world."

I didn't even have to think about it. I reached into my pocket, bringing out my personal scar. Dommy smiled.

"That is perfect, Birdman. You keep that with you always. You will have no better reminder."

Wrapping my fingers around the worn slingshot, I felt centered and whole. I was in the soul of the wasp's nest.

The world dripped outside the bridge. Under the sun, icicles cried from fire escapes and lampposts while rivulets flowed from shrinking snow piles to sewer drains. It was still cold, but the temperature was rising and although the city had been sunken by the storm, it was steadily swimming back up to the surface. Cars moved quickly now as gray sludge fell from their wheel walls and crumbled onto the black, glistening streets.

The four of us — Joey, Roxanne, Domingo and I — began walking towards South Station. Joey's crew had dispersed; they would all hide out for a few days and then make their way to New York.

"From what I hear, that's the *real* Place o' Plenty!" he laughed and skipped a few steps forward, then back. I had a hard time imagining Joey in New York City, but if anything, he was resourceful.

"There's gotta be a hundred give or take a few things for us to do. Don't you worry, no not at all! And you know what the best part will be?"

"What's that, Joey?"

He looked over his shoulder, then whispered with a conspiratorial grin:

"I'll get to ride the train all the way, without stopping 'til I gets there!"

Roxanne laughed.

"You know, I might see you around there, Joey," she said.

"You will go to Manhattan?" Domingo asked.

"Maybe. A girl I knew at Playland used to go to New York and dance at one of the clubs. There's big money in those places. She'd go once a month for three days and make more than she made in three weeks here."

"You don't think that will be dangerous, Roxanne? I mean, the whole point of your getting out of town is to get away from anyone who could recognize you. What about this friend?"

From the look she gave me, I realized the friend was Cheetah.

"I'm sorry...."

Domingo watched his feet as they made slush paths on the pavement.

"Look, it happened," Roxanne said. "What the fuck am I gonna do about it? Go to the cops? That's not exactly the way to disappear. Anyway...the guy's dead."

Domingo looked at her.

"At least Cheetah still has some sort of chance. That's more than that bastard Santos will ever have. You still could have helped her, Domingo, but we all gotta look after ourselves, don't we?"

"*Si.*" Domingo agreed, almost abruptly.

"Listen," Roxanne said after a pause. "I'm not going to stop blaming you, Domingo. But...I understand why you did it. I know you weren't trying to hurt Cheetah. You were just helping Santos, *your* friend. The thing is, you've been trying to help out a lot of other people — me, Tweets and all the people who worked for Vince. Including Gloria. So, I'm going to disappear and try to forget as much of the bad shit that I can. There's been too much of it. It ain't worth hanging on to it. I won't stay in New York long and I won't see any of you again. The further I go, the better. So...so thanks for helping me. All of you. I appreciate that much."

None of us knew exactly how to respond to Roxanne's goodbye. As she looked at each of us, our faces turned downwards until she grunted softly and began to walk away. Then Joey called after her. She stopped and turned.

"Gloria was glory!" he yelled.

Roxanne smiled and Joey repeated it, over and over, dancing around as if the wet sidewalk was burning his feet. Roxanne's smile widened and she waved to Joey before turning around again and walking out of our sight.

"Hey Joey," I said. "Are you going to be all right riding that train?"

"Sure as sure! I been riding trains for a long time. Nothing will be easier than simple!"

"Joey. Thank you for last night," Domingo said. I nodded and shook his hand.

"Yes. We couldn't have done it without you."

"Aah, it was teamwork. Maybe we'll get to do it again someday?! Yeah, what'll you think?"

"*Non.* I have had enough. It is time for me to go back home," Domingo said.

"Oh, don't be a soiled sort of sport!"

Joey ran ahead yelling, "soiled sort!" as we passed South Station and headed towards Downtown Crossing. A few people stared at him as they walked along the salt-laden sidewalks. He ran towards the Common, then darted back like a hummingbird. He kept this up a few times, jumping out at us, yelling "soiled sort!" and then vanishing, like a child playing tag.

"Do you think he will be all right, Birdman?"

"I think so. Especially when he finds his crew."

"*Si*. And you?"

I stopped and turned to him.

"What about me?"

"What will you do? Where will you go?"

I rubbed my hands together, and then hid them in the insulation of my pockets.

"I don't know. I haven't really had time to think about it."

"It's not safe for you to stay here."

"I know. But I'm going to take that chance for a while."

"Birdman, don't be a fool. It is too dangerous."

"I know, Dommy. But I need to think things through, you know? When I do that, I can move on. But right now, this is where I belong. Understand?"

Domingo nodded, and then gave me his scarred hand.

"Thank you for everything, Birdman."

I nodded, shaking his hand.

"You too, Domingo."

Then he let go and turned away, walking down Washington Street towards the South End and dissipating into the crowd.

I looked around. The city still wept as shoppers bustled in and out of the stores. Food vendors sold sausages and peanuts from sizzling carts and a few cops stood in a circle, laughing at some private joke. I crossed Tremont Street and walked into the Common. The snow had drifted in frozen waves, and children played under the watchful eyes of their mothers and nannies. Further down the path, kids skated on the oval rink near the snow-covered baseball diamond. I sat down on a bench and took it all in. The sun was still bright. I heard the shouts of kids and the music from the rink and the wind that made the branches sway. But, above it all, I heard Joey yelling in the distance, "soiled sort!"

I reached into my pocket and rubbed the slingshot, smiling wistfully at the thought of how much had been soiled and how much had already been sorted out. I knew the sorting would have to continue. But as I tightened my hand on the slingshot, I felt confident that I'd be able to maneuver about the wasp's nest. I gazed around and realized that no matter where I went or what I did, I would always have the assurance that somehow I belonged here.

Because this was my world. And I could feel it.

Acknowledgments

Without the efforts and encouragement of the following people, this book would never have appeared into view. I am deeply indebted to:

Drs. Kenneth Knowles, William Van Haaren and Kenneth Mukamal, for their medical advice and insights.

Avis Sevag, my friend and editor, whose wisdom has always allowed me to see my words more clearly.

Eric Hayes at Team H, for layout, design, and fifteen years of camaraderie.

Ewa and Jurek Miklasinscy, for the beautiful photography.

My family, for their never-ending support.

My wife, Joanna, for her warmth, light and love.